MURDER FANTASTICAL

MURDER FANTASTICAL

Patricia Moyes

Felony & Mayhem Press • New York

All the characters and events portrayed in this work are fictitious.

MURDER FANTASTICAL

A Felony & Mayhem mystery

PRINTING HISTORY
First UK edition (Collins): 1967
First US edition (Holt, Rinehart & Winston): 1967
Felony & Mayhem edition: 2018

ISBN: 978-1-63194-144-3

Manufactured in the United States of America

Library of Congress Cataloging-in-Publication Data

Names: Moyes, Patricia, author.
Title: Murder fantastical / by Patricia Moyes.
Description: Felony & Mayhem edition. | New York : Felony & Mayhem Press, 2018. | "A Felony & Mayhem mystery" --Verso title page. | "First UK edition (Collins): 1967 First US edition (Holt, Rinehart & Winston): 1967" -- Verso title page.
Identifiers: LCCN 2018012269| ISBN 9781631941443 (trade pbk.) | ISBN 9781631941603 (ebook)
Subjects: LCSH: Tibbett, Henry (Fictitious character)--Fiction. | Tibbett, Emmy (Fictitious character)--Fiction. | Married people--Fiction. | Police spouses--Fiction. | Police--Great Britain--Fiction. | England--Fiction. | Domestic fiction. lcsh | GSAFD: Mystery fiction.
Classification: LCC PR6063.O9 M83 2018 | DDC 823/.914--dc23
LC record available at https://lccn.loc.gov/2018012269

Born in Dublin in 1923, Patricia ("Penny") Packenham-Walsh was just 16 when WWII came calling, but she lied about her age and joined the WAAF (the Women's Auxiliary Air Force), eventually becoming a flight officer and an expert in radar. Based on that expertise, she was named technical advisor to a film that Sir Peter Ustinov was making about the discovery of radar, and went on to act as his personal assistant for eight years, followed by five years in the editorial department of British Vogue.

When she was in her late 30s, while recuperating from a skiing accident, she scribbled out her first novel, Dead Men Don't Ski, and a new career was born. Dead Men featured Inspector Henry Tibbett of Scotland Yard, equipped with both a bloodhound's nose for crime and an easy-going wife; the two of them are both a formidable sleuthing team and an image of happy, productive marriage, and it's that double picture that makes the Tibbett series so deeply satisfying. While the Tibbett books were written in the second half of the 20th century, there is something both timeless and classic about them; they feel of a piece with the Golden Age of British Detective Fiction.

Patricia Moyes died in 2000. The New York Times once famously noted that, as a writer, she "made drug dealing look like bad manners rather than bad morals." That comment may once have been rather snarky, but as we are increasingly forced to acknowledge the foulness that can arise from unchecked bad manners, Inspector Henry Tibbett—a man of unflinching good manners, among other estimable traits—becomes a hero we can all get behind.

The icon above says you're holding a copy of a book in the Felony & Mayhem "Vintage" category. These books were originally published prior to about 1965, and feature the kind of twisty, ingenious puzzles beloved by fans of Agatha Christie and John Dickson Carr. If you enjoy this book, you may well like other "Vintage" titles from Felony & Mayhem Press.

For more about these books, and other Felony & Mayhem titles, or to place an order, please visit our website at:

www.FelonyAndMayhem.com

Other "Vintage" titles from

FELONY & MAYHEM

ANTHONY BERKELEY
The Poisoned Chocolates Case

ELIZABETH DALY
Unexpected Night
Deadly Nightshade
Murders in Volume 2
The House without the Door
Evidence of Things Seen
Nothing Can Rescue Me
Arrow Pointing Nowhere
The Book of the Dead
Any Shape or Form
Somewhere in the House
The Wrong Way Down
Night Walk
The Book of the Lion
And Dangerous to Know
Death and Letters
The Book of the Crime

NGAIO MARSH
A Man Lay Dead
Enter a Murderer
The Nursing Home Murders
Death in Ecstasy
Vintage Murder
Artists in Crime
Death in a White Tie
Overture to Death
Death at the Bar
Surfeit of Lampreys
Death and the Dancing Footman
Colour Scheme
Died in the Wool
Final Curtain
Swing, Brother, Swing
Night at the Vulcan
Spinsters in Jeopardy
Scales of Justice
Death of a Fool
Singing in the Shrouds
False Scent
Hand in Glove
Dead Water
Killer Dolphin
Clutch of Constables
When in Rome
Tied Up in Tinsel
Black as He's Painted
Last Ditch
A Grave Mistake
Photo Finish
Light Thickens
Collected Short Mysteries

PATRICA MOYES
Dead Men Don't Ski
The Sunken Sailor
Death on the Agenda
Murder a là Mode
Falling Star
Johnny Under Ground
Death and the Dutch Uncle

LENORE GLEN OFFORD
Skeleton Key
The Glass Mask
The Smiling Tiger
My True Love Lies
The 9 Dark Hours

MURDER FANTASTICAL

CHAPTER ONE

IT WAS A beautiful September evening, warm and golden, with a rich promise of more fine weather to come. In the garden of Cregwell Manor, in the county of Fenshire, the apple trees were bent low under their burden of fragrant fruit, and the bees buzzed lazily among the russet chrysanthemums or made their way heavily and erratically across close-cut green lawns. Serenity reigned, and in all the three acres within the garden walls there was no object more serene than the lord of the manor himself, Sir John Adamson, Chief Constable of Fenshire. He had finished mowing the grass, and was now relaxing in a swing on the terrace, feeling that he had more than earned his pipe and his tankard of beer.

It was with no pleasure at all, therefore, that he became aware of the insistent shrilling of the telephone through the open window of his study. However, a Chief Constable is never off duty. Conscientiously, but with bad grace, Sir John heaved himself out of the comfortable seat and plodded in through the French windows.

"Cregwell 32. Adamson speaking."

"Oh, is it you, John? My word, I'm glad I found you in. This is Manciple, George Manciple."

The last piece of information supplied by the caller was unnecessary. Sir John had recognized at once the slight Irish lilt in the voice, and had identified his nearest neighbor, the owner-resident of Cregwell Grange. "Hello, George," he said. "Nice to hear from you."

This was only partly true. Not that Sir John disliked Major Manciple. On the contrary, he had always found him a sympathetic and entertaining character—until recently. Now, however, he had a strong suspicion that Manciple's call might not be of a purely social nature, and he indulged in a mild mental blasphemy.

"Sorry to bother you at this hour, John," said Manciple. "It's about that fellow Mason. I'm afraid there's nothing for it this time. You'll have to call in Scotland Yard."

Sir John made a great effort to remain calm. "Now listen, George," he said, "I know that Mason has been making a nuisance of himself, and I'm very sorry about it, but you must keep a sense of proportion. Scotland Yard is hardly the…"

George Manciple did not appear to be aware of the interruption. He said, "You see, the fellow was a guest under my roof. Invited himself, of course, but one mustn't split hairs. So I regard it as an obligation. And so does Violet. We must do our utmost. You understand that, don't you? Our utmost. No half-measures."

This time it was Sir John's turn to ignore Manciple's ramblings. "As I was saying," he said, very firmly, "I don't know what he has done to annoy you this time, but it's after six on Friday evening and I suggest that you have a quiet drink and put your feet up while you think it over. After all, Monday will be quite soon enough to…"

"I really don't understand you at all, John." Manciple sounded bewildered. "You're surely not suggesting that I do nothing until Monday?"

"I'm suggesting precisely that."

"But, my dear John, what am I to do with the body? I can't keep it here until Monday. Violet wouldn't like it. Neither would Maud."

"The body? What are you talking about? Whose body?"

"Mason's, of course. Haven't you been listening, John? Of course, if you insist I'll keep him until Monday, but it does seem..."

Sir John made a grab at fast-vanishing reality. He had found on previous occasions that conversation with George Manciple had this distressing effect of dispersing logic, as sunshine disperses fog.

"Just tell me exactly what has happened, George," he said.

"But I've told you. The fellow was visiting us at the time, which is why I feel under an obligation. And so does Violet. Thompson is talking about getting on to Duckett, but I wouldn't have that, not at any price. 'I'll ring Sir John,' I said. Least I could do."

"I presume," said Sir John with commendable restraint, "that by Thompson you mean Dr. Thompson, and that the Doctor has advised you to get in touch with Sergeant Duckett at the police station in Cregwell Village. Am I right?"

"Of course you're right. It's perfectly simple, isn't it? I must say you're making rather heavy weather out of a very straightforward matter, John. There's no other Duckett in Cregwell that I know of, unless you count old Henry Duckett, the vet. But he lives in Kingsmarsh."

Sir John swallowed. "Why," he said, "did Dr. Thompson advise you to call Sergeant Duckett?"

"Well, he can't have shot himself, can he? It stands to reason."

"Are you talking about Raymond Mason now?"

"Of course I am. Goodness me, John, I'm putting it as clearly as I can. It's you that are confusing things, with all this talk about vets. Now, you say that I should keep Mason's body here and do nothing until Monday..."

"I said nothing of the sort!"

"You did, you know. But I can't help feeling that you're mistaken. I thought the police always liked to take action very quickly in these cases."

"George," said Sir John, "would you just tell me what happened?"

"But I am telling you. Mason came around this afternoon—don't ask me what time because I was down at the range, but Violet will know. I don't even know what he came for, but you may be sure it was to make trouble, though God knows I shouldn't say it about the poor man, dead as he is. Well, what it comes to is that when he was leaving the house in that great car of his, he was shot. In the drive. Stone dead, Thompson said, although of course we didn't know it at the time. Violet called Thompson, and Thompson has been going on about shouldn't we ring Sergeant Duckett? But I said, 'No,' I said, 'it's Sir John I'm ringing.' And I feel I must insist on Scotland Yard, John. Now don't say you can't do it, because you can, and I know it. I read it in a book. The Chief Constable can decide to call in the Yard. Isn't that so?"

"Yes, it is, but..."

"Well, there you are then. We're relying on you to get the very best man—I dare say you'll know for whom to ask. Well, I must say that's a relief."

"What is?"

"Why, your having taken full responsibility for the whole affair. I feel altogether easier in my mind. I shall go and tell Thompson that you are now in charge of the situation, and that Scotland Yard will be along at any moment. Most good of you, John. I appreciate it."

"Now wait a minute, George!" Sir John found to his annoyance that he had raised his voice. Indeed, he was almost shouting. "I'm taking responsibility for nothing! Everything must go through the proper channels..."

"Through the what? Speak up, John."

"The PROPER CHANNELS!"

"Oh. Oh, yes. But of course. That's why I rang you."

"The proper channels, George, in this case are Sergeant Duckett and the C.I.D. at Kingsmarsh. Until I get their reports I know nothing about this matter officially. Is that clear?"

"Of course, of course. I quite understand, John. I'll get on to Duckett right away. I've no objection to going through the proper channels now that I've talked to you and gotten everything settled. But there wouldn't have been any sense in speaking to Duckett before I'd gotten things fixed with you, now would there?"

"For the tenth time, George, nothing is fixed. I shall wait for the report from the police and then make my decision."

"Naturally. Naturally. Just so long as we're agreed what your decision will be..."

"George, will you kindly ring off and call Sergeant Duckett?"

"Certainly I will. Sorry to have kept you chattering. You'll be wanting to contact the Yard right away, I imagine. Well, good bye, John—and thank you very much."

Sir John put down the telephone and walked out to the terrace again with the idea of resuming his pipe and his beer while waiting for the proper channels to catch up with him, but it was no use. The peace of the evening had been shattered and could not be raveled up again. He decided to go upstairs, have a bath, and change into more formal attire in which to greet the Detective Inspector from Kingsmarsh.

As he lay back in the warm water Sir John thought about Raymond Mason, who now lay dead less than a mile away at Cregwell Grange. He could not pretend that he had ever liked the fellow. For all his eagerness to play the country gentleman, Raymond Mason had never succeeded in fitting into the cozy social structure of Cregwell. He belonged neither with the Adamsons and the Manciples in their sizeable country houses, nor with Dr. Thompson and the Reverend Herbert Dishforth, who both worked hard ministering to the bodily and spiritual needs of the village, nor yet with the jolly company of the farmers, Tom Rudge and Harry Penfold and the rest. There was no doubt at all where Mason had wished to find his niche; it was his overt ambition to belong to "the county set," which was his irritating way of referring to the Adamsons and the Manciples.

Of course, it was simply not possible. Sir John, as he frequently remarked, hoped that he was not a snob—but it was a vain hope. It was inconceivable that he should establish any real rapport with a man who was not merely in business but the nature of whose business was so very unfortunate. A bookmaker, if you please. A pleasant enough fellow in his own way, and generous, but an ordinary bookie. Not that class counts for anything in this day and age, of course, and one even has the fellow to dine at one's table occasionally, and one hopes one isn't a snob, but…

Of Mason's life before he came to Cregwell Sir John knew very little. Mason often referred to himself, with satisfaction, as a self-made man, but he had never given details of how this interesting exercise in do-it-yourself had been achieved. All that was certain was that he was the founder and proprietor of the firm of Raymond Mason, Turf Accountants, whose London office had progressed, step by step, from humble origins east of the City until it had finally established itself in a proud Mayfair mansion. So successful had the enterprise proved that four years ago, Mason—then in his late forties—had been able to install a general manager and retire to fulfill his dream of becoming a country squire. True, he went to London a couple of times a week to keep an eye on things, but henceforth Cregwell was to be his home and his persona that of a thoroughgoing country gentleman.

His arrival had been welcomed at first by Major George Manciple, for he had rescued the Manciple family from a precarious financial situation by purchasing Cregwell Lodge, the old gatekeeper's cottage belonging to the Grange, together with two acres of land. The selling of the Lodge had been just one more stage in the seemingly endless battle which George Manciple had been fighting for years, the battle to keep his family home intact in the face of inflation, rising prices and costs, penal taxation, and an inadequate fixed income. Yes, Sir John reflected, old George Manciple had been pleased enough with Mason in the early days, had made quite a fuss of his stocky, smooth-faced neighbor, and introduced him to the Village. In fact, the trouble between them was quite recent in origin.

Just what this trouble was, Sir John did not know. It appeared that Mason had been conducting a campaign of minor persecution against Manciple about which Manciple complained unendingly to his friend, the Chief Constable. Mason had lodged an objection to Manciple's private shooting range on the grounds that it was both noisy and dangerous; Mason had accused Manciple of closing an ancient right of way across the grounds of the Grange, a right of way which nobody used and of which George Manciple was quite ignorant; Mason had reported Manciple to Sergeant Duckett for riding his bicycle a hundred yards down a lonely lane at dusk without the statutory lights; Mason had unearthed ancient documents relative to the land on which the Grange stood in an effort to prove that Manciple's new garage was illegal and should be demolished; Mason had... And so it went on.

"But surely, George," Sir John had protested, "there must be some reason for all this. What's gotten into the fellow? Why's he behaving like this? What have you done to upset him, eh?"

But to this very sensible question he never received a satisfactory answer. And now Raymond Mason was dead, and never again would his white Mercedes-Benz—registration number RM1, naturally—scream through Cregwell, terrorizing the hens and delighting the children; never again would those stubby, well-manicured hands pull out a wallet full of fivers in the Saloon Bar of the Viking Inn, seeking to buy what could not be bought: an entree to one of the little groups of contented beer-drinkers, to that Village society which was so free and easy to those who were born to it but so infinitely expensive and difficult to an outsider. Poor Mason. Already the fact of his death had taken root in Sir John's mind, provoking kindlier thoughts than the man had ever evoked while alive. Within a few days, secure in the knowledge that he was gone for good, the whole village would be mourning Mason quite genuinely.

Meanwhile there was the disturbing fact that Mason had died a violent death. An accident, presumably, but most unfortunate that it should have taken place at Cregwell Grange, thus dragging in the Manciple family. All that wild Irish talk of George's about calling in Scotland Yard... Surely he was not implying that Mason had been murdered? If so—but Sir John put the unpleasant thought out of his head. For the moment the only thing to do was to get out of the bath, dry himself, get dressed, and wait for a trickle of information to reach him through the proper channels.

And so, in due course, Detective Inspector Robinson from Kingsmarsh turned up at Cregwell Manor with a worried face and a sheaf of papers in order to put the facts before the Chief Constable. These facts could be set out briefly as follows.

Raymond Mason had driven over to Cregwell Grange in his white Mercedes at about half-past five. He had seen and spoken to Mrs. Manciple, but had not seen the Major, who was practicing on his shooting range on the grounds. Mason had been very friendly and affable, according to Mrs. Manciple, and had brought her some plants for her garden. Shortly before half-past six he had taken his departure; however, a few yards down the drive his car had unaccountably stopped, and he had gotten out to investigate the trouble. What happened next was somewhat confused. He had evidently become aware of some sort of danger, for he had uttered a cry of alarm. A moment later a shot rang out, and Mason fell dead beside the car. The only eye-witness—apart from whoever fired the shot—was Miss Dora Manciple, the Major's nonagenarian aunt. She had followed Mason out of the house, hoping to catch up with him in order to give him some pamphlets on spiritualism. Her evidence, it seemed, was not entirely clear, but Mason had apparently run out from behind the car, waving his arms and shouting, as if in alarm. He had then fallen dead.

A search had revealed a gun—presumably the fatal weapon—lying in the shrubbery beside the wall of the house. It proved to be one of Major Manciple's service pistols, which he used for his target practice; it bore no fingerprints and had apparently been carefully wiped clean. One bullet had been fired.

An inspection of the car revealed that it had been put out of action by the operation of an anti-car-theft device which Mason had recently had put in. This was a switch, hidden under the dashboard, which disconnected the gas supply, the idea being that a thief would be able to drive only a few yards until the fuel in the carburetor was used up. The car would then stop, for no apparent reason, embarrassing the robber and ensuring his speedy apprehension. It was highly unlikely that Mason would have activated this switch when leaving his car in the Manciples' drive, and quite beyond the bounds of possibility that, had he done so, he would have forgotten his action so swiftly that he should open up the hood after the car had stopped to look for the cause of the apparent breakdown.

The inevitable conclusion, said Robinson sadly, seemed to be that the car had been tampered with deliberately in order to force Mason to stop in the drive, where he made a perfect target for anybody concealed in the shrubbery. Taken in conjunction with the carefully-wiped gun and the fact that nobody at the Grange would admit to having fired the shot by mistake—well, it looked like murder.

"Not a pleasant thing to happen, Sir John, but there you are. Can't get away from it. And in the circumstances—what with the Manciples being so well-known in the neighborhood—and, well, one thing and another…"

"I think this is a case for calling in the Yard," said Sir John.

Robinson exhaled a great sigh of relief. "My own view exactly, Sir John. We simply haven't the facilities. Best leave it to the experts."

What he meant, as Sir John very well knew, was—"Best leave it to an outsider. These people are your friends and mine. Especially yours."

"Exactly," said Sir John. "We haven't the facilities."

And so it was that Henry Tibbett, Chief Inspector of the C.I.D, at Scotland Yard, had to abandon his plan of a weekend's sailing with friends in Sussex and take a room at The Viking in Cregwell instead. His wife, Emmy, was naturally disappointed, but cheered up a little when she remembered that an old school friend of hers had married a doctor named Thompson who practiced in Cregwell. So Henry booked a double room, and Emmy was allowed to come along on condition that she kept well out of the way of all police activity. They arrived at the inn just before midnight on Friday night.

CHAPTER TWO

ON SATURDAY MORNING, after a long and friendly session with Inspector Robinson and Sergeant Duckett and a lugubrious hour spent inspecting the remains of the late Mr. Mason as well as those of his car, Henry Tibbett drove to Cregwell Manor to meet the Chief Constable.

For both men it was an intriguing encounter. Sir John had heard a great deal about Chief Inspector Tibbett and the intuitive flair for detection which Henry called his "nose." Sir John looked forward to the meeting with the same sort of curiosity that he would have felt at the prospect of encountering a movie star or a political personality; and, when the meeting actually took place, he could not help feeling just a little disappointed. Surely a celebrated criminal-hunter should be a—well—more of a *character*. This undistinguished, sandy-haired, middle-aged man—pleasant enough, certainly, and those dark blue eyes didn't miss much—but this was not Sir John's idea of the Yard's top man. Decidedly disappointing.

As for Henry, he was sharply interested in the Chief Constable, or, to be more precise, in his attitude to Mason's death. Sir John showed a strange reluctance to talk about the matter at all; in particular, he was evasive when it came to discussing the Manciple family.

Finally, after much throat-clearing, Sir John said, "As a matter of fact, Tibbett, George Manciple rang me this morning. We are neighbors, you see. I've known the family for years, and so has my wife. When she was alive, that is. That's why I—well—the fact is that George—Major Manciple—would be pleased if you would take luncheon at the Grange today, just to get acquainted as it were. It'll be a purely family affair. That's why I didn't suggest that you should take your sergeant or—or anybody else. It'll give you a chance to see, to form your own opinion of…" Sir John stopped, tugging at his gray mustache in some embarrassment. Then he added, "They're Irish, of course."

"The Manciples?" queried Henry politely.

"That's right. It was George's grandfather who first came over and settled in England, I believe. It's a Protestant family. Then there was George's father, the famous Augustus Manciple who was headmaster of Kingsmarsh School. He was quite a character. He bought Cregwell Grange some fifty years ago, and it has been the family home ever since. I think it a good notion that you should lunch there."

"You speak as though they are a large family, sir," said Henry.

"Oh, not really. No, no. In the usual way there are just George and his wife, Violet. Oh, and Aunt Dora, of course. That's Miss Dora Manciple, Augustus' sister. But just at the moment—well—you know what these family reunions are like…"

"Family reunions?"

"Yes. There's by way of being a gathering of the clan at the Grange just now. Brothers and daughters and—well—you'll meet them all at lunch. George is expecting you at half-past twelve, so perhaps you'd better be… Good-bye, Tibbett. And good luck."

Cregwell Grange was an upright, ugly house built of sand-colored stone in the early years of the nineteenth century.

It stood on a small mound just outside the Village, a mound which, in those flat and marshy parts, was undeservedly known as Cregwell Hill. Around the house woods and shrubberies and gardens and pastures threw up a protective camouflage screen, so that the dubious architecture of the residence itself did not break upon the visitor's eye until he had navigated several bends of the winding drive which led from the public road. Henry, having studied sketch maps of the place in Inspector Robinson's office, knew what to expect. He also knew, when his car rounded the final bend which brought the house into view, that he must have arrived at the very spot where the unfortunate Mr. Mason had met his death; and, since there was nobody in sight, Henry decided to stop the car and take a brief look around.

The house lay ahead and slightly to the right. In front of it was a sweep of graveled drive from which weeds and grass sprouted liberally. Shallow stone steps led up to the solid-looking front door. On either side of the steps untended shrubbery seemed to menace the house, like an encroaching jungle. Presumably it was among these dense, dark bushes that the gun had been found. Peeping above the shrubs were several small Gothic windows, vertical slits apparently designed to let in the same minimum light as in the days when their function had been to provide an outlet for arrows. Henry stopped the car and got out. The drive was just wide enough for two vehicles to pass. All around shrubs and trees provided perfect cover for a would-be assassin. The whole place seemed deserted.

Suddenly a voice spoke. It was a deep, authoritative, masculine voice, and it apparently came from the sky above. It said, "Bang, bang! Bang, bang!"

Henry stopped in his tracks and looked around him. He could see nobody.

"Bang, bang!" said the voice again. Then there was a little pause, and it added, "You down there!"

This time Henry was able to identify the source of the sound with more precision. He went to the edge of the drive and, looking up, saw that there was a man sitting among the branches of a big sycamore tree above his head. The man wore faded khaki drill shorts and a khaki shirt and had an old bush hat on his head. He appeared to be in his late fifties. His hair and neat mustache were iron-gray, and his eyes were brown and very bright. In his hands he held a businesslike service pistol, which he was pointing steadily at Henry's heart.

"Stop there," said the man in the tree, "Don't move." He took careful aim.

Officers of the C.I.D. are trained to think and move fast. They do not stand around while armed desperadoes point guns at them. As the man pulled the trigger Henry flung himself face downward on the gravel drive.

At the same moment the man said, "Bang, bang! You're dead!" Then there was a curious rending sound, as something heavy was thrown down from the tree breaking small branches as it fell. Henry stood up brushing the pebbles and sand from his suit. The man was still sitting in the tree, but the gun was now lying on the ground. It had been thrown in the direction of the house and now lay in the undergrowth at the edge of the drive.

The man in the tree said, "Hm. Just possible, I suppose. The gun fell a bit short though." The Irish tinge to the voice was more pronounced now. "I wonder, would you mind very much picking it up and handing it to me? I'd like to try it again."

"I presume it's not loaded," said Henry.

"Of course not. Certainly not. Why, it would be very dangerous to throw it around like that if it were."

"That's what I thought," said Henry. He walked over to the bushes, picked up the gun, and held it up butt foremost.

The man grasped it. "Thank you very much," he said. "Thank you. You'll be the man from London, I dare say."

"My name is Tibbett," said Henry. "I'm from Scotland Yard."

"Delighted to sec you, sir," The tree-squatter beamed. "My name's Manciple. If you'll forgive me, I won't come down. One or two things I have to do up here. Just go on up to the house, if you will; my wife's expecting you. I'll see you at luncheon."

As Henry climbed into his car again he was aware of the carefully aimed pistol and the faint cry of "Bang, bang!" from among the branches. He drove the few yards up to the front door in a state of pleasant anticipation. He felt reasonably certain that he was going to enjoy himself.

The bell was an old-fashioned contraption of wrought iron attached to a rusty wire. Henry grasped it firmly and pulled it downward. After a second of silence he heard the tinkling of a copper bell from the depths of the house. The echoes died away; then came a pattering of footsteps, and the big door swung open. Inside stood a small woman dressed in a crumpled tweed suit. She must have been fifty, but her face was extraordinarily smooth and unlined, and her skin had the fine, peach-bloom paleness which, teamed with her black hair and dark blue eyes, had surely made her the prettiest colleen in her native Irish village.

"Oh," she said. "Inspector Tibbett, isn't it? Do please come in. I'm Violet Manciple. I'm afraid you find us in a mess, as usual."

Henry stepped into the big hall and looked around him with pleasure. Yes, Mrs. Manciple was right in a way. The house could not be called tidy, but it was undeniably appealing. Great bowls of late roses and delphiniums stood on big, beautiful pieces of antique furniture; the curtains were of faded chintz; and beside the fireplace was a battered copper tub filled with small logs. Also in evidence were an assortment of old newspapers, a basket full of green gardening string, a dirty apron, and several piles of old letters. Perhaps the most striking object in the hall was a large, stiffly-posed oil painting of a ferocious-looking old gentleman in academic gown and mortarboard, whose compelling eye seemed to fix the visitor with disapproval from the moment of his entry; but the effect was softened by the fact that someone had hung an old green porkpie hat over one corner of the heavy gilt picture frame.

"I do try," said Violet Manciple, "but with no servants—and now that the family's all here, of course—I do hope you'll forgive us, Chief Inspector. By the way..." In the doorway of the drawing room she stopped and turned to Henry. "Should we call you Chief Inspector or just Mr. Tibbett? I'm afraid I've never entertained a policeman before. I did look it up in Chambers, but it only seems to give bishops and ambassadors. You don't mind my asking?"

"Of course I don't," said Henry. "And you can call me whatever you like. I should think that mister will do very nicely, but you must please yourself."

"So long as you don't mind." Violet Manciple smiled, like a young girl. "Do come into the drawing room and have a drink."

The room was as cheerful and shabby as the hall and equally full of treasures. In the big bay window, looking out over the bright, straggling garden, a gaunt man with white hair was sitting in an armchair reading *The Times*. He got to his feet as Mrs. Manciple ushered Henry into the room. He was wearing a very old pair of gray flannel trousers, tennis shoes, and a cricketing pullover. Rather surprisingly, the V-neck of the latter garment was filled in with a purple grosgrain dickey and topped by a starched white dog-collar.

"Mr. Tibbett," said Violet Manciple, "may I introduce my brother-in-law, the Bishop of Bugolaland? Edwin, this is Mr. Henry Tibbett."

"Delighted," said the Bishop. "Take a seat, won't ye? Beautiful day."

"Will you have a glass of sherry, Mr. Tibbett?"

"Thank you. Mrs. Manciple. With pleasure."

"Well, sit down," said the Bishop with a trace of irritation.

Henry did so, and the Bishop subsided into his own chair once more. Then he said, "Know Bugolaland at all?"

"I'm afraid not, sir."

"Horrible country," said the Bishop. "I miss it very much. Charming people. Appalling climate. Independent now, and very good luck to them. Poor as church mice, of course. I'm organizing an appeal—all I can do now, you see. Retired last year. Doctor's orders."

"I expect you're glad of a chance to take things easy," said Henry.

"Easy? Ha!" The Bishop laughed, not sardonically but with real amusement. He then retreated behind his newspaper once more.

Mrs. Manciple came over with a glass of sherry, which she placed at Henry's elbow. "If you'll excuse me, Mr. Tibbett," she said, "I must go and see to lunch. I'll leave you to have a chat with Edwin."

Henry watched her go with the emotion of a castaway who sees his ship disappearing over the horizon. It was apparent to him that chatting with Edwin was going to be a formidable occupation.

After some moments of silence the Bishop said "Ha!" again. This time there was unmistakable satisfaction in his voice. Then he lowered *The Times*, and said, "Lazy type, the policeman. You need help."

"I certainly do," said Henry, surprised.

"Lazy type," repeated the Bishop very distinctly. "Policeman."

"I'm sorry you find us lacking in energy, sir," said Henry.

"You need help. Help. Just think."

"I'm trying to." Like most people coming into contact with the Manciple family for the first time Henry had the impression of struggling through cotton.

"Help! Help!"

"What sort of help?"

"That's what I'm asking you. Very ingenious. Think."

Henry gave up. "I'm afraid I don't understand, sir, what you…"

"Aid," said the Bishop. "Aid."

"Aid for Bugolaland, you mean?"

"Aid. A-I-D. You start with the three-toed South American sloth…"

"I beg your pardon?"

"I should have told you sooner. Three letters."

"I thought you said three toes."

"That's the sloth. The lazy type. Ai."

"What?"

"Ai. A-I. The three-toed South American sloth. Don't you know him? A most useful little fellow. Don't know what the compilers would do without him. That leaves D. D means a penny. A penny is a copper. A copper is a policeman. A-I-D. Aid. Means help. That's what you need. Ingenious, isn't it?" The Bishop thrust his copy of *The Times* under Henry's nose. It was folded so as to display the crossword puzzle to advantage. "Fourteen down."

"Most ingenious," Henry agreed.

"Of course," said the Bishop kindly, "not everybody has a crossword brain. It's a knack." It was clear that he was trying to find the most charitable explanation for Henry's obtuseness. "I don't get much chance to do them at home. When I stay with George, I've got time on my hands."

"Are you making a long stay in Cregwell, sir?" Henry asked.

"Heavens, no. Just a few days." The Bishop laughed again. "Poor young fellow. Must be a bit of an ordeal. But we're not so bad when you get to know us. The family, I mean. Now, the Head, he was a different kettle of fish. You never knew my father, did you?"

"I'm afraid not."

"Remarkable old man. Most remarkable. What you would call a character. Between you and me, he became a little eccentric in his later years, although his brain remained crystal clear right to the end. He was eighty-two when he died..."

"That's a very good age," said Henry.

"A good age?" echoed the Bishop, astonished. "My dear sir, in our family a man is considered a youngster until he is ninety. Look at Aunt Dora, the Head's sister. You'll be meeting her in a minute. Ninety-three and as bright as a button. No, no. The Head would have lived for another twenty years at least had nature been allowed to run her course. I thought you knew."

"Knew what?"

"That he was killed in a car smash. Not his fault, of course. The other driver was to blame."

"You mean, your father was driving? At his age?"

"Certainly."

"I've always thought," said Henry, "that it's rather risky to go on driving after seventy."

"Goodness me, what a bizarre idea. The Head didn't learn until he was seventy-five. He was a most remarkable driver."

"I can imagine that." Henry was thinking of the portrait in the hall.

"If he had a fault behind the wheel it was his reluctance to keep to the left. He considered it dangerous to drive too close to the curb, preferred the middle of the road where he felt safer. After all, as he frequently pointed out, as a taxpayer the highway was his property. Unfortunately, this very point of view was shared by his greatest friend, old Arthur Pringle, who was the Head's solicitor. On this occasion, apparently, their two cars were approaching each other at some speed traveling in opposite directions. Neither driver would concede right of way to the other, and the vehicles met in a head-on collision. A great tragedy. Pringle was killed outright, and the Head died a few hours later in the hospital." The Bishop sighed. "Ah, well, it's all a long time ago now. Fifteen years or more. I always say..."

At this point the drawing-room door opened and a girl came in, a tiny, blonde girl who walked like a dancer. Despite the fact that she wore a plain blue linen dress and no ornaments of any kind Henry was reminded of the fairy doll on a Christmas tree. There was the same pink-and-white perfection, the same sparkle.

"Ah, there y'are, Maud," said the Bishop approvingly. "Mr. Tibbett. My niece, Maud Manciple. Here's one for you, Maud. Lazy type, the policeman. You need help."

"How many letters?" Maud asked without hesitation.

"Three,"

She wrinkled her small forehead. "Lazy type. Sloth. Ai. Policeman, copper, D. Aid. Am I right?"

"Well done! Capital," exclaimed the Bishop. To Henry he added, "Can't catch this girl out. She's got the Manciple brain, all right. First class honors in..."

"Oh, honestly, Uncle Edwin," protested Maud. "Do you mind?" She smiled dazzlingly at Henry. "How do you do?" she said. "You must be John Adamson's detective from London."

"Yes, I am," said Henry.

"I suppose you'll want to talk to us all about Raymond Mason."

"I'm afraid so. But later on."

"Thanks for the respite."

The Bishop, who had returned to his crossword puzzle, looked up. "Where's your young man then, Maud?"

"I wish I knew," said Maud. "I thought he might be here."

"Probably down on the range with George."

"Oh, help. I'd better go and rescue him. I'm convinced that Daddy will kill somebody one of these days..." She stopped suddenly, scarlet-faced. Then, to Henry, she said very deliberately, "That was a joke. The shooting range is perfectly safe."

"I'm glad to hear it," said Henry. "Anyway, I don't think that your father is there. I met him in the garden just now..."

The door opened again, and Violet Manciple looked in. She had put on a butler's apron and carried a wooden spoon.

"Has anybody seen George?" she asked.

"Mr. Tibbett says he's in the garden," said Maud.

"Was he shooting at tennis balls?" Mrs. Manciple asked Henry.

"No," said Henry. "He was up a tree." After as little as ten minutes in Cregwell Grange this exchange of remarks seemed quite normal to him.

"Oh, I *am* glad. Experimenting again, I suppose. I'll go and call him." Mrs. Manciple withdrew.

Maud looked at Henry with distinct amusement. "Are you Irish by any chance, Mr. Tibbett?" she asked.

"No, I'm a Londoner. I believe my family came from Cornwall originally."

"Ah, Celtic. That explains it."

"Explains what?"

"The fact that you seem to understand what we're talking about."

"I wouldn't bank on that," said Henry.

"I'm afraid we *are* rather strange," said Maud.

At this the Bishop looked up from his newspaper. "Strange? What d'you mean, strange?"

"All the Manciples," said Maud, "are mad."

"What utter rubbish," retorted the Bishop with spirit. "Now, that fellow Mason, he was definitely deranged. Should have been locked up."

"Really?" Henry was interested. "What makes you say that, sir?"

"I'll tell you. First time I met the man, two years ago…"

Again the door opened, cutting short the Bishop's reminiscence. The man who came in was younger than either the Major or the Bishop, but his long face and angular jaw marked him unmistakably as a Manciple. He wore a suit made of rough tweed, which might easily have been homespun, and he was accompanied by a middle-aged woman who might easily have spun it. She had the dark hair and skin of a gypsy, and she was dressed in a peasant blouse and dirndl skirt; her sandals, clumsily sewn with thick leather thongs, were almost certainly home-made; and she wore a necklace of massive, hand-baked pottery beads.

"Aha," said the man, "here you all are. Ramona and I have been for a splendid tramp. Five miles across rough country."

"Marsh marigold and stinking hellebore," announced Ramona in a deep and very lovely voice. "Two more beauties for my collection. And we saw a pair of black-tailed godwits."

"Took the glasses, of course," added the man. "For a moment I thought I'd spotted a long-eared owl in the garden, but it turned out to be George."

"He's up a tree, I understand," said the Bishop.

"Yes. The big sycamore in the drive. I was quite disappointed. You don't often see a long-eared owl in these parts."

"Mr. Tibbett," said Maud, "may I introduce my uncle and aunt, Sir Claud and Lady Manciple. Aunt Ramona, Uncle Claud, this is Mr. Tibbett from Scotland Yard."

Henry regarded the newcomers with considerable interest. He had taken the trouble to find out that Sir Claud Manciple, director of the Atomic Research Station at Bradwood, was a younger brother of the Major Manciple concerned in the case; but, even so, Sir Claud surprised him. He could not have said exactly what he expected from one of the nation's foremost physicists, but it certainly was not this.

"So glad you were able to come," said Sir Claud politely, shaking Henry's hand. "It will be a relief to get this business of Mason out of the way. A couple of days should see you through I imagine?" He spoke as though Henry had been called in to cope with woodworm in the attic, an expert who could be relied upon to do his job quickly and efficiently without inconveniencing others,

Henry felt strangely flattered. "I hope so," said Henry. "I've hardly started as yet."

"Quite. I'm afraid George is wasting your time—lunches and so forth. I've no time for social functions myself."

"Pay no attention to Uncle Claud," said Maud Manciple. "He does a great act of being an absent-minded professor, but in fact he simply adores the fleshpots."

"What nonsense," said Sir Claud, beaming fondly at his niece. "Are you not going to get us something to drink, Maud dear? I'll have a whisky and soda. What about you, Ramona?"

"Oh, just a tomato juice or an orange for me, Maud. Nature's thirst quenchers. And Claud will have the same."

"But, my dear…"

"Are you keen on wild life, Mr. Tibbett?" Lady Manciple ignored her husband's protest.

"I know very little about it, I'm afraid," said Henry.

"Then we must instruct you. Cregwell is an ideal center for nature study. If you take my advice you will start a book of pressed wildflowers while you are here. An ordinary school exercise book will do admirably. You can buy one from Mrs. Richards in the General Stores. It will be a joy forever, I assure you, Mr. Tibbett."

"Orange juice, Aunt Ramona," said Maud, putting a tall glass on the table. "And here's yours, Uncle Claud." There was a hint of suppressed amusement in her voice, which made Henry glance at the drink she had handed to her uncle. Sure enough, it was a deep, clear amber, and did not in the least resemble either orange or tomato juice.

"You are very kind, my dear," said Sir Claud gravely.

Lady Manciple did not appear to notice. She went on talking to Henry. "The marshes around here, Mr. Tibbett, are a paradise for wild fowl—godwit, oyster-catcher, tern, and lapwing. Occasionally we are honored by a visit from heron—there's a magnificent sight for you. It is only twenty minutes' walk across the fields to the estuary of Cregwell River. Ah, the happy hours that Claud and I have spent on the mudflats with a pair of binoculars and a thermos! Perhaps we can persuade you to come out with us this afternoon."

"I wish you could, Lady Manciple," said Henry. "Unfortunately, I have to work."

"Work? On a Saturday?"

"I'm here to investigate the death of Raymond Mason," Henry reminded her.

Lady Manciple dismissed the topic briefly. "All very sad, I am sure," she said, "but it would be hypocritical to pretend that he is any great loss. A thoroughly unpleasant man. Setting his cap for a girl half his age! I made my views quite clear to Violet. 'You should not allow that man in the house,' I said. 'You should be ashamed of yourself, selling your daughter for a few primulae auriculae!'"

"I beg your pardon?" said Henry, taken aback.

Lady Manciple looked at him impatiently, and then explained, as if to a retarded child. "Raymond Mason was paying court to Maud. Violet was continually threatening to forbid him the house, but then he would get around her by bringing her rare rock plants from his garden. Violet has a *faiblesse* for rock plants, which she is apparently unable to control. Mind you, I am interested in alpine flora myself, and Mason had some remarkable specimens, but I feel that Violet should have put her daughter first, don't you? Of course, everything is rather different, now that Maud is engaged."

"Engaged? Is she?"

"Of course she is. That's why we are all here, to meet the young man. Julian Something-or-other. I have such a bad memory for names. Perhaps Maud will remember. Maud, dear!"

"Yes, Aunt Ramona?"

"Mr. Tibbett is anxious to know the name of your young man. Can you remember it?"

Maud grinned at Henry. "Just about," she said. "Julian Manning-Richards."

"Manning-Richards? Are you sure? I had an idea that it began with a C."

"I'm quite sure, Aunt Ramona. After all, I am going to marry him."

"Perhaps you're right," said Lady Manciple doubtfully.

"Have you seen him, by the way?" Maud asked. "He went out just after breakfast and now he's going to be late for lunch."

"No, dear, we certainly didn't meet him. We've been down on the marshes,"

"Oh, well, I suppose he'll turn up," said Maud philosophically.

"He's never been known to miss a meal yet."

"Mr. Tibbett? It *is* Mr. Tibbett, isn't it?" The voice came from behind Henry's back. It was a cracked, penetrating female voice such as one associates with the very old and deaf.

Turning, Henry saw a small, rotund woman dressed in ankle-length black. Her face was as round, wrinkled, and rosy as a long-stored apple. This could only be Aunt Dora, the nonagenarian sister of the legendary Head. The Bishop had described her as "bright as a button," and Henry found himself in full agreement. "Yes, my name is Tibbett," he said.

"Mine's Manciple. No need to tell you that. Dora Manciple. Never married. You're not Maud's young man, are you?"

"No, I'm not."

"That's what I thought. Not Maud's young man. Pity."

"Why do you say that, Miss Manciple?"

Aunt Dora sniffed, but did not answer directly. "My memory isn't quite what it was," she said. "They told me you were coming, but the reason for your visit escapes me. Are you one of Claud's scientific gentlemen?"

"No. I'm…"

"I have it. One of Edwin's missionaries. Of course. How is Bugolaland these days? Haven't been there for years. Horrible country."

"But I'm…"

"I went out there to keep house for Edwin, you know. Before he married. That must be—let me see—forty-five years ago. We had a bungalow on the banks of the Bobamba River, swamplands not unlike Fenshire in many ways, except for the crocodiles—the people are a different color…more attractive, to my mind, don't you agree? Where's your mission station?"

"Miss Manciple, I…"

"Alimumba, I suppose. Yes, it would be. I expect you and Edwin have a lot to talk about. Ah, George…"

Henry turned to see that the tree-squatter had joined the party. Major George Manciple, still in his threadbare khaki shorts, radiated a slightly woolly bonhomie as he surveyed his assembled relatives.

"How are you today, Aunt Dora? Bearing up?" He rubbed his hands together.

"I never touch the stuff. You should know that, George," replied Miss Manciple severely.

George Manciple sighed. Raising his voice he said, "Hadn't you better get your hearing aid, Aunt Dora?"

"Lemonade is just as bad. I've enough acid in my system as it is."

"Your hearing aid!" bellowed the Major.

"I was just about to introduce you, George. There's no need to shout. This is Mr. Tibbett, one of Edwin's missionaries from Alimumba. Mr. Tibbett, my nephew George."

"I think we have met already," said Henry. He grinned at Major Manciple, who shook his head gloomily.

"When she does wear it, it whistles," the major remarked. He glanced around the room. "Have you met everyone, Tibbett? Let's see, that's my brother Edwin over by the window talking to my sister-in-law, Ramona. The fellow pouring himself a whiskey is her husband, my brother Claud. My daughter Maud—oh, there you are, my dear. Just talking about you. Get Aunt Dora wired up for lunch, will you, like a dear girl? Where's Julian?"

"I don't know," said Maud. "I've been wondering."

"Ah, well, I wouldn't worry. But we can't hold luncheon for him. I happen to know that Vi has prepared something rather special."

At that moment all further conversation became impossible. From the hall outside came the deep, booming notes of some hollow brass object being struck by a muffled implement.

The Bishop dropped his crossword and was on his feet in a trice. "Lunch!" he exclaimed, with enthusiasm.

"Lunch," said Lady Manciple to her husband, quietly removing the glass from his hand.

"Lunch, Aunt Dora!" screamed Maud to the old lady.

"Lunch. Ah, to be sure, lunch," said Major Manciple to Henry. Then he added, "My brother Edwin brought it back from Bugolaland."

"Indeed?"

"Audible for ten miles through the jungle on a clear day. Remarkable. Well, lunch..."

"Lunch, everybody," said Violet Manciple, putting her head around the door. "We won't wait for Julian..."

"Lunch, Edwin," said Sir Claud to his brother.

"I believe, Mr. Tibbett," said Aunt Dora, with the air of one imparting important news, "that luncheon is served."

"Yes," said Henry, "I had rather gathered that."

CHAPTER THREE

THE DINING ROOM was large and well-proportioned, and furnished with a handsome mahogany table and a set of graceful Hepplewhite chairs, whose seats were in need of re-upholstery. The heavy, crested silver cutlery and the occasional pieces of finely cut Waterford glass contrasted strangely with the plastic table mats and paper napkins. The dinner service was—or had been—exquisite Crown Derby, with hand-painted bouquets of flowers on gold-rimmed plates, but nearly every piece was cracked or chipped, and some items, such as the vegetable dishes, had disappeared altogether and had been replaced by others in thick, serviceable white pottery. The Manciples themselves seemed quite unaware of these anomalies. In fact, Sir Claud spent some time during the meal in congratulating his hostess on the practical and esthetic qualities of the bilious plastic mats and inquiring where they could be bought.

Henry found himself directed to the place of honor on Violet Manciple's right hand. Next to him was the Bishop, and beyond him a vacant seat for Maud. Major Manciple took the head of the table, while Sir Claud was placed opposite Henry, flanked by his wife on one hand and Aunt Dora's empty chair on the other. Another unoccupied seat presumably represented Maud's absent young man.

On the sideboard steaming dishes of delicious vegetables from the garden of the Grange were grouped, like bit-part actors in a musical comedy, around the star turn, a pair of small broiler chickens proudly enthroned on an electric plate warmer. As Major Manciple passed the side table he beamed and rubbed his hands.

"I say, Vi. Chicken, eh? A regular feast!"

"Yes." Violet Manciple sounded almost ashamed. "I was rather extravagant, I'm afraid. They're from the deep-freezing apparatus at Rigley's in Kingsmarsh. I believe they come from America."

"America, by Jove!" exclaimed the Bishop, greatly surprised. "What will they think of next! Fowls all the way from America! Fancy that!"

"I do hope they'll be nice," said Mrs. Manciple anxiously. "At least they'll be a change from salmon. Just imagine, Mr. Tibbett, Edwin and George caught no less than six large salmon last week. We were eating it for breakfast, lunch, and tea. And if it's not salmon, it's oysters from the estuary. I'm afraid we country-dwellers haven't a very varied diet."

Before Henry could marshal his thoughts in reply the door opened and Aunt Dora came in, preceded by a high-pitched whistling sound. She now wore around her neck a complicated system of electric wires and a large pendant object which resembled a transistor radio. Maud followed. She looked resigned.

"Whistling again," said Major Manciple. "I told you so."

"I can't help it, Father;' said Maud. "She won't let me fix it."

"Then for heaven's sake, switch her off," said Sir Claud. "We can't have that row all through lunch."

"Okay." Maud leaned forward and pressed a switch somewhere behind Aunt Dora's right ear. The noise ceased abruptly.

"Thank you, dear," said Mrs. Manciple. "Right, Edwin. If you would..."

Each member of the party was now standing behind his or her chair, head reverently bent forward. Henry hastened to follow suit. The Bishop cleared his throat and then pronounced a long Latin grace in a resonant voice. At the end there was a fractional pause and then a cheerful scraping of chairs and outburst of conversation as the Manciple family settled down to enjoy its lunch. The Major went to the sideboard, picked up a huge horn-handled carving knife, sharpened it on a ribbed steel, and began to dismember the puny frozen chickens with as much gusto as if they had been a baron of beef.

"Chicken, I see, Violet," said Aunt Dora. "Quite a treat."

"Water, Aunt Dora?" inquired Mrs. Manciple in a penetrating voice. Without waiting for a reply, she began pouring water into Aunt Dora's glass, which was rather larger than the others and of a distinctive design. "The last of the Head's beautiful set of Waterford glass," she explained to Henry. "We always give it to Aunt Dora. It seems only right."

"A little water, yes please, dear. There's no need to shout, you know. My hearing aid works very well." Aunt Dora patted the dead transistor on her chest complacently.

As luncheon progressed, Henry resolved not to press the subject of Raymond Mason. Far better, he decided, to leave business until afterward and to concentrate on trying to get to know these unusual but pleasant people. However, the decision was taken out of his hands, for his next-door neighbor, the Bishop, suddenly said, "You're interested in Mason, are you, Mr. Tibbett?"

"Yes, I am, sir."

"Mad as a hatter. I was telling you before lunch."

"Oh, come now, Edwin," put in Mrs. Manciple. "I don't think that's quite fair."

"My dear Violet, if you're going to maintain that his behavior was that of a sane man..."

"I do agree that he behaved very oddly that day, Edwin. But I feel sure it was just an isolated lapse."

The Bishop turned to Henry. "It was like this, Mr. Tibbett. Just over two years ago I was home from Bugolaland on leave. Came to stay here with George and Violet. They told me this fellow Mason had bought the Lodge, but of course I hadn't met him. Well, now, all I did was to ring his front doorbell and ask him perfectly civilly for the loan of half a pound of margarine, and he shouted some gibberish at me and slammed the door in my face!"

"You'd better explain about the margarine, Edwin," said Violet Manciple. "You see, Mr. Tibbett, it was August Bank Holiday Monday and all the shops were shut..."

The Bishop took up the tale. "That's right. Violet found herself short of margarine. Well, I was going to walk down past the Lodge and through the fields to the river for a dip before lunch, I remember I had already changed into my bathing suit, and I was just putting on my Wellington boots..."

"Wellington boots?" Henry did his best not to sound surprised.

"Of course. You have to cross some marshy land to get to the river by the short cut. I was just pulling on my boots when Violet came and asked me would I stop by at the Lodge and ask Mason for some margarine? I wasn't very keen, I remember. I pointed out to Violet that I already had the sunshade and my clarinet to carry..."

"Sunshade?"

"Edwin has always been liable to sunstroke," put in Violet. "That was why he found Bugolaland so trying. It was a very hot day and he had foolishly left his solar topee in London. So I insisted that he should take the little Japanese sunshade that I use in the garden. I suppose the flower design *was* rather feminine for a bishop, but one mustn't take risks with one's health, must one?"

"And the clarinet?" Henry was past surprise.

"Oh, didn't you know?" The Bishop beamed. "My great hobby is playing the clarinet. Unfortunately, I am not very expert, and Violet does not like me to practice in the house for fear of disturbing other people. In Bugolaland, of course, it was easy to get out into the jungle for practice, so long as one can avoid the buffalo, but it's more difficult to find seclusion here at home. So, as I was going down to a lonely stretch of the river, I naturally..."

"In any case," said Violet, "I gave him a string bag to carry the margarine home in."

"So I went and rang this chap's doorbell..."

"Just a minute," said Henry. "Let me get this right. You were wearing swimming trunks..."

"Oh dear me, no. I prefer the old-fashioned type of costume, with knee-length legs and short sleeves. I feel it is more becoming to my cloth and years. Naturally, I would not walk on the public highway in such attire, but across the fields..."

"An old-fashioned bathing costume," said Henry, "and Wellington boots. You were carrying a flowered Japanese sunshade, a clarinet, and a string bag. You rang Mason's doorbell. He had no idea who you were..."

"But I announced my identity at once. As soon as he opened the door, I said, 'I am the Bishop of Bugolaland, and I want half a pound of margarine...'"

"And what," Henry asked faintly, "did he say?"

"That's the whole point, my dear fellow. He looked at me in a distinctly unbalanced way for a moment and then he made a most extraordinary remark. I shall never forget it. 'And I'm a poached egg,' he said, 'and I want a piece of toast.' And with that he slammed the door and I heard the key turning in the lock. Well now, I happen to know," went on the Bishop triumphantly, "that it is a recognized delusion of the mentally deranged to fancy themselves to be poached eggs. A curious fact, but true. Is that not so, Claud?"

"I believe it has been known," replied Sir Claud. "Pass the potatoes, would you, Ramona?"

"And that wasn't the end of it," pursued Edwin. "Strange as the man's manner was, I did not want to go home empty-handed. So I made my way around to the back of the house and looked in through the window of the room which he was pleased to call his library. He was standing there, drinking what appeared to be a glass of neat whiskey. I was somewhat encumbered, of course, but I banged on the window with the sunshade and gestured to him with my clarinet. He saw me, started violently, dropped his glass on the floor, and appeared to try to climb behind the sofa. I have not seen such deranged behavior since one of my cook-boys went berserk in Alimumba in 1935. It was then that I decided that it would be positively unsafe to have to do with such a maniac, and so I made my way home—without the margarine, alas. I wanted Violet to telephone to the police or the doctor, but she was against it."

"What an extraordinary story, Edwin," remarked Lady Manciple, fixing the Bishop with her great dark eyes. "The man was clearly unbalanced."

"Out of his mind."

"Did you not notice it on other occasions, Violet?" asked Ramona.

"No, never," said Mrs. Manciple. "That's why I think it was just an isolated lapse, as I said to Edwin."

"Well, I don't know what you mean by 'never,' Violet," said the Bishop, helping himself to beans. "He was unusual, to say the least of it, the next time we met. It was in this house, if you remember, a few days later. Mason was having a drink in the drawing room with George when I came in. Once again he started violently and very nearly overturned his glass. Then George said, 'Ah, Mason, have you met my brother, the Bishop of Bugolaland?' Or words to that effect. And Mason fairly goggled at me in that same half-witted way and then said—to George, mind you, not to me, 'You mean he's really a Bishop?' And this, after he had been told my identity twice, once by George and once by myself. I can't help feeling. Violet, that you are glossing over the facts when you maintain that the man was mentally normal. Thank you, Maud, another sausage would be most welcome."

"I had clean forgotten that incident," said Major Manciple. "Yes, the explanation for all his goings-on may have been nothing more nor less than feeble-mindedness."

"It doesn't explain who shot him." Aunt Dora spoke in her usual fortissimo cracked soprano.

"It was just an accident, Aunt Dora," said Sir Claud. "You must not distress yourself by thinking about it."

"It certainly was not an accident," replied Aunt Dora with spirit. "I would remind you, Claud, that I was there and you were not. In fact, I was the only person there, so I feel entitled to my opinion. Is there a little more chicken, Violet?"

"I'm afraid there's not, Aunt Dora," said Mrs. Manciple, embarrassed. "Well, I'll clear away now. If you'd just give me a hand, Maud dear. Please don't move anybody else."

"It was most delicious, Mrs. Manciple," said Henry, surrendering his plate.

"I'm so glad. I must get some more."

"Not like the chickens we used to have from the home farm in the old days," said Aunt Dora on a slightly querulous note.

"Well, it's a change from salmon anyway." said Violet Manciple firmly, as she pushed a stack of dirty plates through the serving hatch. This was a statement which nobody could dispute.

The meal progressed through trifle to cheese, after which the company adjourned to the drawing room for coffee. The Bishop went back to his newspaper; Mrs. Manciple and Maud retired to do the washing up; and Sir Claud and his wife began to discuss their plans for bird-watching later in the afternoon. Henry took the opportunity of having a quiet word with Major Manciple.

"Of course, my dear Tibbett. I shall be only too glad—I suggest that I put my study at your disposal. Which of us would you like to talk to first? Oh, I see. Well, if you'll just allow me to finish some typing. I'll be with you inside five minutes—and I dare say you'll want to see the shooting range and so on. I'll just tell Violet—shan't be a moment." The Major hurried out.

The Bishop looked up from his paper and addressed Henry directly. "Einstein's theory under fire again in the States recently," he said.

This time Henry was determined not to be caught out. "Let's see," he said, "Einstein's theory—relativity. Again—re. Recently—lately. In the States. That's U.S., I suppose. How many letters?"

"I beg your pardon, Mr. Tibbett?" The Bishop was regarding Henry over his spectacles.

"How many letters?"

"Oh, just two."

"Two? Surely there must be more than two?"

"Not in today's *Times*. One is from a professor at some research laboratory in Alabama and the other from the editor of a scientific journal in New York. Both attacking Einstein's conclusions. It's the old story of the 1923 Mount Palomar experiments all over again. Utter rubbish, don't you agree, Claud? My brother Claud is the expert on this sort of thing, of course."

In no time the two brothers were involved in a discussion on physics and metaphysics, which soared above Henry's head; he was heartily glad when the Major returned announcing that he was now ready to put himself entirely at the Chief Inspector's disposal, and if he would come along to the study...

It was as the drawing-room door was closing behind him that Henry heard the Bishop saying to Claud in a stage whisper. "First Mason and now this fellow Tibbett. I simply mentioned those two letters to the editor of *The Times* and he answered me with the most extraordinary..." The door closed.

Major Manciple's study was, if anything, untidier and shabbier than the rest of the house, but it was also comfortable and looked lived-in. The walls were lined with what appeared to Henry to be a considerable library of fine leather-bound books, each spine embossed in gold with the same dismembered hand clutching some circular object, which Henry had noticed engraved on the table silver.

George Manciple followed Henry's gaze to the books and said, "My father's library. Or what remains of it. The Head had a magnificent collection, but we've sold a lot of it, mostly the Greek and Latin volumes. None of us are classics, more's the pity. I was sad to see the books go, but we needed the space, and…" He did not add, "and the money." But as if pursuing the same train of thought he went on. "That's the Manciple crest. A hand holding a bag of gold. A sort of pun on the name, I suppose—'manciple' is the old word for a purveyor or purchaser." He laughed shortly. "Somewhat ironic these days. Selling is more in our line now, so long as we've anything left to sell. Well, sit down, Inspector, and tell me how I can help you."

They seated themselves one on each side of the massive Victorian mahogany desk under the stern eye of a large tinted photograph of the Head. Henry had just opened his mouth to reply to Major Manciple's question, when he realized that it had been purely rhetorical. Having quickly sorted out some papers on the desk, George Manciple went on.

"I've been doing some spadework for you, since I knew you were coming. I know how precise you fellows like to be. Now I've drawn up several tabulated lists of all the people who were here yesterday, with notes on their motive, opportunity, and so forth. That's the way you like it done, isn't it? I've read about it in books."

"Well," Henry began. "the way I always like to work is…"

"We begin," the Major rolled on, quite unperturbed, "with a list of the occupants of this house as of six o'clock yesterday evening. I've a copy here for you…" He pushed a paper toward Henry. "Myself and my wife, Edwin, Claud, Ramona, Maud and Julian—that's Maud's young man—and Aunt Dora. Now, here's a second list, which I've headed 'Motive.' These are all the people with motives for killing Mason. There may be others, of course, that I don't know about. You'll see that the list reads myself, Violet, Maud, Julian, and Mason Junior."

"Mason Junior?" Henry repeated, surprised.

"The son. Did you not know that he had a son?"

"I did, as a matter of fact," said Henry. "Detective Inspector Robinson told me this morning that they had traced the fact that Mason had a grown-up son by a marriage which was dissolved many years ago. But I understood that he had never visited his father here, and that most people in the Village were unaware of his existence." He ended on a faint note of inquiry, but George Manciple did not respond.

Instead, the Major went on. "Well, I put him on the list because presumably he inherits from his father. Although until the will is read we can't be sure of that."

"And what are the motives of the other people?"

"We'll come to that later," said Major Manciple briskly. "First, I'd like you to look at the third list. This one is headed 'Opportunity.' You'll see it consists of myself, Claud, Ramona, and Aunt Dora. Everybody else has a complete alibi. If you'll just glance at this fourth list, it shows you. Violet, indoors telephoning to Rigley, the grocer; Edwin, indoors and with Violet—he had been resting in his room and was just coming downstairs into the hall where Violet was phoning when Mason was shot; Maud and Julian, together down by the river; Mason Junior, presumably nowhere near Cregwell at all. Now, I dare say that something has already suggested itself to you concerning those lists,"

"Yes," said Henry. "It occurs to me that only one name appears on both the 'Motive' and 'Opportunity' lists. Yours."

Major Manciple beamed his approval. "Quite right. Quite right. I am clearly the prime suspect, amn't I? And then, of course, there's the matter of the missing gun."

"The gun is not missing," said Henry. "It was found in the shrubbery."

"I am not referring to that gun," said the Major with a trace of impatience. "Sergeant Duckett must have told you that

I reported a gun missing some weeks ago. If he didn't, he was failing in his duty."

"Yes," said Henry, "he did."

"Well, there you are. You must make whatever you like of it."

"I shall," Henry assured him. "It was similar to the gun which shot Mason, I understand."

"That's right. I have half-a-dozen of them for my shooting practice. You shall see them later on. Or five of them. That is to say, four. The police have the one which killed Mason."

"Sergeant Duckett tells me," said Henry, "that you reported one of your service pistols missing ten days ago."

"That's right. Noticed it one morning gone from the rack."

"No idea who could have taken it?"

"Anybody. Anybody at all, my dear fellow. John Adamson had been over here the afternoon before. And Mason had been up here looking for Maud. That was the day that he and Julian—well, anyway, he was here. And Dr. Thompson had been up to see Aunt Dora. And the Vicar had called to talk to Violet about the Fête. It's no use asking me what happened to the gun. I simply noticed it was missing and reported it. I had a feeling," the Major added, with a slight twinkle, "that Duckett didn't take the matter very seriously."

Henry, who had formed the same opinion, said nothing.

Major Manciple went on, "Mind you, now, if I were guilty I might have invented this missing gun, mightn't I, just to confuse you?"

"I suppose you might."

"Well, then, I'll let you go on from there," said George Manciple kindly. He sat back in his chair. "I suggest that you start by questioning me—always remembering that my replies may not be truthful."

Henry forced himself to be stern. "This isn't a game, Major Manciple," he said. "Nor is it a crossword puzzle. A man has been killed."

Manciple looked shocked. "A crossword puzzle!" he repeated. "I never do them myself. I leave that sort of thing to Edwin and Maud. I can't think what gave you the idea that I was keen on crossword puzzles."

Henry sighed. "Forget it," he said. "Tell me about Raymond Mason and why you had such a strong motive for wanting to kill him."

"It may not sound like a very strong motive to you, Inspector," said Manciple, "but the fact is, the man was persecuting me. Trying to turn me out of my own house."

"Turn you out?"

"I can't prove it, of course, but it was obvious enough. He started off perfectly civilly, answering my advertisement about the Lodge. I thought he seemed a decent enough fellow. Helped him to get the Lodge fitted up, and so forth. Then, out of the blue, about a year ago, he came to see me and said he wanted to buy this house. Made me a very substantial offer for it in fact. When I turned him down he wouldn't take no for an answer. Just kept on putting up his offer. I told him over and over again that it wasn't a question of money. I wasn't prepared to sell at any price. Finally he turned nasty. Made insulting remarks about my not being able to afford to keep the place up and so on. We had an unpleasant scene, I'm afraid."

"If you don't mind my asking," said Henry, "why were you so adamant about not selling? If he offered you such a good price…"

"*Sell* this house? Sell *this* house?" Major Manciple bristled. "Couldn't consider it. Never would consider it. I'd starve first—and so would Violet." Seeing Henry's slightly skeptical expression he continued. "Perhaps I'd better explain. It means going back quite a bit."

"That," said Henry, "is just what I would like you to do."

CHAPTER FOUR

GEORGE MANCIPLE CONSIDERED. "Hardly know where to start. With my grandfather, I suppose, the Head's father. He was the first Manciple to come over from the Old Country. Fell on bad times, got involved in religious squabbles, had to sell up the family home in Killarney, and came to England to make his fortune. Funnily enough, he succeeded. By the time my grandfather died, he was a wealthy man; and my father inherited a very substantial estate. When I say estate I mean money, of course. No house or land. My father always had a great urge to establish a family seat here in England, but he had no possible reason for doing so. He was a bachelor, and by the time he inherited, he was already Headmaster of Kingsmarsh School, where a perfectly adequate house was provided for him."

"You say he was a bachelor when his father died?" Henry asked.

"Yes indeed. And considered a confirmed one, by most people. Like most confirmed bachelors, when he did fall, he fell hard. When he was in his late forties he went over to Ireland for his summer holiday, as usual—and came back with a bride less than half his age. A beautiful girl from a small village in

Mallow. My mother." There was a pause. Major Manciple lit his pipe. Then he pulled open a drawer in the desk and brought out a sepia-tinted photograph. He pushed it across to Henry with the diffident pride of a father exhibiting a snapshot of his firstborn.

Henry took the photograph. It showed a young woman standing self-consciously beside a large aspidistra. She was wasp-waisted and wore her fair hair piled on the top of her head. Her elaborate silk dress sported a small bustle and a low neckline filled in with a lace fichu which rose to form a choker around her slender neck. Over this fichu she wore an elaborate, sparkling necklace composed of fern-shaped fronds, which matched her earrings. She was outstandingly pretty, with a bold, almost flirtatious smile on her generous mouth. A marked contrast, Henry thought, to the austere good looks of Augustus Manciple.

George Manciple seemed to follow Henry's train of thought. He said. "A strange marriage it was in some ways, I suppose, but happy. Ideally happy, for as long as it lasted. I'm afraid the Head spoiled his wife outrageously. He delighted in buying things for her and giving her lavish presents—and since he could well afford it, where was the harm?" Manciple looked at Henry aggressively, as though the latter had criticized his father's generosity.

Henry said, "No harm at all that I can see."

"None, none at all," agreed Manciple, mollified. "Well now, first of all he bought this house for her. The Head had to live in school himself during the term time, of course, so Mother used to divide her time between here and Kingsmarsh. It's only a few miles away, as you probably know. We children lived here all the year around with a procession of nannies and housekeepers and what-have-you. In the holidays we were all here together. My father loved this house. Next to his family, it meant more to him than anything in the world.

"A couple of years after my parents married, Edwin was born. I came next, barely eighteen months later. Then there was a gap of six years before young Claud made his appearance. My mother had developed a passion for jewelry, and each new baby was the excuse for a really slap-up present from the Head. Not that he was short of pretexts when it came to buying jewels for her. Christmases and wedding anniversaries were almost as good as babies. But the really splendid pieces—the ruby and diamond parure, the three-strand matched pearl necklace, the fern-pattern diamonds you saw in the photograph—they were all birthday presents. *Our* birthdays, that is. I suppose altogether the Head must have spent more than twenty thousand pounds on jewelry. And sixty years ago that was a lot of money."

"It still is," said Henry. He was by now considerably intrigued to know what had become of these treasures. Was it possible that Major Manciple, in spite of his precarious financial situation, still refused to sell his mother's jewels on sentimental grounds? Or had they been sold long ago and the money spent?

Manciple went on. "Two years after Claud was born—when I was eight and Edwin nearly ten—there was great excitement in the family. I can remember it well. We children were packed off to stay with Aunt Dora at Bexhill for six weeks, and we were promised that when we got home we'd find a new little brother or sister waiting for us.

"I don't know what went wrong. The Head would never speak about it. All I do know is that the baby arrived prematurely, stillborn. And my mother died. My father never got over it. Before his marriage he had been rather a withdrawn man, not given to easy friendships. With marriage he had blossomed, become sociable and almost gay. When Mother died, he went right back into his shell. Worse than that, he began to distrust everybody outside his immediate family circle. It began with the doctors, whom he blamed for my mother's death. Then it spread to include his colleagues at the school, his servants at home, and eventually his friends and neighbors.

"Of course, it was a gradual process and we children were too young to be aware of it at the time. Aunt Dora sold her cottage and came to live here, to run the house. I can just remember my mother and our life when she was alive. It's a golden haze in my memory, like a long, glorious summer's afternoon. And then everything changed.

"Not that we were unhappy, don't think that. Aunt Dora couldn't have been kinder, and as for the Head—well—we idolized him, even if we were a little scared of him. And he loved us dearly. But—he tended to cut himself off more and more from the world outside this house... Which meant that we were cut off from it, too, and that's not a good thing for growing boys. As soon as we were old enough we all made our way out into the world, away from Cregwell, but we were constantly aware of it. Wherever we might go in life Cregwell was always our home.

"Now, the Head retired not long after Mother's death. I told you that he was finding it difficult to get on with his colleagues. He lived here with Aunt Dora, and as he grew older, he became more and more distrustful of outsiders. He imagined that his stockbrokers were ruining him, that the tradesmen were cheating him, that his doctor was lying to him—you know the sort of thing. In the end the only friend he had left was his solicitor, old Arthur Pringle. They'd known each other since college days. The only honest man in England, my father called Pringle."

"And then they both died in the same car smash," said Henry.

"Oh, you know about that, do you?"

"Your brother told me."

"Yes—the Head and poor old Pringle did each other in, in the end. Ironic, wasn't it? Unfortunately, I was abroad at the time; in fact, we all were. I was in the Far East with my regiment; Edwin was in Bugolaland, and Claud in New York. As soon as I heard the news I resigned my commission and hurried home."

"Resigned your commission?" Henry repeated, surprised.

"Oh, yes. That was the whole idea you see." Manciple paused. "I'd better explain. You must realize that from an early age it was clear that Edwin and Claud had inherited the Manciple brain. The Head was one of the greatest classical scholars of his day, you know. His commentaries on the later Roman poets are now considered definitive. To his sorrow, none of us followed in his academic footsteps. Edwin realized his missionary vocation while still in his teens, and Claud was messing around with chemistry sets in the nursery. However, as I said, both of them had brains. I took after my mother in mental ability—without, alas, inheriting her looks. So there was really nothing for me except to go into the Army."

Manciple spoke blandly, without a trace of self-consciousness. He was obviously stating a simple fact which had long ago been acknowledged by the whole family.

He went on. "As a matter of fact, the arrangement suited the Head very well. He was absolutely determined that one of us should make his home here at Cregwell Grange and preserve the house as a nucleus for the family. Edwin would clearly be unable to do so, and Claud had to be prepared to live wherever his work dictated. I didn't care one way or the other about the Army; it gave me an opportunity for some shooting and polo, but otherwise, quite frankly, it bored me. So I was ideally situated.

"The Head explained all this to the three of us some years before he died. He was going to leave me this place and the bulk of his money, not to mention Mother's jewelry, on condition that at his death I would chuck the Army and come to live here. The others agreed at once. Claud was already doing famously in his profession, and Edwin had no use for money in the jungle. So that was the agreement.

"Well, after Father's death the will was read, and it was all just as he had said. He named Pringle as his executor and left him some money, but as Pringle died before the Head that was automatically annulled. For the rest, one quarter of his money, as represented by stocks and shares, was to be divided equally between Edwin and Claud. The remaining three-quarters came to me together with this house and its entire contents and the strongbox containing Mother's jewelry, which was kept at the bank. All this on two conditions. First, that I should give Aunt Dora a permanent home here, and second that I should live in this house and maintain it as a center to which my brothers and their families could come at any time. The will ended: 'I charge my son George never to sell the said dwelling house, Cregwell Grange, but to pass it on to his children or to his brothers' children. I have left him ample means to maintain the property.'" The Major paused.

Henry said, "So you retired from the Army and came to live here."

"You make it sound very simple and straightforward," said George Manciple dryly. "In fact, it was nothing of the sort. After the will had been proved, we began the business of trying to sort out Father's affairs. It was a nightmare. Pringle had been the only person in his confidence, and apparently Pringle had been instructed to put as little as possible in writing. Pringle's files on the Head's affairs were full of scraps of paper with cryptic numbers and initials scribbled on them—presumably as aids to memory. But Pringle was no longer there to interpret them. In any case, my father had long since refused to take advice from anybody, but managed his own affairs—if managed is the right word. To cut a long story short—and it was a long story, Tibbett, I can assure you—when everything was sorted out we found that my father had run through the best part of his fortune in wild and hopeless speculation on the stock exchange.

"The stockbroker who transacted his business had become resigned years since to the fact that if he recommended my father to buy more of a good stock, he would immediately sell what he had of it and put the money into whatever rickety shares his broker had particularly warned him against. It was all part of his conviction that everyone was trying to cheat him. So what it all added up to was a couple of tons of virtually worthless share certificates. Not totally worthless, of course—he had had the sense to hang on to a few sound investments—but it was nothing like the fortune we had been led to expect. It was all the more of a blow because he had never seemed short of money in his lifetime.

"Well, the shares were sold; Claud and Edwin received their meager portions; and the rest was sensibly re-invested. This, together with my small Army pension, produced just enough for me to live here with my family, but nowhere near enough to maintain the place in its old style. There seemed nothing for it but to sell at least part of my mother's jewelry." Again Manciple paused.

Henry said, "A very sensible idea, I should have thought. There was nothing in the provisions of the will to stop you."

"Just what I thought. I went to the bank, got out the strong box, and took the stuff to a big jeweler in London to be valued. You can imagine my feelings when he told me that the whole lot was fake. Paste and glass. Not a real stone among the lot."

"Good heavens!" Henry was taken aback. He had certainly not expected that.

"I went back and questioned the bank manager. It seemed that over a period of ten years or more before his death the Head had been in the habit of visiting the bank at intervals and taking out the box. Naturally, he did not permit anyone to see what he took out of the box—or put into it. Once, the manager did venture to ask whether the listed contents of the box remained the same—and he had his head bitten off for his pains. I then found some unspecified receipts from a London jeweler among Father's papers. I visited the man and discovered that over the years the Head had been bringing him the items of real jewelry one by one, and having them copied in paste—all in strict secrecy of course. He must then have replaced the real piece with the fake and sold the genuine article. It explains why he was never short of money."

"Then," Henry began. "he must have known that he was leaving you nothing but worthless…"

Manciple sighed. "Oh, yes, he knew all right. I suppose he simply couldn't face telling me, poor old man. He expected to live for many years longer than he actually did, and I dare say he always hoped that one of his mad speculations would turn up trumps and restore his fortunes. As a matter of fact, before he died in the hospital he was asking for me. The doctor wrote and told me. Apparently he was not very coherent, but he was trying to tell me something. All very sad.

"I suppose you might say that in the circumstances I was not bound to keep the house, whatever the will said. In fact my lawyers advised me that there would be no obstacle to selling. But—well—I talked it over with Violet and my brothers, and we all agreed that if it were humanly possible we should carry out the Head's wishes.

"It hasn't been easy, I can assure you. I have had to sell a lot of the original land, and finally the Lodge itself; and a lot of the better pieces of furniture and pictures have gone, to say nothing of my father's library, as I told you. But we manage, you know. We manage.

"I may say, however, that I have never regretted my decision to stay on here, never for a single moment. And we're over the hump now. My daughter Maud, who has blessedly inherited the brains that by-passed me, has at last finished her expensive education and has gotten herself a good job. So things are looking up, you see.

"As far as I am concerned, I have achieved what I set out to do, what the Head charged me to do. This house is still the center of the family, the focal point, as Father wished. Maud was brought up here, and when I am gone, she and her husband will take over the place and bring their children up here. Do you understand now, Mr. Tibbett, why I turned down Mason's offer?"

"Yes," said Henry slowly. "Yes, Major Manciple, I understand. What I don't understand is why was Raymond Mason so keen to buy this house?"

Manciple shifted in his chair a shade uneasily. "I hardly like to say this, Tibbett," he said, "but the man was a social climber. As I told you, I found him pleasant enough at first, but people like John Adamson never really took to him. He tried to impress people, you see. John's told me, for instance, that if Mason spotted him coming up to the Lodge he'd quickly shove away the lurid paperback he was reading under a cushion and whip down some learned-looking tome, so that he could greet John with—'Ah, Sir John. I was just dipping into Horace,' or some such nonsense. That was just the sort of thing that annoyed John, but then he's a bit of a snob I fear. English, of course. One has to make allowances. And then the Village people—they didn't regard Mason as—as well…" Manciple cleared his throat loudly. "You know what villagers are like. Worst snobs of the lot. I suppose Mason imagined that if he owned Cregwell Grange they'd *have* to accept him as a landed gent."

"He could surely have bought a large country house anywhere in Britain," said Henry.

Manciple smiled and shook his head, "Oh, no. Dear me, no. That wouldn't have done at all. I can tell that you never knew Mason or you'd realize that the one thing he would never accept was defeat. Cregwell it was that had given him the cold shoulder, so Cregwell it was that had to be conquered. I never saw a man's mind more set on anything. It was as if the devil himself was driving him."

It seemed to Henry that the Irish brogue was growing more pronounced.

"Now, what are the big houses around here? Well, there's Kingsmarsh Hall, which has been the seat of the earls of Fenshire since the sixteenth century. Mason could hardly have bought that. There's Priorsfield House, but that includes several hundred acres of arable farming land, and Mason had no mind to be a farmer. So that leaves Cregwell Manor, John Adamson's home, and this place. Now, John's a wealthy man and certainly wouldn't dream of selling. Whereas, I—well—let's say that I looked a pretty fair bet."

"I see what you mean," said Henry.

They looked at each other and there was the suspicion of a twinkle on each side of the desk.

"So," Manciple went on, "Mr. Raymond Mason made up his mind that he would buy Cregwell Grange. And then he found that it wasn't for sale. So what did he do?"

"Proposed to your daughter," said Henry.

"No, no, no. That came later. His next move was a campaign of deliberate persecution directed against me, trying to make my life such a misery that I'd up and leave the place of my own accord."

"What sort of persecution?"

"Every sort you can think of. First of all, it was the little bit of a garage that I had Harry Simmonds build for Maud's little car. Mason tried to prove we'd no right to put up more buildings on the land. Then he found some right of way or other across the fields from the Village to the river and accused me of blocking it. Fortunately, I was able to prove that not a living soul had used it for a hundred years so that it had safely lapsed. But it was all very unpleasant. Then he started on about my range. He knew very well that shooting was my great hobby, clay-pigeon shooting. Well—not precisely clay pigeons, because they're so devilishly expensive; I've invented a device of my own I'll show you later. Anyhow, he knew how keen I was and that I had this range built in the garden. Miles away from Mason's cottage, of course, but still he had to complain—about the noise. About it being dangerous. Petitioned the Council about it. Well, of course, I had him there. I simply rang John Adamson and Arthur Fenshire, who pretty well run the Council between them, and his petition was dismissed. Still—it wasn't nice, you know.

"Then he began reporting me to Sergeant Duckett for riding my bike without lights; said my chimneys were smoking; objected to my compost heap; claimed I had no license for the new boxer pup, and her only three months old. I really can't describe what I suffered at that man's hands, Tibbett. That was why I was so prompt about reporting it to Duckett when that gun disappeared. I wouldn't have put it past Mason to take it himself and then run me in for not reporting it."

"I thought that things were better lately," said Henry.

"I don't think I'd call it better," said Manciple gloomily. "Out of the frying pan into the fire. When he found his foul schemes weren't working, he suddenly changed his tactics to something even more sinister. Became charming and affable, the good neighbor. He flattered my wife, brought her plants for the rock garden, and so on. And then it came out that he was making up to Maud. Can you imagine the bare-faced cheek of it? He actually proposed to her!"

"She's a very attractive young woman," said Henry. "I can understand any man falling in love with…"

"Falling in love be damned!" Major Manciple was vehement. "The fellow simply calculated that a suitable wife would be even more effective and much cheaper than a suitable house. And he knew that Maud would inherit this place one day. Of course Maud just laughed at him. Told him that she was unofficially engaged to Julian and that it would soon enough be official. You haven't met Julian, have you?"

"Not yet," said Henry.

"Delightful young man. Quite delightful. Anyhow, even that bit of news didn't deter Mason. He kept on pestering my daughter."

"I imagine she was quite able to deal with him," said Henry. "Miss Manciple strikes me as being extremely capable."

"That's the funny thing," said George Manciple. "I'd have said the same. But the last few days, I've had a curious feeling that—well—that she was afraid of Mason."

"Afraid?"

"Yes. You'll have to ask her about it yourself. I haven't liked to; it was all rather awkward you see. Ten days ago Julian had this great row with Mason, and threatened to—that is…"

"Threatened to do what, Major Manciple?"

"Oh, nothing. Just a figure of speech. Julian simply warned him off pretty sharply, and told him that if he came bothering Maud again, he'd…" Again Manciple stopped.

Henry grinned. "I can imagine the dialogue," he said. "Fortunately threats like that are seldom meant seriously, otherwise the murder rate would be a lot higher than it is. However, I now understand why you put Maud and her fiancé on your list of people with motives."

"Well," said Manciple, "there you are. That's how things stood."

"You put Mrs. Manciple on the 'Motive' list," said Henry. "Why?"

"Why? Why? Because she's my wife, of course. Her reasons would be the same as mine."

"I see," said Henry. "Now, will you tell me exactly what happened yesterday? From your point of view."

"Very little to tell. I'd invited the family for the weekend to meet Julian, before we put it in *The Times* and made it official. Edwin arrived on Thursday and spent nearly the whole of Friday down on the estuary in a punt, fishing."

"And playing his clarinet?"

"That's right. I wonder Mason didn't complain about *that*. I spent yesterday afternoon in the garden, doing some weeding, and I saw Edwin come back from the river about five. He had his clarinet with him and he had caught a fine salmon trout. It was a pity he put the clarinet in the creel and the fish in the music case, but Violet thinks she can save it. He said he was going to his room to have a kip, or ky-eep, as they say in Bugolaland, and he went indoors.

"Claud and Ramona arrived from Bradwood on the 3:45. The local taxi brought them up from Cregwell Halt. When they had unpacked—about half-past four, it must have been—they came out into the garden and said they were going to potter about a bit. Ramona said something about making friends with the trees, which I didn't quite follow. That's why I put them on the 'Opportunity' list, y'see. They were in the garden.

"Well, around half-past five I heard the roar of that great, ugly car of Mason's coming up the drive. I had no desire to speak to the fellow, so I grabbed a gun from the cloakroom and went off down to the range as fast as I could. I met Maud and Julian, who were walking up from the river, 'I wouldn't go back to the house just yet,' I told them. 'You-know-who has just arrived in his Mercedes.'

"Maud went quite pale, poor child, but Julian was very angry. 'I'll go and see him off the premises,' he said. 'No, darling,' said Maud. 'Be sensible. Let's go down to the river again and keep clear until he's gone.' Well, Julian was raring for a fight, but Maud persuaded him in the end and they went off down to the river again.

"I carried on around to the range and had a bit of target practice. I was keeping an ear cocked to hear the car leaving, and sure enough, about an hour or so later the engine started up. 'Fine,' thought I. 'Capital. Now I can go into my own house and have a quiet bottle of stout without interruption.'"

"Did you hear Mason's engine cut out again?" Henry asked.

"Can't say that I did—consciously. The noise stopped, but I assumed that he'd driven off down the drive. Then I heard a shot. I was very surprised. I had my own gun with me and nobody is allowed to fire outside of the target range. I was afraid there might have been an accident, so I took the quickest way back to the front of the house. That is to say, I came through the shrubbery and out into the drive. There I saw the car standing with its hood open. And Mason, lying on the ground beside it."

"You didn't see anybody else?"

"Only Aunt Dora. She was coming across the drive from the house waving some of those damned pamphlets of hers, if you'll forgive my French, and shouting out 'Mr. Mason! Mr. Mason!' I don't suppose she realized at all what had happened. Then Violet and Edwin came running out of the house.

"'What's happened?' Violet said. 'Mason's been shot, by the look of it,' said I. 'Oh, George,' she said, 'what have you done?' 'Don't be a fool, Vi,' I said. 'I haven't done anything. Go and phone Dr. Thompson.' And so she did."

Henry had been taking notes unobtrusively while Manciple spoke. Now, in silence, he finished a scribbled page and drew a firm line across the bottom.

"How much of that did you believe?" asked Major Manciple. "What I mean is—did it sound convincing at all?"

"You surely don't imagine that I'd tell you, do you?" said Henry. He looked at his watch. "It's getting late. Let's go and take a look at this famous shooting range of yours."

CHAPTER FIVE

AS THEY CROSSED the hall Major Manciple said, "Are you a marksman yourself?" And before Henry could reply, added, "Of course you are. Silly of me. Part of your training. We'll take a couple of guns with us."

He disappeared through a massive oaken door and came back a few moments later carrying two pistols. He handed one to Henry.

"I look forward," said George Manciple, "to showing you my little invention. I flatter myself that it is quite ingenious, a fair substitute for a bird in flight. The local tennis club are very cooperative, you understand."

Henry, who did not understand, said, "I suppose you get a lot of shooting around here?"

"Certainly. I usually spend at least an hour a day on the range."

"Game, I mean. Pheasant and..."

"Game?" Manciple sounded deeply shocked. "Certainly not. I strongly disapprove of blood sports—except fishing, which doesn't count. I can assure you, sir, that no bird or beast is hunted or shot on my lands. If you want to kill or mutilate living creatures for sport you have come to the wrong place.

You should go to a barbarian like John Adamson for that sort of thing." The Major had gone very red and was breathing hard.

"I'm very sorry, Major Manciple," said Henry. "I didn't mean to upset you. As a matter of fact, I'm against blood sports myself. It was just the fact that you are so keen on shooting..."

"That's all right, Tibbett," said the Major, mollified. "This way. Down the steps and through the shrubbery. Perhaps I should explain. When I was in the Army I went through a crisis of conscience. The only part of my profession which I really enjoyed, and at which I excelled, was sniping, sharp-shooting. Whatever you like to call it. And then, one day, I was having a bit of target practice in the garden of the mess with a friend of mine, when he suddenly said, 'There she goes! Watch this, Manciple!' And he aimed up into the trees at the end of the compound, and shot a monkey. Have you ever shot a monkey, Tibbett?"

"No, I haven't," said Henry.

"They cry, like babies. They..." The Major cleared his throat. "It doesn't matter. Only, from that moment on I knew I would never raise a gun in anger against a living creature. A fine frame of mind for a soldier, you'll agree. That was why I was so delighted to be able to resign my commission; and ever since, I have greatly enjoyed using my lethal skill in an entirely harmless manner."

"I wonder," said Henry, "whether you are trying to convince me that you would never have shot Raymond Mason."

The Major looked at him sidelong, and then laughed hugely, "Perhaps I am," he agreed with great good humor. "Perhaps I am. Here we are."

The shooting range was a bleak place. It was, in fact, no more than a bare tract of land which ran slightly downhill away from the east wall of the house. At the far end was a twenty-foot-high concrete wall pitted with the scars of many shots. In front of the wall stood four mysterious-looking boxes, spaced at intervals of several feet from each other and connected one to the other with what looked like string.

The Major said, "You'll take a couple of shots?"

"No, thank you," said Henry. "I'll just watch you, if I may."

"Just as you wish; just as you wish. In that case, keep well back, near the wall of the house. That's right. Now..."

Major Manciple walked up to the row of boxes and knelt down beside the left one. Henry, to his surprise, saw him pull a cigarette lighter out of his pocket and ignite the string. Then the Major stood up and strolled back to where Henry was standing.

"Fuse," he explained shortly. He then took his stance, pistol cocked and ready.

"But what...?"

"Quiet, if you please!"

Henry became quiet. He was straining his eyes, fascinated, to see how the fuse was burning gradually nearer and nearer to the wooden box. Suddenly, with no noise and no warning, a sort of silent explosion took place. The box sprang open, and out of it, like a jack-in-the-box, a small circular object flew upward and outward. At the same moment, the Major fired; and with the sound of the shot the small flying object appeared to explode in mid-air. Henry had no time to comment before the second box behaved in a similar manner. Another shot rang out, but this time the flying object continued unharmed on its upward trajectory, hung poised for a moment, and then fell to the ground.

The Major had just time to say, "Missed, dammit!" before the third and fourth jack-in-the-boxes leaped out. Two brisk shots dispatched these in rapid succession.

The Major turned to Henry. "Three out of four," he said. "Not too bad, I suppose, but I'd liked to have shown you a full hand. Never mind. I'll go and set up a fresh lot."

Henry followed Manciple to the wall at the far end of the range. The one object which had escaped the deadly revolver fire was lying like a gray rat in the scrubby grass. Henry approached it with a certain amount of trepidation, and then he saw that it was a very old, very worn tennis ball.

The Major picked it up. "The local tennis club gives them to me for nothing, as I was telling you," he said. "Past playing with, you see, but still very resilient. Just the job for the Manciple traps."

"How on earth do they work?" Henry asked,

"Perfectly simple. I make them myself. Stout wooden box, lid secured with string. Inside the box, powerful metal spring with tennis ball on top. Fuse burns slowly toward string—giving me time to get back to my gun, y'see, when I'm on my own. Once the fuse burns as far as the string, box flies open, spring throws ball out. Meanwhile, fuse burns on to second box, and so on. What d'you think of it, eh?"

"It's amazing," said Henry faintly. "I thought you said you hadn't inherited the Manciple brain."

The Major looked pleased, but he said, "Brains are one thing, ingenuity's another. Take Claud. He couldn't invent a thing like this; no good with his hands. But give him a couple of pages of mathematical formulae—that's the way it goes, you see. Yes, I flatter myself that my traps are ingenious. All the advantages of clay pigeons without the exorbitant expense. Of course, I have to take them back indoors and reset them once they're sprung, but I always keep some in readiness." He was busy clearing away the four used boxes and bringing out a further set from a dilapidated garden shed near the end of the wall.

"So this," said Henry, "is what you were doing when Mason was shot."

"Not exactly," said Manciple. "I was just setting up a new four, as a matter of fact, when I heard his car starting up and decided to go indoors. Now, if you'll stand well back, I'll try to get four out of four for you this time."

That time, indeed, four out of four tennis balls disintegrated in mid-air, and the Major smirked complacently.

"Practice makes perfect," he said, forestalling compliments.

"This range," Henry sounded hesitant. "Is it completely safe?"

"Safe? Safe? Of course it's safe." The Major's color was rising again. "Unless some lunatic turns around and fires away from the target and toward the house. That's what Mason kept on about—shots going astray. Now, I ask you, sir, is anything safe by that reckoning? A car is dangerous, if you drive it over a precipice. A window is dangerous, if you throw yourself out of it. A pillow is dangerous, if you smother yourself with it. And I'll tell you something else, Tibbett." The Major shook a bony finger in Henry's face. "Whoever killed Raymond Mason was deliberately trying to discredit my shooting range."

"What do you mean by that?"

"A clumsy attempt," said Major Manciple, "to make it look as though the man had been accidentally shot by someone firing on the range. By me, in fact."

"Can you think of anyone who would want to do such a thing?"

"Nobody. That's what is so mysterious. Except Mason himself, of course." Manciple gave a short bark of ironic laughter.

"Nevertheless," said Henry, "you mean that it would have been possible for the shot that killed Mason to have been fired from the range?"

"Possible, yes."

"But," Henry went on, "it would have meant the marksman turning around and firing away from the target, which is hardly likely, not to mention the fact that the gun was found in the shrubbery near the front door. And any shot that was fired from the range would have been quite at random. You can't see the drive at all from here because of the bushes."

"You're a sensible fellow, whatever Edwin may think," remarked the Major. "I'm glad you appreciate the point I was making."

"Yes," said Henry slowly, "yes, I think I do. Thank you for showing me the range."

"A pleasure, a pleasure. Well, we'd better be getting indoors again. I dare say you'll be wanting a word with Violet."

Henry looked at his watch. "It's nearly six," he said. "I dare say that tomorrow will be time enough…"

"Just as you wish, just as you wish." The Major cleared his throat. "I'm afraid you may not find Violet a very reliable witness. She is inclined to be emotional, especially where Maud is concerned."

"I'll make allowances for that," Henry promised.

Violet Manciple met them in the hall in a state of some agitation. "Oh, there you are! I've been looking everywhere for you, George. Mr. Tibbett, a sergeant has arrived asking for you. I've put him in the morning room. Perhaps you'd like to have a word with him. The tea's cold, I'm afraid. I made it some time ago, but I didn't want to disturb you. And the puppy's been sick. I think Ramona has been feeding her again, although I asked her not to. There's no sign of Julian, George, and Maud is getting quite worried. Oh dear, there's the telephone…"

She hurried away, and George Manciple said, "Women always make a bit of a fuss over things I'm afraid."

"All this must mean a lot of extra work for Mrs. Manciple," said Henry.

"Work?" George Manciple sounded as though he had never heard of the word. "What do you mean, work?"

"Well—cooking and washing up and extra people in the house…"

"Oh, the house. Yes, I suppose it does mean a bit more for Violet to do."

"She runs this place entirely alone, does she?"

"I suppose she does, now I come to think of it. Normally old Mrs. Rudge comes in two mornings a week, but she's off in Kingsmarsh at the moment, staying with a sick daughter. Heaven knows when we'll see her back."

"And how many servants did there used to be in the old days?"

"The old days?" A pleased smile illuminated George's face, as it always did when he contemplated the golden past. "Let me see. Cook, of course, and Jimson the butler, and a housemaid, and a parlormaid indoors. Outdoors, the Head kept two full-time gardeners and a boy. And very contented they all were. Pity they had to go, but they all got too old to carry on and frankly, Tibbett, you can't get the people these days. Not for the money one can afford to pay."

"So your wife is doing the work of four people?"

George Manciple looked surprised and not a little offended. "I don't know what you mean," he said. "It's only the house, after all. And Violet doesn't wait at table or bring around the jars of hot water to the bedrooms in the mornings, the way the house maid used to do. Work? Violet has never worked in her life. She is my wife, and I can assure you, sir, that she has never done a hand's turn for reward, which is what I understand by the word work. Goodness me, anybody would think that she was being exploited, like a Victorian factory girl." The Major paused, and breathed heavily, as though expelling an unpleasant suspicion from his mind. Then he indicated a door and said, "That's the morning room. You'll find your fellow in there."

The sergeant was apologetic for disturbing Henry, but thought that the Chief Inspector ought to know that Frank Mason, the dead man's son, had arrived in Cregwell and was demanding to see Henry at once. He was being a bit troublesome, in fact, and was making certain wild accusations and—well—quite apart from all that, the sergeant went on rapidly, and with some relief, some further technical information had come through.

The bullet which killed Mason, for instance, had definitely been fired from the gun found in the shrubbery. The Mercedes had been minutely examined, but had revealed no identifiable fingerprints other than those of Mason himself; these were particularly well-defined and fresh on the switch which operated the gas cut-off. Lastly, the sergeant wondered whether Henry needed a shorthand writer for his interviews; he presumed that the Chief Inspector *was* conducting interviews at Cregwell Grange...?

Henry grinned. "I think I've done enough here for today," he said. "I'll just make up my notes and then I'll go along to Cregwell Lodge and see young Mr. Mason. You might warn him to expect me."

"I'll see he's waiting for you, sir," said the sergeant. And added, "You're—all right, are you, sir?"

"What do you mean, all right?"

"Well," the sergeant was embarrassed, "there are some funny types around here. Not quite right in the head, if you ask me."

"Oh, really?" said Henry innocently.

"Well, I ask you, sir, I was waiting in here while Mrs. Manciple went looking for you and the Major, and a tall, skinny old gentleman comes in, very raggedly dressed but wearing a dog-collar. 'Are you a policeman?' he says. 'Yes, sir,' I says. 'Then you should get it,' he says, and then he starts some rigmarole about three-toed sloths and lazy types and wanting help. I thought he was trying to make a complaint of some sort..."

"Lazy type, the policeman," said Henry, with reprehensible relish. "You need help."

The sergeant began to look seriously alarmed. "That's what he said. And I said..."

"Three letters," said Henry. "Start with the three-toed sloth."

The sergeant had risen and was edging toward the door. "Yes—well—time I was getting along, sir..."

"D is a penny," pursued Henry relentlessly. "A penny is a copper. A copper is a policeman."

It was at this moment that the door opened behind the sergeant and Ramona Manciple said in her deep voice, "Ah, Mr. Tibbett. I have brought you some hellebore and toadflax, and you owe me sixpence. Did you know that George was up in his tree again?"

The sergeant gave a low moan and fled. Henry accepted the school exercise book with becoming gratitude. On the first page Ramona had written in a fine Italian script. "Henry

Tibbett, His Book of Wild Flowers," and underneath "… blossom by blossom the spring begins…" Henry's particular spring had been sent off to a flying start by a handful of drooping flora wrapped in blotting paper.

"It's extremely kind of you, Lady Manciple."

"Not kind at all. You owe me sixpence for the book."

Henry produced a sixpence, which Lady Manciple dropped into the pocket of her dirndl. "I hear you wish to speak to Violet," she said.

"Not until tomorrow," said Henry. "I'm going to leave you all in peace for the moment."

"Well for heaven's sake, keep her off rock plants. She becomes quite unbalanced on the subject. Was that one of your men?"

"Who was in here with me? Yes."

"An odd young man, rushing off like that. You should teach him his manners."

"I'll try, Lady Manciple," Henry promised.

Ramona saw Henry to the front door, and he was saying good-bye to her on the steps when he saw a young man walking quickly up the drive. As the newcomer passed the sycamore tree a voice bellowed, "Julian!"

The young man stopped abruptly and looked around in some bewilderment.

Ramona called out, "Up in the tree, Julian! It's George!" To Henry, she added, "That's Julian. Maud's fiancé. I'm so glad he's back. Maud was getting quite worried."

"Where've you been, Julian?" Major Manciple's disembodied voice was stern and godlike as it floated down from the treetops.

The young man hesitated. Then he said, "I had to run up to London on business, Major Manciple."

"London? London? London and back all in one day? Never heard of such a thing. Why didn't you tell Maud?"

"I—I had a reason, sir. Anyhow, I was only away for a few hours…"

"You missed chicken for lunch," came the oracular tones of the Major. He seemed to imply that this in itself was sufficient punishment for any misdemeanor, for his voice was friendlier as he added, "And a policeman."

"For lunch?"

"Yes. Fellow by the name of Tibbett. Not a bad chap, although Edwin doesn't reckon him very bright."

Henry felt that the time had come to interrupt the conversation before it became too personal. Loudly he said, "Well, good-bye for now, Lady Manciple." He walked quickly down the steps and along the few yards of drive to the sycamore tree. "Good-bye, Major Manciple," he called up into the leafy heights. Then, to the young man he said, "You must be Mr. Manning-Richards. My name is Tibbett. I'm from Scotland Yard."

"I'm delighted to meet you, sir," said Julian Manning-Richards. At these close quarters Henry was able to see that he had dark hair, a sunburned skin, deep blue eyes, and an attractive smile. He and Maud, Henry reflected, must make an extremely handsome couple.

"I suppose," Julian went on, "that you've come about this terrible business of Raymond Mason."

"Yes, I have."

"Well," Julian hesitated, "I—I'd welcome a word with you sometime, if that's possible, sir. You see, I..."

"What's that? What did you say?" Major Manciple sounded touchy. "Speak up, can't you, boy?"

"I'll be back tomorrow morning and I'll be interviewing everybody then," said Henry. He made his way quickly down the drive to his car,

"Of course," said Isobel Thompson, "they're all quite mad. Rather charming in a way, but absolutely insane. More tea, Emmy?"

"Thank you," said Emmy Tibbett. Then she laughed, and said, "Henry has a genius for getting himself mixed up with odd characters. I expect he's enjoying himself a lot."

Isobel, pouring tea, considered this remark gravely. Then she said, "The Manciples are a lot of fun, if you don't have to try to make sense of them."

"Surely they're not *really* mad?" Emmy asked. "I mean, not certifiable?"

"Good Lord, no. They're brilliant, most of them. Sir Claud is head of the Atomic Research Station at Bradwood, and Maud is positively hung around with first-class honors degrees, and Edwin is a bishop—or was, until he retired. George and Violet aren't intellectual giants, certainly, but…"

"They seem to be an enormous family," said Emmy. "Do they all live here at Cregwell Grange?"

"Oh goodness no. This is a family gathering, to vet young Julian Manning-Richards."

"To do what?"

"To approve the young man before he and Maud announce their engagement officially. It's supposed to be a secret," Isobel added a little smugly.

"I'm not sure I like the sound of that," said Emmy.

"The Manciples are eccentrics," Isobel went on. "They follow paths of logic that other people don't. At least, that's what my husband says."

"What sort of paths of logic?"

"Well—take this obsession about the house. That comes from the old man, of course. The Head, they used to call him."

"Major Manciple's father, you mean?"

"That's right. He was Headmaster of Kingsmarsh. Mad as a coot. I mean, take the way he died just as an example. He would insist on driving in the middle of the road, and so did old Pringle, his solicitor. One day the two cars met, head on. Neither would give way, and—it would be funny if it weren't tragic. They were both killed. Alec's father was the local G.P. in those days, and he was the last person to see old Manciple alive, at the hospital. Apparently, he kept rambling on about George and the house, and Alec's father noted it all down word for word, and wrote to tell George Manciple. Whereupon George promptly chucked up his commission in the Army and came to live here. I believe he and Violet would starve before they sold that ugly great house. I wouldn't have it as a gift myself. It may seem logical to them, but," Isobel Thompson shrugged her pretty shoulders.

"How well did you know Raymond Mason?" Emmy asked.

"My dear—hardly at all. He was absolutely impossible. I suppose I shouldn't say it, now that the poor man is dead, but he was so vulgar and common. That wouldn't have mattered if he hadn't always been pushing himself forward, trying to gate-crash the Village. People were extraordinarily kind to him, considering, even Sir John Adamson and the Fenshires had him to dinner once or twice; I can't think why. The only person who really seemed to like him at all was Violet Manciple, but then she's a seraph, and she doesn't seem to be aware at all of—well—of social distinctions. He used to have his nails manicured in a barber's shop," added Mrs. Thompson. It was clear that she could think of no more damning statement to make.

"Is that so awful?" Emmy was smiling.

Isobel said, "Do you remember, Emmy, when we were at school you were always sick when you ate bananas?"

"What on earth has that got to do with it?"

"Well, you used to say, 'I like bananas, but they don't like me.' That's how it was with Raymond Mason and Cregwell. He liked Cregwell, but Cregwell didn't like him. The difference was that you had the sense to steer clear of bananas, while Mason..."

"You mean that Cregwell...?"

"Spewed him out," said Isobel. "Just that. And frankly I'm not surprised."

"You don't mean," Emmy felt suddenly frightened by what she knew she must say, "you don't mean that you know who killed him?"

"No," said Isobel, "I don't. If I did, I'd tell you. But I doubt if anyone else in Cregwell would, except Violet Manciple."

"She can't possibly know," said Emmy, "or she'd have told your local police yesterday. Henry is only called in on a case like this when the local people feel that..."

"That they can't cope?" Isobel sounded amused.

"I didn't exactly mean that. But Scotland Yard has so many facilities that local forces don't have..."

"My dear Emmy," said Isobel, "your husband has been called in because our Chief Constable is well aware that this case is much too close to home to be comfortable. He's the Manciples' nearest neighbor and one of their best friends. He knew Mason as well as anybody—and disliked him more than most. It would have been altogether too tricky for him to handle it himself."

"Yes," said Emmy, "yes. I suppose it would."

"Anyway," Isobel went on, "the Village is simply seething with rumors and gossip, I can assure you." Her eyes lit up with innocent delight at the thought. "So what I propose is this: I'll keep my ear to the ground and I'll tell you *everything*. Otherwise your husband might never get to hear what people are saying. They all know who he is, you see."

"Well," Emmy hesitated. Unlike her old school friend she had a rooted dislike of gossip and abominated any form of snooping. Nevertheless, what Isobel said was perfectly true. As the local doctor's wife she was splendidly placed to pick up any whispers which were going around and they might well be useful to Henry. Emmy said, "That'll be fine, Isobel, Thank you."

"I'll enjoy it," said Isobel frankly. "Just look in any time you're passing and I'll give you the latest bulletin. As for the current situation, opinion in the General Stores this morning was unanimous that George Manciple's was the finger that pulled the trigger—although not a soul would dream of saying so to your husband. About fifty percent thought it was an accident caused by the shooting range, which they've always had their doubts about. The other half thought George had killed Mason deliberately, because of all the rows they'd been having recently. If it had been an accident, they said, Scotland Yard wouldn't be here, which seemed a pretty good argument. Of this lot I'd say nine out of ten were on George's side. So you can tell your Henry that if he decides to arrest Major Manciple, he'll be lucky to get out of Cregwell without being lynched."

"Thanks," said Emmy, "I'll tell him."

CHAPTER SIX

FRANK MASON WAS an aggressive young man with red hair, a strong jaw, and a marked Cockney accent, which he seemed to accentuate with a sort of perverse pride. He faced Henry angrily across his father's desk in Cregwell Lodge, and said, "It's no use coming the old pals act on me. I know who killed my old man and I demand justice!"

"Mr. Mason," said Henry, "I..."

"Double-barreled fancy names," said Frank Mason scornfully. "Think they can get away with murder. Plain bloody murder. Well, they can't. They've got me to reckon with."

Henry began to lose patience. "If you'd just sit down, Mr. Mason, and tell me..."

"I'll say what I damn well like. You can't stop me!"

"Sit down!" said Henry. He did not speak very loudly, but his voice carried the unmistakable mark of authority.

Mason paused, surprised. Then he sat down.

"That's better," said Henry. "Now." He took out his notebook. "Your name is Frank Mason. You are twenty-five years old and the son of the late Raymond Mason."

"That's right."

"His only child, I believe."

"As far as I know." Frank Mason seemed a little more relaxed. "The only legitimate one at any rate. My mother died ten years ago."

"And what is your profession. Mr. Mason?"

For the first time Mason smiled. "Profession? None. I'm a gentleman of leisure, Inspector."

"You mean—you do nothing?"

"I mean nothing of the sort. I read Philosophy at college, and now I'm writing a book: *The Philosophical Theory of Xenophanes Reconsidered in the Light of Dialectic Materialism.* That's just the working title. I'm spared the irksome necessity of earning a living by the fact that I own a half-share in the firm of Raymond Mason, Turf Accountants. In fact, I even go into the office once or twice a month to watch the shekels being raked in."

"Let's be accurate," said Henry. "You *used* to own a half-share in the business."

"What do you mean by that?" Frank Mason suddenly looked thoroughly rattled.

"Just," said Henry, "that since your father's death, I presume that you own the entire enterprise."

There was a long pause. Then Frank Mason said, almost to himself, "I never thought of that."

"Didn't you?" Henry sounded skeptical. It was not the sort of thing that people generally overlook, even at the moment of bereavement. "I suppose that you are the chief beneficiary under your father's will?"

Mason flushed angrily. "What are you implying?"

"I'm implying nothing. I'm asking you a question. Are you the chief beneficiary?"

"The only one, as far as I know, and you can make what you like of it."

Henry made a note. Then he said, "Perhaps you'd now tell me just what you did yesterday, say, from lunchtime onward."

"That has nothing to do with it. I came down here to tell you..."

"You'll kindly tell me what I ask."

"Now, you listen to me..."

Henry shut his notebook with a snap. "I'm sorry, Mr. Mason. I shall have to ask you to come to the police station."

"What do you mean?"

"I had hoped," said Henry, "that we could have an informal talk here. But if you persist in your attitude..."

"Oh, very well." Mason slumped down behind the desk. "If I answer your fool questions, will you listen to what I have to say?"

"Of course."

"All right then. Yesterday, I spent the morning working on my book at home. I live in London, as you probably know. Got a service flat, Victoria way. Went out to my local pub for lunch. Afterward, I looked in to the office to see how things were going. Left there about half-past three and went along to the Reading Room of the British Museum to do a bit of research. Came home, via the local, getting in about half-past seven. That was when the local police got hold of me to tell me about the old man. They'd been ringing for some time, they said. No reply, of course. I told them I'd be along at once, but they said there wasn't much point in coming down here until today. So I drove down from London this morning, and here I am. Satisfied?"

"Yes," said Henry. "Thank you. That seems quite straightforward. Now..." He sat back and looked at Mason. "What's all this about knowing who killed your father?"

"I'll tell you, in two words: Julian Manning-Richards."

"That's a very serious accusation, Mr. Mason."

"You bet your sweet life it is."

"Very well. Go on."

Mason frowned. He picked up a carved ivory paper knife from the desk and fiddled abstractedly with it, picking his words. He said, "My father and I weren't very close. I'm not pretending we were. We went our own ways. I suppose I was a disappointment to him, because he wanted me to go into the business full-time. He just couldn't understand that I preferred an academic life to making money. We disagreed about politics, too, I need hardly say. In fact, we disagreed about everything. But we agreed to disagree. We didn't fight. D'you understand that?"

"Yes," said Henry.

"We didn't see much of each other. In fact, when he came to live down here it was more or less a complete break between us. I came down to see him once, and I was pretty sickened, I can tell you. It was pathetic. Poor old Dad, swanking around trying to be Lord of the Manor and fawning like a blasted toady all over die-hard old Fascists like Adamson. I swore I wouldn't come again and I never have, until now." He paused.

Henry said. "So it's some time since you last met your father?"

"Well, no, not so long. The one point of contact we had, you see, was the office. The old firm. I've told you that I go along there every week or so and Dad used to do the same. A couple of weeks ago we happened to turn up there on the same day, and so we went out and had lunch together. We were pretty friendly so long as we didn't see too much of each other." There was another hesitation, and then Mason went on. "As a matter of fact, though, I soon began to suspect that Dad had found out from the office manager when I was expected and had deliberately engineered for us to meet in what would look like an accidental way. He hemmed and hawed all through the soup and fish, but it wasn't until the coffee and brandy that he plucked up courage to come out into the open and spill the beans."

"What beans?"

"That he was thinking of getting married again. Married! I ask you. And to some ghastly debutante half his age. This Manciple girl. I was absolutely disgusted, and I told him so. It was bad enough his having turned into a snob and a social climber, I said, without being a dirty old man into the bargain."

"That must have pleased him," said Henry drily.

Frank Mason slapped the desk with his hand. "The really bloody thing was," he said, "that I didn't seem able to get it into his thick skull that I was trying to insult him."

"No? I should have thought…"

"He would misunderstand me. He'd made up his mind, you see, that I'd be against the marriage simply because I'd see my inheritance disappearing—or at any rate, having to be shared with the little woman and any unspeakable step-brothers or sisters who might put in an appearance. He judged everybody by himself, you see. Couldn't conceive that I'd be interested in anything but the financial aspect. The more I tried to point out to him how repellent the whole idea was, the more he kept assuring me that I'd be better off, not worse. 'I'm very fond of Maud,' he kept on saying, 'but at the same time, I know which side my bread's buttered on. And yours, my boy.' It made me puke. I suppose the blasted girl's family is rolling in filthy inherited capital."

Henry made no comment. After a moment Mason continued. "Anyhow, I made my views as plain as I could, and we parted on fairly rough terms. Then, last week—Tuesday evening, it was—the old man telephoned me. First time in years he'd done such a thing. 'Well, Frank,' he said, 'it looks as though things are going to work out your way after all.' I asked him what he meant, and he said, 'I've been turned down. The lady won't have me.' 'Bloody good thing too,' I said. 'Not only that,' he went on, 'but it seems she's engaged already, to a young man by the name of Manning-Richards.' Well now, that rang a bell at once. I'd met this pustule Manning-Richards at the university; he comes from Bugolaland, as you may know, of fine old Imperialist stock, and he was over in England doing a post-graduate course of some sort. We'd had a couple of smashing old ding-dongs one way and another, and it seemed to me that if the girl was silly enough to contemplate marrying him, she was only getting what she deserved.

"Dad was very interested to hear that I knew Julian Manning-Richards. 'In that case, son,' he said, 'you'll do well to know that he threatened me with physical violence. Said that if I didn't leave Maud alone he'd see that things got unhealthy for me. Now you remember that, Frank boy. Then, if anything happens to me, you'll know who to blame.'" Frank Mason, having reached the climax of his story, sat back with an angry snort. "You see, Inspector? Do you understand now why I…?"

"Wasn't it rather odd, your father telephoning to tell you about Manning-Richards?"

For a moment Mason hesitated. Then he said, aggressively, "Seems to me it was the most sensible thing he ever did, as it turned out."

"That," said Henry, "remains to be seen. Well, thank you very much, Mr. Mason. Now, since I'm here, I wonder if I may take a look around this house?"

"You mean, you're not going to arrest Manning-Richards?"

"Not just at the moment."

Mason looked at Henry with a sneer. "Whose pocket are you in, Inspector? Who's making it worth your while to lay off the Establishment? I suppose you'll find some poor bloody working man to put the blame on…"

Henry sighed, and stood up. "I'll be back with a search warrant to look over the house," he said.

"Oh, for God's sake, look at anything you like. I'm going out for a walk. This place suffocates me."

Henry watched the spiky figure in its shabby duffle coat as it strode away through the gathering dusk of the September garden. Then he turned his attention to Cregwell Lodge.

The house had been built as a gatekeeper's lodge to Cregwell Grange in the days when the main road ran to the east rather than to the west of the big house. With the construction of the new road, around the turn of the century, the present carriage drive to Cregwell Grange had been laid out, and the Lodge left in isolation. The old driveway was completely overgrown with grass, and the splendid wrought-iron gates beside the Lodge led only to a rutted, leafy lane. Beyond the lane marshy fields stretched away toward the river.

The Lodge was small but compact, functional and more satisfying architecturally than the main house. It had been immaculately restored and redecorated by Raymond Mason. Henry, visualizing the dilapidated state in which Mason had certainly bought it, assumed that he must have spent thousands rather than hundreds of pounds to put it into its present condition.

The ground floor consisted almost entirely of the large library-drawing room, from whose bay window Henry now watched Frank Mason's retreating figure. Several small rooms had clearly been thrown together to make this imposing apartment. It was furnished in a deliberately expensive, masculine style—deep leather armchairs, a great fireplace capable of engulfing young trees in its huge maw, a deep red carpet, a vast mahogany desk with classic brass handles and an inlaid surface of red-and-gold tooled leather. On either side of the fireplace, from floor to ceiling, bookshelves were burdened with fine, leather-bound volumes, many of which bore the clenched fist of the Manciple crest in gold on their massive spines.

Henry glanced at the titles. Nearly all of them seemed to be Greek or Latin, either in the original language or in translation. Gibbon's *Decline and Fall of the Roman Empire* was there, too, together with learned commentaries on Homer, Sophocles, and Virgil by eminent Victorian authorities. These were the books that Mason had pretended to read for Sir John Adamson's benefit, but a small bookcase filled with paperbacks of the more lurid kind gave a better clue to the late householder's real literary tastes.

Henry next turned his attention to the desk. For all its massive size it had apparently served little useful purpose, for most of the drawers were empty. One contained writing paper—large sheets of deep blue, rough-edged mock-parchment with the address die-stamped in flamboyant lettering at the top right-hand corner. Another revealed a file of receipts from local tradespeople, which showed that Raymond Mason had settled every bill promptly and without wrangling. This trait, Henry reflected, which should have endeared him to the Villagers, probably did no more than confirm their suspicion that he was "not gentry." Gentry did not pay cash on the barrelhead.

The only real object of interest was a diary for the current year, and this Henry opened eagerly. It was, like everything else in the room, conspicuously opulent: large, leather-covered, and embellished with the initials R.M. in gold on the cover. Inside, each day of the year was allotted a double-page spread, and each page was divided into two sections—the left-hand marked Morning and Afternoon and the right-hand Evening and Notes. Unfortunately, Raymond Mason had neglected to make use of this acreage of paper. The entries were laconic and sparse.

A few, a very few, were written carefully and with evident pride. "Dinner with Sir John Adamson" occurred on July 16th, and "Luncheon with the Headmaster of Kingsmarsh College to discuss foundation of Mason Scholarship" had made a very special date of August 14th. And Henry could almost feel the bated breath with which Mason had written, on August 25th, "Cocktails at Kingsmarsh Hall with Lord and Lady Fenshire." The most recent of these red-letter-day entries was for September 12th, which Henry realized, with a slight sense of shock, was the day after tomorrow—Monday. It read, "Tea with Mrs. Manciple, Lady Fenshire, and the Rev. Dishforth to discuss arrangements for the Fête."

The other entries were scribbled, almost shamefacedly, it seemed to Henry. "Meeting, R.M. Ltd. Dividend agreed." "See Bellson about rt. of way. Legal position?" "Attend Council meeting."

At the beginning of the diary there were a number of pages on which the owner was invited to inscribe various data, ranging from the telephone numbers of his friends to his own size in shirts. Surprisingly, Raymond Mason had filled in these personal details meticulously.

Address: Cregwell Lodge, Cregwell
Tel. No.: Cregwell 79
Passport No.: 383714
Car. Reg. No.: BK6P82
Shoe size: 10
Collar size: 15-1/2
Blood Group: A
In case of accident, please inform:
General Manager
Raymond Mason Ltd.,
14, Dell Street, W.1

On the following pages, which provided space for names and addresses of friends, Henry found a list of the most aristocratic and/or wealthy families in the district, carefully written in Mason's writing. Some of these had been ticked off in a slightly smug way, and Henry was interested to see that the names so ticked corresponded exactly to those appearing in the carefully-noted diary entries. In fact, the list represented Mason's social aspirations, and the ticks his successes to date.

Henry sighed, and returned the diary to the desk. Then he went on with his exploration of the house. It was unrewarding. On the ground floor only a small kitchen and a cloakroom. Upstairs one large bedroom, luxuriously furnished, and one small one—spare in every sense of the word—in which Frank Mason had now established residence. The bathroom was characterized by a lot of expensive bottles containing ozone-scented after shave lotion, aromatic pine bath salts, and talcum powder perfumed, if the label was to be believed, with essence of old leather riding boots.

If Henry had been less conscientious, he might have been tempted to leave it at that. However, he had noticed the trap door in the bathroom ceiling, and realized, from his observation of the outside of the house, that there must be a sizeable attic. So, without much enthusiasm, he procured a chair, pushed up the trap door, and hauled himself up into the dim dustiness above.

At first sight the loft appeared to be much like any other loft; there were the dusty trunks and boxes, the empty cardboard cartons, the old Wellington boots, the three-legged kitchen chair. And then Henry noticed the gun. It lay on the kitchen chair, half-hidden by an old newspaper, and it looked surprisingly clean and polished among the dusty relics. It was a twin to those which Henry had seen earlier at Cregwell Grange, and around its trigger was tied a stout piece of string.

Henry pulled a clean handkerchief out of his pocket, wrapped it around the pistol, and, very gently, opened the weapon. It was not loaded. With meticulous care he then replaced it in the exact position in which he had found it. Now that he knew where Major Manciple's missing gun was, he felt it would prove more interesting to use it as bait rather than as evidence.

Downstairs there was no sign of Frank Mason. Henry pulled the front door shut behind him, heard the Yale lock click into position, and hoped for Mason's sake that he had not gone out without his key. Then he drove to the police station, and after that headed for The Viking Inn, Emmy, and a glass of beer.

The Viking was a cheerful, comfortable little inn built of the white weatherboard that was typical of the district. Henry found Emmy in their bedroom, which was small but cozy, overburdened with massive Victorian furniture but prettily tricked out in fresh, flowery chintz. Emmy was sitting at the dressing table brushing her short, dark hair energetically. She smiled at Henry in the mirror as he came in.

"Hello, darling. How did it go? Is the mystery solved?"

"I think so," said Henry.

Emmy swung around in surprise. "No. Honestly? So soon? Have you made an arrest?"

"No, no, no," said Henry.

"Then what…"

Henry sat down on the bed. "I'm sorry, love," he said. "I had no right to say that. Nothing is solved yet, and I shan't know for certain until tomorrow at the earliest, but I have a hunch… Oh well, you know I'm not allowed to say anything about anything at this stage."

"You're a beast." said Emmy. "I'm sure other men tell their wives all sorts of state secrets. I thought that telling your wife didn't count."

"Well it does," said Henry. "Now, what sort of a day did you have?"

"Oh, quite amusing. I had tea with Isobel Thompson, the doctor's wife. We were at school together, but I haven't seen her for more than twenty years,"

"And how was she?"

Emmy smiled. "Just the same. Very domestic and gossipy. She's kept her figure better than I have," she added ruefully.

Henry came over and kissed the back of her neck. "You know I adore fat women," he said. "Probably because at the age of six months I was subconsciously in love with the cook, who weighed almost two hundred pounds."

"Mind my hair, idiot," said Emmy. "Anyhow, Isobel is all set to pass on the local gossip, in case it might help you. But if you've solved the case…"

"I'd still like to hear what the Village is saying," said Henry.

Emmy passed on Isobel Thompson's assessment of opinion in Cregwell.

"Very interesting," said Henry. "So your friend is married to the son of the doctor who attended Augustus Manciple?"

"That's right. She was telling me about the old man. Is it true that the whole family is slightly deranged?"

"Not at all," said Henry. "Far from it, very far from it." He paused, and then said, "Well, let's go down to the bar and sample a bit of local opinion ourselves, not to mention the local ale."

At half-past nine the following morning, Henry was once more ringing the wrought-iron bell beside the front door of Cregwell

Grange. It turned out that his desire to interview Violet Manciple and Aunt Dora was most opportune, for the other members of the family were intending to be otherwise occupied on that fine, cold Sunday morning. Claud and Ramona, as staunch atheists and nature-worshippers, were already out on the marshes equipped with field glasses and specimen box; while George, Edwin, Maud, and Julian were proposing, as always, to attend Matins in the Village church. Aunt Dora had, with great reluctance, given up church-going several years ago and now made do by listening to the religious services on the B.B.C.

"And as for me," Violet explained to Henry with her sweet smile, "I am just too busy getting lunch to think very much about God. That is," she added quickly, with a blush, "I think about Him a great deal, but it's nearly always when I'm washing up or in the bath. I know that Edwin is rather shocked that I don't go to church. He's a little like St. Paul in some ways. I feel sure in my own mind that God understands about housework."

"I'm sure you're right, Mrs. Manciple," said Henry.

"Well now, I'll ask Maud to get Aunt Dora ready to see you. If you'd like to go into the study I'll be with you in a few minutes."

Henry had established himself behind Major Manciple's desk and had his notebooks and pencils neatly laid out in front of him when Violet Manciple came in at her usual half-run, trying to smooth her hair and remove her apron simultaneously. "Oh dear, Mr. Tibbett," she said, "this isn't very comfortable for you, I'm afraid. George said you were all right in here, but I could have cleared one of the spare bedrooms for you..."

"I'm perfectly happy here, Mrs. Manciple," said Henry. "Now, do sit down and..."

"Oh, but you need a better chair than that! Goodness me, that's George's old one that I told him to throw away last year..."

"This chair is quite all right," said Henry with a trace of desperation.

"It isn't, you know," said Violet Manciple. And at that moment, as he shifted his weight, Henry felt an ominous cracking and sagging beneath him.

"Hold on to the desk with both hands or you'll go right through," commanded Mrs. Manciple with the crispness of an experienced field commander issuing vital orders. Obediently Henry hung on, as the webbing of the chair seat disintegrated under his weight. He felt glad that his sergeant was not there.

Mrs. Manciple ducked apologetically, removed the wrecked seat by brute force from Henry's buttocks, and brought a simple but sturdy wooden chair from the kitchen as a substitute. Then she sat down meekly on the swivel chair in front of the desk and asked Henry how she could help him over this terrible business of poor Mr. Mason.

It was fortunate that Henry was not one of those policemen who rely on the trappings of officialdom to maintain their dignity. He thanked Mrs. Manciple for her help, gave her a broad and infectious grin, and then asked her what she knew about Raymond Mason.

"What I know about him?" Mrs. Manciple looked positively alarmed. "Why nothing, Mr. Tibbett. What should I know about him? He hadn't done anything wrong, had he?"

"Not that I know of," said Henry. "I simply meant, when did you first meet him, and how?"

"Why, when he answered the advertisement about the Lodge, of course. That was four years ago."

"You hadn't met him before?"

"No, no. We advertised the Lodge in *Country Life*, and Mr. Mason actually sent a telegram only a few hours after the announcement appeared, saying that he was interested and would we give him first refusal? He came down in his car that very day, took one look at the Lodge, and bought it. Sat down in that very chair you are sitting in and wrote out the check—well—no, not that very chair, of course, the one that so unfortunately broke just now. It's my opinion that it was Mr. Mason cracked it in the first place. He was a heavy man, you know. I was telling him only the other day that he should go on a high-protein diet, but he said that too much protein affected his liver, and that…" Violet Manciple broke off, looking bewildered. "Are you really interested in Mr. Mason's diet, Mr. Tibbett?"

"Not really," said Henry.

"Then what am I talking about?"

"About Mason buying the Lodge."

"Ah, that's right. Well, there's no more to tell. He wrote the check then and there, and George and I were delighted. Quite frankly, Mr. Tibbett, we needed the money badly. John Adamson was very upset, I remember. He had a friend—a Lady Something-or-other—who quite fancied the Lodge. She wouldn't have been able to pay so much, he said, but she would have been what John called the right sort of person. I've never been able to understand just what he means by that, although it's one of his favorite expressions. Do you understand it, Mr. Tibbett?"

"I presume," said Henry, as delicately as he could, "that Sir John was drawing a distinction between those who are gently bred and those who are—not."

"Gently bred?" For a moment Violet Manciple seemed baffled. Then she said, "You don't mean that John Adamson is so vulgar as to be a—a *snob*, Mr. Tibbett?"

Henry found himself becoming a little irritated. "For heaven's sake, Mrs. Manciple," he said, "you must know what I mean. You can hear the difference in the way that people speak, for instance. I imagine that Mason had a—a regional accent."

"A delightful tinge of East London," said Mrs. Manciple promptly. And she added, "Mine is South Dublin. I can detect remnants of Killarney in George's voice, even though he was born here in Cregwell. His father's influence, of course. Aunt Dora, now, is a different matter. She came originally from Killarney, like her brother, but as a young girl she went back to Cork, and…"

"Could we get back to Mr. Mason?"

"Of course, Mr. Tibbett. I'm so sorry. I'm afraid I tend to ramble off at tangents, if I'm not mixing my metaphors. The Head used to be most particular about accuracy of speech in the family, and of course when I married George I became a Manciple, and—oh dear." Violet blushed becomingly. "There I go again. Now—Mr. Mason. Well, as I was saying, he wrote a check on the spot and bought the Lodge. He had the place completely renovated, and moved in as soon as it was ready. Later on, he told us he needed extra furniture and—and so on. He gave us an extremely good price for several pieces which we—we had no further use for. For which we had no further use, I should say. The Head was always adamant that the preposition…"

"Mr. Mason, Mrs. Manciple."

"Oh yes, of course. Well—furniture, as I said, and quite a number of the Head's books, the leather-bound ones from the old library. I was glad that they hadn't left Cregwell altogether, and since none of us read Greek or Latin, it seemed…"

Henry interrupted the flow. "You were on good terms with Mr. Mason at this time?"

"Oh indeed, yes. In fact, you mustn't think that we ever quarreled, Mr. Tibbett. The trouble between George and Mr. Mason only started a year ago, when Mr. Mason made that very generous offer for this house and George was so angry. I always stand by George in public, but between ourselves it seemed to me that he was rather hard on poor Mr. Mason. After all, how was he to know that we regard this house as a sacred trust? All he did was to make an offer…"

"Which your husband refused?"

"Naturally. That was when the misunderstanding started. Mr. Mason got the impression that George was holding out for more money, and he kept raising his offer. Each time he did so George got even angrier, and refused him even more bluntly. By the time Mr. Mason had grasped the fact that we weren't prepared to sell at any price, the two of them were at dagger's edge. All quite unnecessary, it seemed to me. Then Mr. Mason started on what George called his campaign of persecution—I dare say he has told you about it."

"Yes," said Henry, "he has."

"So childish. But all the time Mr. Mason was coming to see me every so often and bringing me plants for my rock garden. He shared my fondness for alpine flowers, you see, and he was lucky enough to be able to order all sorts of rare specimens from Kew and elsewhere. He was so kind, Mr. Tibbett, bringing me cuttings and roots even when George was threatening him with solicitors' letters over the right-of-way business."

"I understand," said Henry, "that Mason wished to marry your daughter."

"Oh you've heard that, have you? Well now, Mr. Tibbett, it's all a bit of a mountain in a teacup, if you ask me. Out of a molehill, I should say. Just like the house all over again. He wanted to buy the house; he made a good offer; and he was turned down. Then he wanted to marry Maud; he made a good—that is—a perfectly honorable offer; and once again he was turned down. I think the poor man was to be pitied rather than blamed. What had he done wrong?"

"Nothing, as far as I can make out," said Henry. "But it was a bit sudden, wasn't it? His falling in love with Maud, I mean?"

"I suppose you might call it sudden, but then, he hardly knew her until recently. Before, she was at the university, and then she went to the Sorbonne for a year. It was only when she took this job at Bradwood last year and started spending weekends at home..."

"At Bradwood?"

"Yes, the Atomic Research Station."

"So Maud works for her uncle, does she?"

"In a way, yes. But there's no question of nepotism, I do assure you, Mr. Tibbett. Maud is a fully qualified physicist, and she applied for the job and got it without Claud's knowledge. He was quite dumfounded, he told us, when her name appeared on his desk as having been unanimously recommended for the job." Violet Manciple hesitated for a moment, and then added, "I don't feel *quite* so happy about Julian. Of course, I don't interfere in any way, and Maud is old enough to make up her own mind. Don't you agree, Mr. Tibbett, that if young people are not encouraged to use their initiative they will never..."

"Mrs. Manciple," said Henry, "could we please get back to Mr. Mason?"

"Oh dear, there I go again. Yes of course. Mr. Mason. Well, what else can I tell you? The poor man was very struck by Maud, even though she is so much younger than he. And he was old-fashioned enough to come to *me* to ask my permission before he proposed to her. I thought it rather charming. Naturally I told him that it was entirely for Maud to say. I believe—I don't like saying it, but one must be truthful—I believe that Maud was rather unkind to him. Laughed at him. So unmannerly. After all, Mr. Mason was paying her a great compliment, as I tried to explain to her. She seemed to find the whole thing ludicrous and a little disgusting. I think that is why she showed such a—a lack of courtesy. I'm afraid Mr. Mason was deeply hurt."

"And angry?"

"Oh no. *Julian* was furious. I suppose that is understandable, but, after all, the engagement isn't official yet, and Mr. Mason couldn't have been expected to know about it. I said all this to Maud, but young people..."

"Now," said Henry firmly, "we come to the day before yesterday in the afternoon and Mr. Mason's visit. Will you tell me exactly what happened?"

"But nothing happened, Mr. Tibbett. That's what makes it all so extraordinary."

"Was Mason expected?"

"No, no. He simply turned up in his big car, at about half-past five. I heard the car from the kitchen and I came out into the hall, just in time to see George grabbing a gun from the cloak room and making off into the garden as fast as he could. He would go to any lengths to avoid poor Mr. Mason. Claud and Ramona were in the garden, and Maud and Julian had gone for a walk, so that Aunt Dora and I were alone in the house—except for Edwin, but he was having a nap upstairs.

"I went out to meet Mr. Mason and he told me he had brought me some cuttings for my rock garden. We brought them indoors together and talked for a while about alpine plants. Then Aunt Dora came downstairs and gave Mr. Mason a great pile of pamphlets from a spiritualist society that she's very keen on. Between ourselves, I don't think he was really keen on the subject, but he was very polite, as always. It did occur to me, though, that it *might* not have been an accident that he left the pamphlets behind when he got up to leave. For that reason, I didn't say anything about them. I thought it would be more tactful, especially as Aunt Dora had gone upstairs again by then."

"What did you talk about, Mrs. Manciple? Can you remember?"

Violet Manciple wrinkled her brow. "Nothing, Mr. Tibbett. Nothing important. Mr. Mason asked me was George down on the shooting range and I said he was. Mr. Mason said, wasn't it dangerous at all, and I told him that it certainly wasn't, or I wouldn't allow it, and that anyway the Council had agreed it was safe. He changed the subject then—I expect he was a little embarrassed, since it was he that had lodged the complaint in the first place—and he asked me about Maud. Then Aunt Dora came in, and we had a conversation about the possibility of the survival of animals in psychic or astral form. It wasn't very easy, because Aunt Dora kept on whistling."

It took Henry no more than a split second to interpret this remark. "Her hearing aid, you mean?"

"That's right. George blames it all on the National Health, but I think that she just won't adjust it right. However..."

"Then your aunt went upstairs again, and Mr. Mason left. Is that correct?"

"Yes. I saw him out. He got into his car, started it up, and set off down the drive. I came back into the hall, and there was Aunt Dora coming out of the drawing room with the pamphlets. 'Mr. Mason has forgotten these,' she said, 'and he was *so* interested. I must try to catch him.' 'He's gone now, Aunt Dora,' I said, but she was at the front door by then and she called out, 'No he hasn't, dear. He's stopped the car.' And she went out and down the steps, calling to him..."

Henry, who had been making some notes, frowned and said, "How agile is your aunt, Mrs. Manciple?"

Violet looked surprised. "Well, you've met her, Mr. Tibbett. She gets about wonderfully, considering her age and her weak heart. Dr. Thompson has warned her not to..."

"What I mean is," said Henry, "that she must have nipped upstairs and then down again very fast to get back to the drawing room and find the pamphlets before Mr. Mason had gotten further than..."

Mrs. Manciple looked embarrassed, "Oh, well—there was a short interval, a few minutes..."

"What do you mean, Mrs. Manciple?"

Reluctantly, touching on a subject which was not usually mentioned, Mrs. Manciple said, "Mr. Mason asked me if he might—em—wash his hands before he left..."

Henry grinned, "I see," he said, "So Mason went into the downstairs cloakroom. Was he there long?"

"Really, Mr. Tibbett, I didn't stand outside with a stop watch. What extraordinary questions you do ask. As a matter of fact, it *did* strike me that perhaps he took a little longer than—than usual. Anyhow, when he came out I saw him to the front door, and I had gone back into the hall to telephone to Rigley's, the grocers, when Aunt Dora came down, as I told you. And then, just as Mr. Rigley had answered the phone, I heard the shot."

"And ran straight out to the drive?"

"Not immediately, I'm afraid. The shot didn't alarm me—one gets used to the sound of gunfire in this house, Mr.

Tibbett. No, it was Aunt Dora crying out which caught my attention. I rang off at once, and just then Edwin came downstairs—he'd been resting in his room, as I told you—and he said, 'Aunt Dora's raising Cain in the drive. What's up?' 'I don't know,' I said; and we both went out together."

"And what did you find?"

"Oh, it was dreadful. Poor Mr. Mason was lying on the ground in front of his car. The bonnet was still open—he'd been looking inside, it seems, to find out what made it stop. Aunt Dora was quite bewildered, poor old thing. She kept saying that he'd waved his arms and shouted. I really don't think she knew what had happened. George came up through the shrubbery almost at once, and then, of course, he took charge. Maud and Julian soon came running up, and so did Claud and Ramona. So I left them to cope with poor Mr. Mason and took Aunt Dora indoors. Ramona wanted me to give her one of those sleeping pills that she takes, to soothe her, but I told her that Dr. Thompson had most emphatically forbidden Aunt Dora to take anything of the sort because of her heart. So I made her a nice cup of tea instead. That's really all."

"Thank you, Mrs. Manciple. You've been very helpful."

"Have I?" Violet Manciple sounded surprised and almost dismayed, as if it had not been her intention to be helpful.

"Perhaps I could have a word with your aunt now, before lunch?"

"Yes, of course. I told Maud to get her settled in the drawing room for you. She'll be delighted to see you. Just keep her off psychic research, if you can, and you'll find her astonishingly lucid. Quite remarkable for her age."

CHAPTER SEVEN

AUNT DORA MANCIPLE had been carefully installed by Maud in the drawing room, a rug tucked around her plump knees and her hearing aid adjusted—despite her protests—so that it did not whistle. It was obvious that she took a very poor view of the whole proceeding.

"So there you are, young man," she began, before Henry had time to close the door behind him. "Why do we have to talk in here, eh? Why not in the study, where it's warm?"

"If you'd prefer the study, Miss Manciple," said Henry pacifically, "I'm sure that…"

"Violet said it had to be in here, and of course this is Violet's house now. Not that I have anything against Violet. She's a good girl, and she's made George a good wife, which is more than could be said of some people. All the same, it's not like the old days."

"You must have lived a great many years in this house, Miss Manciple," said Henry, feeling that Aunt Dora's ruffled feathers would have to be smoothed before any real sense could be extracted from her.

"I came to live here fifty-two years ago this month," replied the old lady promptly. "Augustus sent for me as soon as Rose died. Rose was his wife, of course. I don't suppose you knew her."

"No, I didn't," Henry admitted.

Aunt Dora's lips clamped together into a thin line. Her normally good-natured face became quite fierce. "A little hussy," she said, "a spoiled, greedy, grasping little madam—and I'm not ashamed to say it, even if the is dead. She ruined my brother, ruined him."

"Financially, do you mean?"

"In every way. Look at all that jewelry she made him buy her, with money that should have been used to provide for his family."

"Yes, but," Henry hesitated. "She couldn't take it with her, could she, Miss Manciple? I understand that it was after her death that your brother was obliged to sell..."

"That's what we're told now." Aunt Dora bridled, shook herself, and settled down into her chair like an angry hen. "Augustus was infatuated with her, of course. That was the trouble. Arthur Pringle could have told you a very different story, if he'd lived. You mark my words."

Henry did not attempt to unravel this remark. Instead, he said, "Well, that's all a long time ago now, isn't it, Miss Manciple? I'm really more interested in recent events."

"Poor Mr. Mason, you mean. I wondered when you were going to get around to him," said Miss Manciple with a note of reproach in her voice. "Well, what can I tell you?"

"If you'd just give me your account of what happened on Friday..."

"Certainly. I had my rest after luncheon and I think I must have dropped off, which is *very* unusual for me. I don't approve of sleeping in the daytime. It lowers the resistance. At all events, it must have been about half-past five when I heard the sound of the car outside."

"Were you wearing your hearing aid, Miss Manciple?"

"No, no, of course not. Cumbersome thing."

"Then how did you hear the car?"

Aunt Dora looked pityingly at Henry. "Not being hard of hearing yourself," she said, "you wouldn't understand. Certain sounds, like engines, come through perfectly clearly. The doctor says it is a question of vibrations. I am speaking now of earthly vibrations, you understand, rather than psychic vibrations,"

"Yes, yes," said Henry. "So you heard the car…"

"Quite correct. I got up and looked out of my window in time to see Mr. Mason going into the house with Violet. Now, Mr.—I fear I didn't catch your name…"

"Tibbett, Miss Manciple."

"Tibbett, Tibbett, hang him from a gibbet," said Aunt Dora.

Henry started in spite of himself. "I beg your pardon?"

"A mnemonic," explained Aunt Dora, "a device of my brother's. He insisted that a successful man—or woman, for that matter—should never forget a name, and he evolved this trick of rhyming couplets. I can assure you, Mr. Tibbett, that I shall never forget your name again. Unfortunately, I have a very poor memory for faces, so it is quite likely that I may not recognize you in the future. But your name is now indelibly inscribed in my mind. What was I saying?"

"You saw Mr. Mason going into the house," said Henry.

"Ah, yes. As I was saying—you, Mr. Tibbett, are not interested in psychic vibrations. I know this. Your aura changed color in a distinctly hostile manner when I mentioned the subject just now."

"Did it?" said Henry. "I'm sorry."

"You cannot help it," replied Miss Manciple graciously. "You are powerless to control your vibrations and emanations—at least, without a long course of meditation. Mr. Mason, on the other hand, was most interested in the science of the supernatural. His aura was blue, I need hardly tell you. I had promised to lend him some pamphlets on *Astral Manifestations of the Lower Forms of Life*—dogs, cats, and so on. He was telling me that a friend of his had once seen the astral form of an elephant. It had happened in London, curiously enough; in Bugolaland, it would not have been surprising.

It was in the early hours of the morning, when Mr. Mason's friend was returning from a celebration of some sort."

"Not a pink elephant, by any chance?" Henry asked. He was beginning to form a high estimate of Raymond Mason.

"How strange that you should say so. Yes, it appears that the animal had a distinctly rosy aura, which of course signifies an earthly rather than a spiritual astral state, but that is only to be expected from an elephant. But perhaps I am boring you?"

"Far from it," Henry assured her. "Do please go on."

"Well, as soon as I saw Mr. Mason come into the house I got up, made a somewhat sketchy toilette, collected the pamphlets, and came downstairs. I found Mr. Mason in here with Violet, and we had an interesting chat. However, I could tell that Violet was anxious to return to the subject of plants—Mr. Mason had brought her some specimens for her rock garden, you see. Now I realize that this is Violet's house, and I always take particular care never to intrude upon her friends. So I bade Mr. Mason good-by and returned to my room.

"I suppose it must have been about a quarter of an hour later that I heard the car starting, and judged that I might come downstairs again without interrupting Violet and her caller. It was then that I found the pamphlets, which Mr. Mason had forgetfully left behind. I knew how disappointed he would be not to have them, so I hurried out into the drive after him. I believe Violet was in the hall, telephoning.

"As you must know, the car had only moved a few yards. It was standing in the drive with its hood open, and Mr. Mason was peering at the motor. I called to him—I can't remember the exact words I used—and waved the pamphlets to attract his attention. I hurried down the front steps and toward the car. Mr. Mason looked up, saw me, ran out from behind the car, and began waving his arms quite wildly."

"Did he say anything?" Henry asked.

"I fear I cannot tell you. My wretched hearing aid had somehow become maladjusted, and all I could hear was a whistling sound. I am sure of one thing, however. Mr. Mason had seen something which alarmed him very much. The next thing I knew was that he had fallen to the ground beside the car."

"You heard the shot?"

"I have already told you, Mr. Tibbett, that I heard nothing except that curious whistling sound, which—ah—listen!" Miss Manciple had been fiddling with the black box hanging on her chest. Now it began to emit an ear-splitting noise such as might be made by drawing a squeaky chalk over a blackboard. "That's the noise!" she yelled, drowning the cacophony. "Do you hear it?"

"Yes, thank you," shouted Henry.

"Oh, don't you? I'll try to get it louder." She did.

"I can hear it!" Henry bellowed.

"This is the volume control, I think..."

Desperately Henry shouted at the top of his lungs, "Stop it please, Miss Manciple!"

Simultaneously two things happened. Aunt Dora switched off the hearing aid, restoring a blessed and decorous silence, and the door opened to reveal a white-faced Violet Manciple.

"Oh—Mr. Tibbett—is everything all right? I thought I heard somebody shouting..."

"Yes, Mrs. Manciple, you did," said Henry.

"Oh dear, Aunt Dora hasn't been overexcited, has she? We have to be so careful, with her heart..."

"I was demonstrating my hearing aid to Mr. Tibbett, Violet," said Aunt Dora. "However, he failed to hear it." She sounded a little smug.

"Well," Violet Manciple looked uncertainly from Henry to Dora. "If you're sure you're all right, and not too tired..."

"Pray don't worry about me, Violet," replied Miss Manciple, and added, with penetrating truth, "I think it is Mr. Tibbett who is a little fatigued."

"Well, then—I'll get back to the lunch," said Violet, and disappeared.

Henry and Aunt Dora looked at each other in silence for a moment. Then Aunt Dora said, "Of course, there's always Maud's young man."

"What about him?"

"I find him very hard to remember. The face is unfamiliar. Manning-Richards, canning pilchards. Not very good, I'm afraid, but it serves. You have met Maud's young man?"

"Once," said Henry, "for a moment."

"I knew a Humphrey Manning-Richards at one time," said Miss Manciple. She said it slowly, in a wondering voice, as if she had just made a discovery of some importance. Henry, looking up, was surprised to see a tear creeping from the corner of one bright brown eye. Aunt Dora was evidently equally surprised. She flicked the tear angrily away, and added, gruffly, "You had better speak to Edwin about all that." And then she went on, "I *am* a little tired, Mr. Tibbett. Violet is quite right. My heart is not as sound as it was. Perhaps…?"

"Certainly, Miss Manciple." Henry was on his feet in a moment.

"If you'd just help me up—drat this rug—oh, excuse me, Mr. Tibbett; we were used to plain speaking in the jungle, I'm afraid. No, no, that's quite all right, I can manage—if you'd just open the door for me. Thank you so much…"

As he held the door open Henry said, "Miss Manciple, about Mr. Manning-Richards…"

"It has been a pleasure, Mr. Tibbett," said Miss Manciple very firmly. And with that, she touched the switch on her hearing aid and passed from the room enveloped in a cone of high treble sound.

It was a minute or so later that Violet Manciple came back into the drawing room. Henry explained that Miss Manciple had felt a little tired and had gone to her room.

"I heard her," said Violet, giving Henry a curious look. "Oh, by the way, Mr. Tibbett, Julian is most anxious to speak to you when he gets back from church."

"Certainly, I'll be delighted to see him this afternoon. And the Bishop. if I may."

"Edwin? I can't think that Edwin will be able to help you, Mr. Tibbett."

"You never know," said Henry.

"Very seldom, I'm afraid," Violet Manciple agreed seriously. And she added, "You'll stay to lunch, won't you?"

"It's very kind of you, Mrs. Manciple, but I think not. They're expecting me at The Viking, and I want to call in at the police station. I'll be back about half-past two, if that suits you."

Half-past two. The Bishop arrived in the study in great form. He was carrying his clarinet, but otherwise looked remarkably episcopal in the dark suit which he had worn to church in the morning. He seemed surprised when Henry mentioned Julian Manning-Richards.

"Julian? Julian? What about Julian? Charming boy. Son of old friends of ours from Bugolaland. Grandson of Aunt Dora's beau. What makes you so interested in Julian?"

"I believe he was on bad terms with Raymond Mason."

The Bishop snorted slightly. "The man was mentally defective," he said. "The more mature of us were able to view the man's aberrations with Christian charity, but when a high-spirited young man like Julian hears that his fiancée is being pestered by a man who imagines himself to be a poached egg—and twice her age at that…"

With some difficulty Henry guided the conversation back to the Manning-Richards family. Soon, Edwin had settled down comfortably into a mood of reminiscence.

"Humphrey Manning-Richards," he said, "was a district commissioner in Bugolaland when I first went out there as a young man. Mind if I smoke?" Henry nodded his assent, and the Bishop brought out a tattered oilskin tobacco pouch and began to fill his pipe with leisurely enjoyment. "Yes, he was quite a chap. Big-game hunter, handsome, cricket blue—Oxford, of course—quite fearless, and delightfully modest with it—the best type of English man. A lot older than I, of course. He was married to a charming woman, and they had a son."

"Julian?"

"No, no. Tony. Julian's father. About fifteen, Tony was, when I first went out to Bugolaland. It was a couple of years later that the tragedy happened. Mrs. Manning-Richards came down with a fever. Dead in a matter of days. Aunt Dora had come out by then to keep house for me, and naturally she did what she could for poor Humphrey and the boy. In fact, between ourselves, it seemed only a question of leaving a decent interval after the wife's death, before... Very suitable, in every way. Both of them in their late forties, a motherless boy to care for, and I was by that time engaged to my future wife, and to tell the truth I was a little worried about Aunt Dora's future. But," Edwin sighed, "it was not to be."

There was a pause and Henry said tentatively, "Another tragedy?"

"If you like to call it so," said the Bishop. "Humphrey Manning-Richards went on home leave. I personally am convinced that he would have proposed to Dora the day before his boat sailed, had it not been for the fact that the rains broke early that year and put an end to the farewell picnic which I had organized for him. At any rate, be that as it may, Manning-Richards sailed for home without—er—speaking to Dora. And the next thing we heard was that he had married a young person from the chorus of a musical comedy, which was currently playing in London. A foreigner, into the bargain. Serbo-Croat or Yugo-Slav"—the Bishop pronounced it Juggo—"or one of those Balkan countries which were changing their names so rapidly at that time. Magda, her name was."

Edwin paused again, and then snorted. "Magda Manning-Richards. He brought her back to Bugolaland with him, but I fear she was not well received. Oh, she was an attractive little thing, I agree, but a good twenty years younger than he; more his son's age than his, to be truthful. I'll be frank with you, Mr. Tibbett. Nobody liked Magda Manning-Richards, and few people took any trouble to conceal the fact. We were a small European community in Alimumba at the time, and Aunt Dora was greatly loved. There was a lot of resentment, and the Manning-Richards were more or less ostracized socially. That meant a lot in those days.

"Well, to cut a long story short, Humphrey soon cottoned on to what was up, and he did the only sensible thing. He applied for a posting, and was transferred to East Bugolaland some hundreds of miles away—he and his wife and the little boy, Tony. Not so little by then either.

"We quite lost touch with the whole family. The next thing I heard was about ten years later—that Humphrey had died of a heart attack. Then Violet wrote and told me that she'd seen the announcement of Tony's marriage in *The Times*. He'd stayed on in Bugolaland and was farming there. Married a local girl, a clergyman's daughter, I believe. I thought no more about them until I read one day that Tony and his wife had both been killed in a car smash somewhere up in the eastern hills. He'd stayed in the east, very sensibly. Much better climate—almost cold in the winter. Well, it was very sad, of course, but I hadn't seen Tony since he was a schoolboy and I'd never met his wife. So that seemed to be that.

"You can imagine how surprised I was when Violet told me that Maud had met this young man called Manning-Richards at the Sorbonne in Paris. 'Bless my soul,' I remember saying, 'I wonder if he's related to the family we knew in Bugolaland?' He was, of course, Tony's son. He'd been orphaned by that car smash when he was only six, and brought up in Bugolaland by his step-grandmother until she died recently. He'd come over to Europe to finish his studies in England and Paris. And met Maud, by a strange chance." Edwin puffed at his pipe. "I can't think of anything else. Is that what you wanted to know?"

Henry smiled. "Yes and no," he said. "It's all very straightforward. I had an idea that perhaps—but obviously I was wrong."

"Wrong—wrong—and mature, at that," remarked the Bishop, knocking his pipe on a large pewter ash tray.

Henry thought quickly. Then he said, "Five letters?"

"Of course."

"Grown. Mature. Anagram of wrong."

The Bishop beamed. "I misjudged you, Tibbett," he said generously. "Well, I won't take up any more of your time. I expect you'd like to see Julian. He's been asking for you."

Maud and Julian came into the study together, hand in hand, like children.

"Well now," said Henry, "what can I do for you?"

"Julian didn't want me to come with him," said Maud, "but I was determined..."

"She thought that if we both came, you might take it more seriously, you see, sir," said Julian. "I mean, I know it sounds a bit thin..."

"Now, now, one at a time," said Henry. "Why don't you sit down for a start?"

Reluctantly, Julian released Maud's hand and ushered her into a chair, as gently as if she had been made of egg shell. Then he sat down himself, and said, "It's about Frank Mason."

"I thought it might be," said Henry.

"You mean—you know?"

"I've met young Mr. Mason," said Henry.

"I—I knew him slightly at London University."

"I gathered that much from him," said Henry. "I also gathered that you and he didn't exactly hit it off."

"That's putting it mildly," said Julian. "He was a thoroughly unpleasant type of man. Too many of them around these days, if you ask me. It's not socialism per se that I object to, it's the lack of mental discipline which contents itself with woolly theories of pie in the sky and never bothers to work out the cost."

I suppose, Henry thought, that he can't help sounding pompous. He's young, after all. Aloud, he said, "I don't quite see what all this has to do with…"

"I'll explain," said Julian. "For a start, one of the things I objected to most strongly in Mason was his attitude to his father. Taking as much money as he could from him with one hand and kicking him with the other. Sorry about the mixed metaphor, but you see what I mean. As soon as Mason had had a couple of drinks, he began to tear down his old man and all he stood for in a disgustingly hypocritical way." Julian almost choked at the memory, as though his vocal cords had become tied in knots.

"One day I couldn't stand it any longer, and I put it to him, fair and square, how he had the nerve to live on the profits from his father's business while professing the political and social ideas that he did. And I'll tell you what he said. He said that the only possible justification for a man like his father was that his ill-gotten gains should pass eventually into the hands of somebody who would use them to promote world revolution. 'Like you, I suppose?' I said, and he said, 'Precisely.' 'Which means,' I said, 'that you are looking forward eagerly to your father's death, does it?' And, believe it or not, he actually said, 'But of course, old man. I'd bump him off tomorrow if I thought I could get away with it.'"

"How very interesting," said Henry.

"I know it's true," Maud burst out, "because Julian wrote and told me, and I've still got the letter, only it's not here, it's at Bradwood; and so you see that *proves*…"

"Oh, I believe you," said Henry. He smiled. "I can almost hear young Mr. Mason saying it. So you think he murdered his father."

Julian looked a little taken aback, "I didn't mean to put it as strongly as that," he said.

There was a little pause, and then Maud said, "Go on, darling. Tell him the rest."

Julian still hesitated. "I don't know whether I…"

"If you won't, then I will," said Maud. Her small jaw was set in a determined line, and Henry was vividly reminded of the portrait of the Head which hung in the hall. She leaned forward. "Mr. Tibbett, this terrible Mason man is almost certainly going to accuse Julian of killing his father."

"Really?" Remembering his conversation with Frank Mason the previous evening, Henry was intrigued. He decided to give nothing away. "Whatever makes you think that?"

"Well, you see, when Maud turned him down—you'd heard that old Mason had the effrontery to propose to her, I suppose?"

"I'd heard," said Henry.

"Naturally, Maud refused him, but he kept on pestering her. And so I—well—I had a row with him."

"What exactly do you mean by 'pestering'?" Henry asked.

There was a vibrant silence.

Julian said, "Well—coming to see her, telephoning…"

"Miss Manciple," said Henry, "you are a very modern young woman, with a very strong personality, if I may say so. Did you really need this sort of Victorian chivalry?"

"You're laughing at me," said Maud angrily.

"Yes," said Henry. "And I shall continue to do so until you tell me what it was that *really* upset you about Raymond Mason."

The glance that the two young people exchanged was as eloquent as a page of written statement. Then Maud said, "Oh, very well. It was about Julian."

"What about Julian?"

"Well, not about Julian really. About Uncle Claud."

"Could you be a little more explicit, Miss Manciple?" Henry asked politely.

"I've applied for a job at Bradwood as Sir Claud's personal assistant," said Julian loudly. It was almost a shout of defiance. "I heard last week that I've gotten it. Is there any harm in that?"

Henry remembered something that Violet Manciple had said. "You mean," he said, "that Mason was hinting at nepotism?" There was a dead silence. Henry elaborated. "Marry the niece and make sure of the job with the uncle. Is that it?" Silence again. "Just what are your qualifications, Mr. Manning-Richards?"

This goaded Maud into angry speech. "He's got all the qualifications he needs. It's an administrative job, after all. It's not supposed to be a position for a physicist, just for an able organizer with a good knowledge of science and physics, which is exactly what Julian has. I don't see why we should all be put at a disadvantage, just because Uncle Claud happens to be the Director-General at Bradwood!"

"Nobody has made any insinuations against you, have they, Miss Manciple?" Henry asked. "I've been told that you got your job entirely on your own merit, and that Sir Claud didn't even know you had applied until..."

"It's rather a different case, sir," said Julian. He spoke stiffly. "This particular appointment—the one I hope to get—is in Sir Claud's personal gift. He chooses the chap he wants," he added, lapsing into the vernacular.

"I see," said Henry. "And this was upsetting Raymond Mason."

"It wasn't upsetting him at all," said Julian. "He was reveling in it. Using it to pursue Maud with these vile insinuations that I was only marrying her because—well—you can imagine. That was why I had that row with him."

"And threatened to kill him?"

"I did nothing of the sort. I just—well—I made it clear that it would be healthier for him to keep away from Cregwell Grange in the future."

"Oh, well," said Henry, "that gives me a very complete picture of the state of affairs as of Friday evening. I wouldn't worry too much..."

"There's more to come," said Maud ominously. "Tell him, darling."

"Yesterday morning," said Julian, "I had to go up to London, as I think you know. When I got back to Cregwell in the afternoon I called in at the Lodge."

"Why did you do that?" Henry asked.

Julian looked a little embarrassed. "I—well—I was taking the short cut back from the station, which passes the Lodge, and I saw Frank Mason's car there. I felt a bit badly about the whole thing—I mean, Mason being dead, and having had that row with him, and so on. So I thought I'd go in and make my peace, as it were, offer my condolences."

"I see. And did you?"

"I didn't get the chance. As soon as Frank saw me, he started to abuse me. It seems that his father had telephoned him and told him all about the fight we'd had, and he said," Julian swallowed, "he said that he was going to tell you that I had killed Raymond Mason."

"Which is a black lie!" Maud burst out. "How could Julian have killed him? He was with me down by the river when it happened."

"I think," said Henry, "that you've both worked yourselves up quite unnecessarily. As a matter of fact, Julian *could* have killed Raymond Mason, but I'm pretty sure he didn't. In fact, I don't think..." He checked himself, changing his mind. "I don't think," he resumed, "that there's anything more I can do here this afternoon. I'm very grateful for all you've told me; it fills in the corners of the puzzle. By the way, Mr. Manning-Richards, just why did you go to London on Saturday?"

Julian was obviously embarrassed. He went a dull red and asked if Henry insisted that he should answer the question. Henry, intrigued, said that while he couldn't compel an answer he thought that it would be wise to give one. Grudgingly, Julian then divulged his dark secret. He had been to the jewelers, he said, to buy Maud's engagement ring. It was supposed to be a secret surprise, but now—and he sheepishly brought out from his pocket a small box embellished with the insignia of one of London's most celebrated jewelers. Inside was a very beautiful but not very large diamond solitaire ring. Whereupon Maud threw her arms around Julian's neck, and Henry found no difficulty whatsoever in withdrawing unnoticed from the study.

In the hall he met Violet Manciple. "Ah, Mr. Tibbett? Is everything all right? Have you seen everybody you need to? Goodness me, I see it's five o'clock already. Won't you come into the drawing room and have a glass of sherry? George is still down at the range, but he'll be in soon. It was so kind of you to make such a fuss of Aunt Dora. She does appreciate it. She tells me that you are intensely interested in psychic phenomena, although you put up an outward resistance to it. Something to do with your aura. You should feel flattered. According to Aunt Dora, it's not everybody who has one. Now, do come and have a..."

"Really, Mrs. Manciple," said Henry, "you are most kind, but I must get back now. My wife will be waiting for me at The Viking."

"Your *wife*? Goodness me, Mr. Tibbett, I never realized you had a wife. Not in Cregwell, at any rate. Why, you must bring her to lunch tomorrow. We'd be delighted. Delighted. You must think me very rude not to have invited her sooner, but I had no idea..."

"Her visit here is quite unofficial, Mrs. Manciple," said Henry. "Unlike mine, alas."

"The working day is *over*," said Mrs. Manciple firmly. "In any case, Sunday is not a working day, is it? I quite see that you must get back to your wife now, but tomorrow, without fail. I'm afraid it will only be salmon, but at least it'll be fresh out of the river. Edwin is down there fishing at the moment..."

Henry thanked Mrs. Manciple again, and accepted the invitation for Emmy and himself. Then he added, "I wonder if I might—wash my hands before I go?"

Violet Manciple went pink. "But of course. How thoughtless of me—I should have offered. I *do* hope you haven't been—em—this way, just along here..."

The cloakroom was as large as a public bathhouse and ornamented in flowered tiles. The outer room housed, besides the washbasin and towels, the raw materials of George Manciple's patent home-made clay pigeons. Boxes of old tennis balls, wooden canisters, springs, and balls of string were everywhere. There was also a rack, set high on the wall, where the guns were kept. There were spaces for six weapons, three of which were empty.

Henry looked around with interest, and then went into the lavatory beyond. This, too, was a large apartment, with an elaborate throne enclosed in solid mahogany, standing on a raised dais at one end of it. A small amount of waning daylight filtered in through the mock-Gothic arrow-slit of a window. Henry went over and peered out of it. The thin, vertical slit was open, and Henry found himself looking out through the shrubbery and toward the front drive.

When he emerged into the hall again Henry found Violet Manciple waiting to bid him good-bye at the front door. She looked considerably taken aback when he said, "Forgive me for asking, Mrs. Manciple, but have you cleaned your downstairs lavatory lately?"

"Have I…?" Mrs. Manciple blushed violently. "You don't mean that it was…? Oh, Mr. Tibbett, I *am* so sorry…"

"It was spotless," Henry reassured her. "I just wondered when it was last cleaned."

"Yesterday morning, Mr. Tibbett. I clean it every morning, except Sundays. I have a terrible job with that cloakroom, because George will keep his shooting equipment in there. It's always full of string and boxes and I *can't* get him to keep it tidy. Only yesterday—I mean, why *should* he want to take string and fuses into the lavatory? I've asked him and asked him, but men are so thoughtless, aren't they?"

"Yes, I'm afraid we are sometimes," said Henry.

"Oh, forgive me. I didn't mean you, Mr, Tibbett. I'm afraid I say foolish things sometimes—George says I'm worse than Aunt Dora. And with all this worry about Mr. Mason…"

"I think you can stop worrying about Mason, Mrs. Manciple," said Henry. He had not meant to say as much, but Mrs. Manciple touched him with her artless anxiety.

"Stop worrying? But how can I, Mr. Tibbett? Quite apart from anything else—oh yes, I knew there was something I had to ask you. What about the Fête?"

"The Fête?"

"The Annual Church Fête and Jumble Sale. It's next Saturday, and George and I always lend the gardens for it. Well—what am I to do? Can I go ahead with the arrangements? I have a working tea party tomorrow with some of the organizers—we have to start preparing the booths quite early in the week, you see, and I just don't know what I'm going to say to everybody. If this terrible mystery isn't cleared up..."

Henry smiled reassuringly. "I think you can safely go ahead with your Fête, Mrs. Manciple. I'm pretty sure that by tomorrow there'll be no mystery left. In fact, I don't think there ever has been one."

Violet Manciple looked bewildered. "Whatever can you mean, Mr. Tibbett?"

"Just that things aren't always what they seem," said Henry cheerfully.

"I hope so," said Mrs. Manciple doubtfully. "I certainly hope so. But I can't help feeling that there is a mystery, all the same."

And here Violet Manciple was right; and so, paradoxically, was Henry Tibbett.

CHAPTER EIGHT

EMMY WAS WAITING for Henry when he got back to The Viking. She had spent the afternoon in Kingsmarsh, where she had visited the fourteenth-century abbey and the local museum. She had just arrived back in Cregwell, after a long and complicated journey by various country buses, and she pronounced herself more than ready for a beer when the bar opened at six.

"Besides," she added, "we may be able to hear what the Villagers are saying about the case."

"You haven't seen your friend Mrs. Thompson again today?" Henry asked.

"No. I thought I'd leave her in peace, as it was Sunday."

The bar was almost empty. A languid platinum blonde polished glasses lethargically behind the counter, an ancient farmer in leather gaiters sat stolidly in a corner drinking his pint with the solemnity of a celebrant of the Japanese tea ceremony, and two middle-aged men in tweeds discussed golf stances and grips in dedicated undertones. Henry bought beer for himself and for Emmy, and they sat down in the high-backed ingle seat beside the fire.

"Not much local gossip going on in here, by the look of it," said Emmy.

"Patience," said Henry, "it may yet arrive."

At that moment the outer door of the bar opened and two people came in. Henry, hidden inside the tall inglenook, said to Emmy, "New arrivals?"

"Yes." Emmy craned to look. "A small fair girl, very pretty, a nice-looking young man and a boxer puppy."

"Maud Manciple and Julian Manning-Richards by the sound of it," said Henry.

"Maud. That's the one who is hung around with first-class honors degrees, according to Isobel. She doesn't look like a bluestocking, I must say. Are you going to go and say hello?"

"I don't think so," said Henry. "They haven't seen me. Let's just sit tight and see what happens."

Nothing very spectacular happened. Julian went up to the bar and exchanged a joke with the platinum blonde, whom he addressed as Mabel. Mabel giggled, and gave him a pint of beer and a gin and tonic. He then made his way back to Maud, and they sat down on the bench which backed the one on which Henry and Emmy were sitting.

As he lowered himself onto the polished oaken bench, Julian said, "I was looking everywhere for you. What on earth made you go off down to the river on your own?"

"I was only giving Tinker her run." Maud sounded a little ill at ease. "Mother asked me to. There was no need to come after me as though I—as though I couldn't look after myself."

"I thought you didn't seem particularly pleased to see me just now," said Julian. And then, warmly, "Don't you understand, darling, I don't like the idea of you wandering around on your own with all the things that have been going on. After all, it's getting quite dark. And I don't care if you laugh at me. You're only a weak woman physically; you can't deny that. You *do* need somebody to look after you."

"Oh, I'm sorry, darling." Maud sounded contrite. "It was sweet of you to come and look for me, and I'm glad you found me." There was a little pause, and then Maud said abruptly, "I wonder if Tibbett believed you."

"He seems quite a reasonable sort of fellow," said Julian. "Better type than you'd expect, for a policeman."

Maud said. "It's so terribly unfair, the things people say. Why shouldn't you get the Bradwood job?"

"No reason," said Julian. "Nevertheless, I wish to God that Sir Claud weren't your uncle. It's bound to give ammunition to—to people who don't like me. Still, there it is and it's no good worrying about it. This business of Mason doesn't help either. Admitting the fact that I'm delighted he's out of the way..."

"Julian! You mustn't say things like that!"

"You know it's true. No good being hypocritical."

"Yes, but—if somebody heard you..."

"Oh, highly suspicious, I agree. Fortunately, however, Tibbett seems to have more sense than would appear from his outward aspect. Your mother was telling me just now that he'd given her the green light to go ahead with the Fête on Saturday. Apparently he hinted broadly that the whole business was pretty well solved, and that he wasn't taking it too seriously."

"I wish I could believe that," said Maud.

"I wonder," said Julian reflectively, "what all the others have been saying to him."

"All what others?"

"The Cregwell Grange collection of nut cases, Aunt Dora and Uncle Edwin and the rest."

"I'm not sure that I like having my family referred to as nut cases," said Maud.

Julian laughed. "Come off it, darling. You're always saying that there's not a sane sprig on your family tree."

Maud gave a little sigh, and Henry could hear the smile in her voice. "Sorry, darling. It's silly, I suppose—it's all right for one of the family to say it, but..."

"Am I not one of the family?"

"Oh yes, darling, yes. Of course you are."

"Maud," Julian's voice dropped, and the rest of the sentence was inaudible.

Emmy, who had been growing steadily more unhappy in her position of captive eavesdropper, was heartily glad when soon afterward an interruption occurred.

The bar door burst open and a young man with red hair came striding in, bringing a rushing draft of cold air with him. He approached the bar like a tornado, rubbing his hands together and shouting for beer. As ill luck would have it, he arrived at the counter at precisely the same moment as Julian Manning-Richards, who had come to order a second round of drinks. There was an electric silence as the two young men faced each other.

Then Frank Mason said to the barmaid, "Cancel that order, dear. I'm not so parched that I'd drink in *any* company."

"You can come outside and say that again, Mason," said Julian.

It sounded to Henry as though the words should have been written in a balloon-shaped space above his head. Frank Mason turned his head slowly and looked at Julian Manning-Richards. "I *beg* your pardon?" he said.

"Come outside and say that again," said Julian. He was very pale.

"I *don't* think," said Mason, "that we have been introduced." His voice was intended to be a parody of the entire Manning-Richards-Manciple complex, but it was not a very good one.

Julian slammed the empty tankard onto the counter. "Bloody coward," he said. And before Mason could answer, he wheeled around and said, "I'm afraid you'll have to wait for your beer until we get home, Maud darling. We're going now."

Maud was standing, gripping her leather jacket too tightly around her slim body with one hand and holding the puppy's leash in the other. Manning-Richards went over to her, reaching her side in one stride, and took her arm. Then he turned back to Mason, and flung out—there was no other word for it—his final taunt. "You're frightened, aren't you, Mason? Frightened of anyone your own size!"

Having thus packed a maximum number of clichés into a minimum number of seconds, he marched Maud and Tinker out of the bar and the door slammed behind them.

In the corner one of the tweed-clad men said, "It's a question of keeping your *left* arm straight, old man. You should think of it as operating in *one piece*..."

The farmer in the leather gaiters stood up slowly and went over to the bar. He said, "Same again, Mabel."

"I think," Henry said to Emmy, "that we might have the same again too, don't you?"

He stood up from the inglenook seat and walked over to the bar. Frank Mason was still standing there with a dazed expression on his face. He looked as though he had just been hit over the head with the proverbial blunt instrument.

"Two halves of bitter, please," said Henry.

"Tibbett." Mason seemed to come to life slowly, as he focused on Henry.

"That's right," said Henry.

Mason grabbed his arm. His grip was very strong. "Who is she?" he demanded.

"Who is who?"

"That girl. With Manning-Richards."

"Maud Manciple, of course. Didn't you gather that?"

"She can't be Maud Manciple."

"I assure you that she is. Why are you so surprised? Have you met her before?"

"No, of course not. I mean, yes. Half an hour ago. I was walking down by the river and she came along with her dog, and..."

"And what?"

"Nothing, damn you. Nothing at all."

"Two halves of bitter," said Mabel, appearing from the beer pumps like Venus from the waves. She smiled sweetly at Henry, and then, in a different tone, she said to Frank Mason, "Did you want a drink or didn't you then?"

"No. I don't want a drink. I don't want anything in this blood-soaked place." Mason turned on his heel and marched out of the bar.

"Charming, I'm sure," said Mabel, giving the counter an unnecessary wipe. "Do you know him then, Mr. Tibbett?"

"Only very slightly," said Henry.

Mabel sighed. "That'll be two and fourpence," she said. "Terrible business about poor Mr. Mason, wasn't it?"

"Terrible," Henry agreed.

"Poor Major Manciple. Who'd have thought that one of his guns would go off accidental like that. They won't put him in prison, will they?"

"I really have no idea," said Henry.

He picked his change off the bar, together with the two mugs, and began to make his way back to Emmy. At that moment the telephone rang somewhere in the depths of the inn, and Mabel disappeared. When she came back she approached Henry with a certain respect.

"Telephone for you, Mr. Tibbett."

"Oh, thank you, Mabel."

"It's Sir John Adamson," said Mabel almost reverently. "Sir John would like to speak to you."

The Chief Constable cleared his throat several times, causing the telephone line to crackle alarmingly, before he finally said, "Well, Tibbett. How did you get on then?"

"I've had a very interesting couple of days, Sir John," said Henry.

"I was wondering—that is—I thought you might have contacted me sooner."

"I've been very busy, I'm afraid," said Henry.

"Yes, yes, yes. Of course you have. And have you come to any—em—any conclusion?"

"Yes. As a matter of fact, I have."

"You have?" Sir John sounded positively alarmed. "You're not proposing to—to, that is, to take immediate action?"

"No, no. There are still a number of loose ends to be tied up. It'll be a day or so before I can make..."

"An arrest?"

"I wasn't going to say that, sir—a full report. That's what I'm hoping to make."

"Oh. Oh, I see. No arrest?"

"I don't think," said Henry carefully, "that it will be necessary."

"But if you know who killed Mason—I gather that you do know?"

"Oh, yes. But I don't know why."

"That's surely beside the point. If you know who killed him..."

"I'm hoping, Sir John," said Henry firmly, "that an arrest may not be necessary. I really can't say more. This is a public telephone line, you know. I shall be making my report to you very soon, tomorrow, I hope."

There was a helpless pause. Then Sir John said, "I see. Very interesting. Yes. Well. Keep in touch, won't you?"

"Of course, Sir John."

The next morning Henry got up early and drove to London. He arrived at Dell Street, Mayfair, early enough to find a parking meter for his car at a reasonable distance from the offices of Raymond Mason Ltd., Turf Accountants, before the Monday morning rush began in earnest.

The firm was established in a pretty Regency house not far from Hyde Park Corner, the only indication of its occupancy being a discreet brass plate fastened to the pilastered, white-painted doorway. Inside, a carpeted hall ended abruptly at a businesslike counter with a frosted-glass panel marked

INQUIRIES which was firmly closed. There was, however, a bell, and Henry pushed it.

There was a sound of scuffling and giggling from behind the frosted glass and then it was drawn back by a pretty blonde girl of about seventeen, who had gone pink from the effort of trying to keep a straight face. Behind her, in a large office, several other teenagers of both sexes pretended to be busy at typewriters and calculating machines. The blonde looked disappointed when she saw Henry.

"Oh," she said, "only you?"

"Were you expecting someone else?" Henry asked.

All the girls giggled, and then the blonde said, "I thought there'd be several of you with photographers and all. You are the gentleman from the *Daily Scoop*, aren't you?"

"No, I'm not."

"Oh. Then you'll be from the *Planet*."

"I'm not a journalist at all, I'm afraid," said Henry.

"Oh. Oh, well, they'll be along soon," The blonde patted her elaborate hair-do complacently.

"Will they really?" Henry asked. He was interested. The police had issued the briefest of statements about Raymond Mason's death, and he was surprised that the sensational press should be so intrigued by it. "Well, it's just as well that I got here before them. I'd like to see the general manager, please."

"Mr. Mumford isn't in yet," said the girl. "You could wait, if you like." It was apparent that her interest in Henry had reached the vanishing point.

"Yes, I will," said Henry. "Can you show me his office?"

"This way," said the blonde. "What name is it?"

"Tibbett."

The girl ushered Henry through the large outer office and into a small inner sanctum which was equipped with a haircord carpet, filing cabinets, an enormous mahogany desk, and a great many charts on the walls. It was only a minute or so later that the door opened and a small, neat man with a black mustache came bustling in. He looked exactly like the chief clerk of a respectable City firm—precise, a little fussy, painstaking, utterly reliable, and above all indomitably conventional. Not at all, Henry thought, the sort of person one would associate with the rip-roaring, slightly rakish profession of bookmaking. Then he remembered that Raymond Mason himself had been the larger-than-life character behind this enterprise. Mr, Mumford was, in fact, no more nor less than an expert accountant, running this business with the same humorless efficiency that he would have brought to the statistics of import/export or the computation of income-tax liability. The Mr. Mumfords of this world do not launch business enterprises; they administer them for other people.

As he came through the door of his office, Mumford was saying over his shoulder, "I absolutely forbid it. Is that understood, Miss Jenkins? If and when they arrive, they are to be shown the door. At once." His head came around with a jerk, and he saw Henry. "Who are you and what do you want?" he snapped.

"I am Chief Inspector Tibbett of Scotland Yard," said Henry, producing his official card. Nothing but hard facts and figures would cut any ice with Mr. Mumford. "I am investigating the death of Mr. Raymond Mason."

Mumford's attitude changed at once. "Oh, I see. Yes, inevitable, I suppose. Please sit down. Perhaps you can do something about this intolerable persecution, Inspector."

"Persecution?"

"The press. They actually telephoned to my home this morning. How they got hold of the number is beyond me. It gave my wife a very nasty shock. These people have absolutely no right to invade the privacy of the individual."

"They're only doing their job, Mr. Mumford," said Henry.

"You call that a job? Ghouls, Inspector. That's what they are. Parasites. I gave them short shrift, I can tell you. But now I hear that they've been telephoning the office, and these feather-brained young girls like Miss Jenkins and Miss Cooper—I don't like to think what will happen if they gain access to the building. You really must help me, Inspector."

"I'm afraid there's nothing I can do, Mr. Mumford, unless they actually commit a trespass or use violence..."

"Violence! I feel like using violence myself!" Mumford settled himself peevishly into his chair. "In any case, this must be your doing. You have been spreading stories about poor Mr. Mason to the press, otherwise how would they know?"

"That's a point which interests me," said Henry. "I can assure you, they've had nothing but a very curt announcement from us."

Mumford looked at Henry disbelievingly. "I have to think of the firm's reputation," he said. "This is a very high-class business, you know, Inspector. Some of the most respected and highest-placed people in the land are among our clients. I can't have them caused embarrassment."

"Sudden death is always embarrassing, Mr. Mumford," said Henry. He had considered avoiding the cliché, but decided that it was the quickest way to Mumford's comprehension. "The best we can do for you is to clear up the whole matter as soon as possible."

"There I agree with you," said Mr. Mumford. "I'll help in any way I can."

"That's very kind of you," said Henry.

"Not at all, Chief Inspector," said Mumford expansively. "I can see that we understand each other, you and I, speak the same language."

Henry winced, in spite of the fact that he had labored to create just this impression. He said aloud, "First of all, I'd be interested to know how you first heard of Mr. Mason's death."

"Why, from Mr. Frank, of course. He telephoned me at my home on Friday evening. It came as a terrible shock."

"I'm sure it did. What time did Mr. Frank Mason telephone you?"

"Let me see. It must have been just before eight in the evening. We were at the table. It quite spoiled my dinner."

"And what did he say?"

"You want his exact words?"

"If you can remember them."

"Well, now—he started off by saying, 'Is that you, Mumford?'—he makes a habit of addressing me by my surname, which I do not consider quite—well, Mr. Raymond Mason always did me the courtesy of calling me Mr. Mumford and I appreciated it. I am sure you take my point, Inspec—that is, Chief Inspector. One's name is one's name."

"Oh, indeed," said Henry. For no very good reason Aunt Dora's mnemonic was running relentless circles in his brain. Tibbett, Tibbett, hang him from a gibbet. Thank goodness, *that* particular nightmare was ended now, thanks to enlightened legislation. Nevertheless, the rhyme ran inside his head like a mouse on a treadmill. He became aware that Mumford was speaking again.

"Mr. Frank said, 'My father has been murdered, Mumford.' And I said…"

Henry was fully alert now. "You're sure he used the word murder?"

"Quite sure, Chief Inspector. I couldn't believe my ears. 'I can't believe my ears, Mr. Frank,' I said. To tell you the truth, I thought at first that he might have had—em—one over the eight, as you might say. It seemed so fantastic, 'Are you sure, Mr. Frank?' I said, and he said, 'Of course I'm sure. The Cregwell police have just telephoned me.' *'Well!'* I said, 'what a dreadful thing!' And it was, I mean, wasn't it, Chief Inspector?"

"Certainly it was," said Henry.

"'What should I do now?' I asked Mr. Frank. 'Just carry on, Mumford,' he said, 'just carry on. You run the office on your own anyway, don't you? No trouble there, I hope?' 'I really don't know what you mean by trouble, Mr. Frank,' I said. He's always been—well—a little difficult, Chief Inspector. Not the man his father was. Not in any way. Then he said a funny thing. 'Heads are going to roll, Mumford,' he said. These were his very words. 'Heads are going to roll, but it's no concern of yours. You just carry on.' 'I certainly intend to, Mr. Frank,' I said. I was considerably upset, but I trust I kept my dignity. Then he rang off." Mr. Mumford paused, and wiped his spectacles. Then he went on. "Sergeant Duckett from Cregwell police station telephoned me soon afterward. He told me that Mr. Mason had been accidentally shot. I appreciated that."

"What do you mean, appreciated it?"

"Well," Mumford coughed, "Mr. Frank had used the word murder, as you pointed out. And since you are here, Chief Inspector, I can only conclude that Mr. Mason's death was not accidental. But it seemed clear to me that the *Cregwell* police"—Mumford gave the word enough emphasis to draw a comparison between Cregwell and Scotland Yard, in the former's favor—"the *Cregwell* police were keeping any unsavory aspects of the matter out of the hands of the public. After all, anybody may have a shooting accident, especially in the country." Mumford spoke as though Fenshire lay beyond the bounds of civilization in the Great Outback. "That is why I was appalled—I do not use the word lightly, Chief Inspector—*appalled* when Miss Jenkins told me this morning..."

"Tell me about Mr. Mason," said Henry.

Mr. Mumford stopped in full spate, surprised. "About him, Chief Inspector? What about him?"

"What sort of man was he?"

"Why," Mumford was aghast at Henry's obtuseness, "why you only have to look around this office. Mr. Mason was a highly successful man. A tycoon, one might almost say."

"Yes, but what sort of man was he?"

"He was a wealthy man, Chief Inspector." Mumford's voice held a note of reproof. It was clear that he suspected Henry of *lèse-majesté*. Raymond Mason had been a rich, successful man, and Mumford's employer. There was no more to be said.

Henry changed his line of approach. "When did you last see Mr. Mason?" he asked.

"Let me see—it must have been about a week ago. He came into the office nearly every week, you see. Kept a close eye on things."

"And you noticed nothing unusual? He seemed perfectly normal?"

"Oh, perfectly, Chief Inspector, perfectly. Mind you, Mr. Mason was a—well—he was a character, if you know what I mean. Always chaffing with the girls in the office—delightful informality, and—well—unconventional." Mr. Mumford cleared his throat. Clearly, behavior which would have scandalized him in any ordinary mortal became charming eccentricity in his employer. "Of course," Mr. Mumford added rather hastily, "he moved in what I can only call elevated circles. A great number of the nobility were among his friends, you know. You'd be surprised, Chief Inspector."

"I dare say I would," said Henry. "The last time he came to the office was the time that he met his son here, was it?"

"No, no. That was on the previous occasion. He particularly asked me to let him know when Mr. Frank was coming in. That was a bit of a poser, of course. I never know when Mr. Frank may not drop in. However, by good luck Mr. Frank did telephone me the day before and I was able to inform Mr. Mason. Frankly, I was a little surprised."

"Really? Why?"

"Oh—no reason," Mr. Mumford fussed with his fountain pen and went a little pink.

"You mustn't worry about betraying confidences, Mr. Mumford," said Henry gently, "not to Scotland Yard. It is your duty as a citizen to tell us all you can."

"Now, please don't read anything sinister into my remarks, Inspector. It was just that—well—Mr. Mason and Mr. Frank generally went out of their way to avoid each other. It was an open secret that they didn't get on well together. Mr. Frank has very *modern* political views, you know."

"Yes, " said Henry. "I know. Well that seems to cover that. Perhaps you'd now show me the files of the business."

"The files? You mean, you want to inspect our accounts?"

"Not at the moment," said Henry. "I'm not a qualified accountant. I'm prepared to take your word for it. I take it that business was flourishing?"

"Indeed it was. In fact, it is." Mr. Mumford relaxed, sat back in his chair, and prepared to enjoy himself. "Our figures over the past ten years have shown a most satisfactory rise in profit rate from season to season. Thanks to efficient and careful management, together with scientifically-calculated laying-off of…"

"I'm afraid it's all rather above my head," said Henry. "Let's just take it that business was good and the bank balance healthy."

"Ah, now," said Mr. Mumford, "that's something I fear I cannot enlighten you about."

"But you just said…"

"Business is excellent," said Mr. Mumford, "and the bank balance *should* be healthy. Indeed, I have no reason to suspect that it is not. But," he hesitated, "as I've told you, Mr. Mason was unconventional. The bank was positively forbidden to divulge the exact position of the firm's account to anyone but Mr. Mason himself. I had authority to draw checks for the day-to-day running of the office—wages and so on—and to pay out winning bets, and I need hardly say that no check was ever dishonored by the bank, but…"

"But Mr. Mason didn't want even you to know what he was taking out of the business privately," said Henry.

"I wouldn't have put it like that," said Mumford stiffly.

"No, I'm sure you wouldn't," said Henry. "Well now, perhaps you'd show me the files."

"I've told you, Chief Inspector…"

"I mean, of course," Henry pursued, "the personal files of your clients. I want to know who was betting with you, and whether any of them were in serious debt to you, or…"

"Our *clients*!" Mr. Mumford spoke as though Henry had uttered some gross obscenity. "Chief Inspector, I would never under any circumstances reveal the name of a client, let alone his financial position on our books. It would be altogether…"

It took a good half-hour and a lot of throwing about of official weight before Mr. Mumford was convinced; and even then, it was with the utmost reluctance that he eventually unlocked the large green filing cabinet and allowed Henry to inspect the written record of the flutters of Raymond Mason's clients. As it turned out, they were of no interest at all. As Mr. Mumford had hinted, there were quite a few illustrious names on the register, and Henry was privately amused at the parsimony with which some of the wealthiest of them placed their bets. There was a black list of defaulters from whom bets were not to be accepted, but none of these names appeared to be in any way relevant. A few unfortunate characters appeared to be fairly deeply in debt to Raymond Mason, but again the names signified nothing, and, in any case, Henry reflected, it would do a debtor no good to remove Raymond Mason from the scene. The firm, and Mr. Mumford, went marching on.

At last he closed the final dossier and said, "Thank you, Mr. Mumford. That's the lot, is it?"

"It is, Chief Inspector. Except for Mr. Mason's personal files. of course."

"His what?"

"His personal files. Mr. Mason had a very limited number of special clients whose affairs he dealt with on a strictly personal basis."

"And where are these personal files?" Henry asked.

"In Mr. Mason's own filing box." Mr. Mumford indicated a smaller green cabinet in the corner. "And it's no use asking me to open it, Chief Inspector, because I have no key to it. Mr. Mason kept that himself." Mumford spoke with considerable satisfaction.

"In that case," said Henry, "the key is probably here. I have Mr. Mason's key ring, which was in his pocket when he died."

Mr. Mumford's jaw dropped in dismay, as Henry walked over to the holy of holies and began trying various keys from the ring which he produced from his pocket. When one of them finally fitted, and the filing cabinet opened, Henry had the impression that Mr. Mumford was piously averting his eyes from the sacrilegious act.

In fact, the contents of the cabinet were not very sensational—a couple of largish cardboard boxes and a handful of files. Henry took one of the boxes out of the cabinet.

"What's in here? he asked.

"I think," said Mumford uneasily. "that Mr. Mason liked to have a little ready cash..."

Henry lifted the lid of the box. It was full of one-pound notes tied in bundles.

The second box was heavier. Henry looked inquiringly at Mumford, who went a becoming shade of blush-rose.

"Mr. Mason was—he was compelled to entertain important clients from time to time..."

The box, unsurprisingly, contained a bottle of whiskey, about half full, and another of gin. The bottles were resting on a book, which had a luridly suggestive jacket. Henry recognized it as one which was banned from public sale in England but which "everybody" had read—or claimed to have read.

He closed the two boxes, put them back in the cabinet, and turned his attention to the files. All of them related to people of high rank and social importance, many from the Cregwell area. In fact, they corresponded pretty closely to the names which had been entered so carefully in Mason's diary. Each betting transaction was carefully entered in Mason's own handwriting, and the state of the client's account was also meticulously noted.

Henry said to Mumford, "A lot of these people seem to be in debt to the company. What action will you take about them?"

"None whatsoever," said Mr. Mumford promptly. "That filing cabinet was a matter for Mr. Mason, and for nobody else. He used to arrange, privately, to collect the debts of his personal clients. In some cases he would decide to waive them and write them off as general expenses. He was quite within his rights to do that," Mumford added defensively.

"And now that Mr. Mason is dead?"

"The point has been worrying me," admitted Mumford, "but I have made up my mind as to the ethical course. Any private client who is owed money will, of course, be paid out in full. Any private client who is in debt—well—the debt will simply be written off—as general expenses. That is what Mr. Mason would have wished."

"I see," said Henry. "Do you think that Mr. Frank will agree?"

"Mr. Frank," said Mumford icily, "will not be consulted."

It was then that pandemonium broke loose in the outer office. Henry and Mumford looked at each other in dismay as giggles, loud-voiced laughter, and, apparently, the shifting of furniture announced the arrival of the gentlemen of the press.

"Oh dear," said Mr. Mumford, "oh, dear. Oh dear. I shall have to go and deal with—oh, dear."

"I'm not anxious to meet the press myself at this stage," said Henry. "So if…"

"I should think not!" exclaimed Mumford. "They'll recognize you, I am sure, and if they get the idea that Scotland Yard has been here—oh, dear…"

"So if there's a back door…"

"Yes, yes. Out this way and down the staircase. There's a door at the bottom out into the mews—that's right, Chief Inspector…"

Out in the narrow street Henry walked thoughtfully back to his car. He was in a state of some perplexity. He was reasonably certain that he had solved the mystery of Raymond Mason's death, and he had no wish to interfere in matters which were irrelevant and might cause distress. On the other hand—was it irrelevant? Could it be irrelevant? The fact that Sir John Adamson had been one of Mason's private clients, and that, according to his dossier, he owed the company no less than three thousand pounds.

Henry was still pondering the problem when he paid his second call, a routine check at the famous jewelers who had supplied Maud's engagement ring. By good luck he quickly found the clerk who remembered the transaction well. Mr. Manning-Richards had come in just after lunch on Saturday, had bought the ring, and paid by check, which had subsequently—that very morning, in fact—been cleared by the bank. When Henry suggested that it might have been risky to accept a check for a valuable ring on a Saturday afternoon, the clerk replied with a smile that Mr. Manning-Richards was an old client, well known to the firm. Henry thanked him, went back to his car, and headed for Cregwell.

CHAPTER NINE

HENRY ARRIVED BACK in Cregwell barely in time to collect Emmy from The Viking and get to the Grange by one o'clock. He was a little disconcerted to see Sir John Adamson's Daimler parked in the drive: In the circumstances, he would have preferred not to have the Chief Constable as a fellow luncheon guest.

Violet Manciple greeted Henry with her usual flustered friendliness, and in no time Emmy was being introduced into the Manciple family circle. Soon, she was borne away by Maud and Julian to meet Ramona, and Violet said to Henry, "Well, I really must get back to the kitchen, Mr. Tibbett. Oh, by the way, Aunt Dora has been asking for you all morning. I rather think she wants to give you some pamphlets."

Henry grinned. "I wouldn't be surprised," he said.

"She was really impressed by your aura," said Violet seriously. "Now, if you'll forgive me…" She hurried off in the direction of the kitchen, and Henry found himself buttonholed by Sir Claud, who was looking, he thought, quite a lot sprightlier than he had the previous day.

"We're off back to Bradwood after lunch," Sir Claud said. "Duty calls, I'm afraid. Still, I hear from Vi that you've cleared up this business of Mason's death. Nice work." He took a gulp of whiskey and nodded approvingly. "That's what I always tell my staff. Marshal your facts, draw your deductions, make your decisions."

"It's rather premature to say that it's cleared up," said Henry. "I've more work to do yet, and the world is full of surprises, you know."

"It should not be," said Sir Claud severely. "Not for the expert. Even the research worker should be relatively immune from surprises if he goes about his job systematically."

"Your field of research is rather more precise than mine, I'm afraid," said Henry. "I deal in human behavior, which is notoriously unpredictable."

"Rubbish," replied Sir Claud. "If the subject were approached from a soundly scientific angle it would be seen to conform to rules, just like any other physical phenomenon. Apparently random behavior, whether in men or in matter, is caused by the inability of the investigator to appreciate the workings of basic laws."

Henry looked at him for a moment. Then he said, "That's a very interesting point of view, Sir Claud."

"What d'you mean, interesting? It's factual, that's all. If I mentioned to you in conversation that the sun would rise tomorrow morning, would you call that an interesting point of view? Of course not. I am forever trying to instill simple, rational thinking into my staff. You'd be surprised how many of them lack mental organization, even the most brilliant physicists among them."

"I understand," said Henry, "that Julian Manning-Richards will soon be joining your staff."

"I hope so. I hope so very much. He's a nice lad."

"But not a physicist surely?"

"No, no. Not necessary for the position I have in mind for him—my personal assistant. What I need is a young man of sound academic training, who is one hundred percent reliable and intelligent enough to understand what I say to him; and that is precisely what Julian is."

"You know him well then?"

Sir Claud looked surprised. "Of course I do," he said. "He is engaged to be married to my niece."

Just then Lady Manciple came up. "And how is your collection, Mr. Tibbett?" she asked.

"My collection?"

"Of wildflowers. I trust you have been out in the hedgerows this fine morning."

"I'm afraid not. I've been working."

"What a pity. God gives the sunshine for man to enjoy, you know."

Sir Claud looked sharply at his wife, appeared about to say something, and then changed his mind.

Swiftly, Ramona said, "I should say—the sunshine is there to be enjoyed."

Henry said, "And work is there to be done, unfortunately."

"But I understood from Violet that you had—what is the phrase you people use—completed your investigations."

"I'm afraid," said Henry, "that Mrs. Manciple may have jumped to a too hasty conclusion. I simply told her that I thought she could safely go ahead with her plans for Saturday's Fête..."

Lady Manciple's face fell. "You mean, the case *isn't* closed?" she asked, with obvious dismay. "But, John Adamson was only just saying..."

"What was Sir John saying?" Henry asked a little sharply.

"Well—nothing definite. I mean, he couldn't, could he, in his position? But he quite clearly gave us the impression that there was no great cause for alarm." Ramona Manciple's troubled eyes searched Henry's face with disconcerting earnestness. "Of course, violent death is all in the day's work to you, Inspector, so perhaps you don't realize how upsetting a thing like this is to ordinary people like us."

Henry smiled. "I do appreciate that," he said. "And yet, I really can't agree that any of the Manciples are ordinary people."

"You're not implying that we are *extra*-ordinary, I hope." Lady Manciple sounded quite annoyed.

"No, no," Henry reassured her, "but I would say that as a family, you are quite exceptional."

"Ah, yes. If you mean the Manciple brain, then I must agree with you. Inherited from the Head, of course. It's a pity about George."

"By the way, Lady Manciple," Henry added, looking around the room, "do you happen to know where Sir John is at the moment? I saw his car in the drive, but he doesn't seem to be here."

"He went down to the range with George a few minutes ago," answered Ramona promptly. "Something about having a private chat. They'll be back for lunch. And now I intend to prise your charming wife away from Edwin. I have only had the chance of a minute's conversation with her, but I gather that she shares my interest in wildlife…"

Left temporarily to his own devices, Henry wandered over to the open French window. Emmy, Ramona, and the Bishop were engrossed in a discussion on local flora and fauna; Sir Claud and Julian were laughing over an erudite scientific pun of some kind; Maud had gone upstairs to help Aunt Dora fix her hearing aid; Violet was in the kitchen. Nobody seemed to notice when Henry stepped quietly out into the garden.

He made his way slowly between the privet hedges to the range, deep in thought. He was convinced that he knew how, and by what agency, Raymond Mason had been killed; and according to his terms of reference his interest in the affair should be at an end. And yet—and yet, there was so much unexplained. In fact, the solution posed more questions than the original problem. And there was something *wrong*…

Henry's colleagues at Scotland Yard were familiar with the intuitive streak which he himself referred to as his "nose."

Frequently it had led him to scrap all preconceived notions of a case and tackle it from a fresh angle. Frequently it had prompted him to a closer investigation of an apparently open-and-shut case to reveal something more sinister beneath the surface. And now it was operating on all cylinders, telling him urgently and unambiguously that the real mystery of Cregwell and the Manciples was yet to be unraveled, that he should not and could not go calmly back to London and forget the whole matter simply because he was convinced that Raymond Mason's death had been caused by…

The voice was surprisingly, almost shockingly loud. It came from the other side of the privet hedge, and it said, "But why, John? *Why*?" The Irish intonation was unmistakably George Manciple's.

Henry stood perfectly still. His usual distaste for eavesdropping was quite forgotten. This might be important.

After a short pause George Manciple went on. "The man didn't like me, and I didn't like him. That's plain enough. But it seems to be taking things to extremes to suggest that he committed suicide on my doorstep, when it's perfectly obvious…"

Henry heard a small rustling of leaves, as though someone were shuffling his feet uneasily. Then, gruffly, Sir John Adamson said, "I'm only telling you what Tibbett said, George. I don't pretend to be able to explain it."

"It wasn't physically possible for Mason to have shot himself," said Manciple. "Aunt Dora's evidence…"

"You surely don't take that seriously, George?"

"I certainly do. Aunt Dora has all her wits very much about her, I can assure you. And if he killed himself, how do you suggest that the gun got into the shrubbery?"

"Look here, George." Sir John sounded exasperated. "I told you this because I thought you'd be pleased. Tibbett definitely said that there would be no arrest, which means either accident or suicide, and I can see no possibility of accident. So there you are. You can forget the whole thing."

"The man was under my roof," said George Manciple stubbornly. "Well, in my drive at any rate. It's my bounden duty to get to the bottom of the matter."

Sir John seemed to be making a great effort to remain calm. He said, "When you telephoned me on Friday evening, George, you suggested that I should call in Scotland Yard in order to get the most expert advice possible. I did that. The case has been investigated by no less a person than Chief Inspector Henry Tibbett. I can't see what more you want. After all, it's not as though the man had been a friend of yours."

"Exactly." George Manciple sounded triumphant, as though he had scored a telling point. "Precisely. That is why I feel an obligation." There was a tiny pause, and then he added, "I suppose you know what they are saying in the Village?"

"I have no idea what they are saying in the Village. It doesn't interest me."

"It interests *me*," said George briskly. "They are saying that I shot Mason accidentally from the range here. At least, that's what the more charitable element are saying. The others—well—you can imagine. It's not at all pleasant, John. The very least that will happen will be a strong local movement to get the Council to condemn the range, and not even Arthur Fenshire will be able to stop it. And you know how much it means to me. No, John, it's simply not good enough for Tibbett to say he's not going to make an arrest and then simply go off, leaving the air full of loose ends. Not good enough."

"I simply don't understand you, George." Sir John sounded exasperated. "I should have thought you'd be delighted to hear that there's to be no arrest. You surely don't want to stir up scandal in your own family, do you?"

"And I don't understand *you*, John," replied George with spirit. "Why are you so keen to hush it all up, eh? Don't you want to know the truth?"

Sir John sighed impatiently. "This is a useless conversation, George," he said. "I'm sorry I ever started it. Until I receive Tibbett's detailed report I can't possibly make any comment."

"Now, John, don't come all over official on me. I've known you long enough to realize when you're up to something. For some reason of your own, you're delighted that this Scotland Yard inquiry is about to fizzle out with no publicity, no scandal, and no proper conclusion. Well, I can only tell you that it doesn't satisfy me, and I intend to speak to Tibbett about it."

"You have no right to do any such thing, George. Tibbett is responsible only to his superiors at the Yard, and to me."

"We'll see about that," said George Manciple.

"Just because you're afraid of losing your precious shooting range…"

Sir John was interrupted by the resonant notes of the dinner gong, which was living up to its reputation for audibility in the jungle. Very quietly Henry made his way back to the house. He found himself in entire agreement with Major Manciple, and was even more determined than ever to have a talk with Sir John at the earliest opportunity.

Luncheon followed the pattern of Saturday's meal. After the Bishop's Latin grace Violet Manciple dispensed large helpings of exquisite, freshly-caught salmon trout and garden vegetables. apologizing profusely for the dullness of the fare. Meanwhile, Maud and Julian handed around tumblers of home-made lemonade, which looked alarming but tasted delicious. The second course consisted of a large dish of canned peaches, which were clearly regarded by the whole family as a great treat. They caused quite a stir.

"In Bugolaland," Edwin confided to Henry, "we always used to open a large can of peaches on Christmas day. Too hot for Christmas pudding, you see. Why, I've had my can of peaches carried by bearers through miles of jungle sooner than miss it for Christmas dinner. Remember, Julian?" he asked suddenly in a penetrating bass.

"Remember what, sir?" Julian, who had been listening politely to one of Ramona's rambles, found himself caught between the fire of two Manciples.

"Peaches for Christmas dinner," bellowed Edwin.

"Ragwort in Three-Acre Meadow," said Lady Manciple.

Julian looked from one to the other. Then, with great aplomb. he said to Ramona, "Yes, Lady Manciple. I have noticed it." He gave her a little bow, indicating courteously that the conversation was over. Then he turned to the Bishop with a smile and said, "In Bugolaland you mean, sir?"

"Of course," said Edwin, "Where else would you have peaches for Christmas, eh?"

"Things are rather different now, of course, sir," said Julian, with just the right note of respect. "I remember the tradition of peaches for Christmas when I was a child, but nowadays people tend to eat ice cream out of the deep freeze."

"Up country," said the Bishop. He sounded far from pleased, as though his authority had been challenged. "Up country. No deep freezes up country."

Julian looked a little uncomfortable. "I expect you're right."

"Of course I'm right." Edwin shot a disapproving look at the young man, the sort of look he might have given a curate whose chanted response was flat. Then he transferred his whole attention to his dish of canned peaches.

Violet Manciple said to Emmy, "I hear you are a friend of Isobel Thompson's. Mrs. Tibbett."

"Yes," said Emmy, "that is, we were at school together."

"A most charming woman," said Violet, "so interested in everything that goes on in the Village."

"A meddling little gossip," said Aunt Dora suddenly and loudly. There was a slightly awkward pause. Then, as if afraid that she might not have been fully understood, Aunt Dora repeated, "Isobel Thompson is a meddling little gossip."

Violet Manciple had gone as pink as a strawberry. "Do have some more peaches, Mrs. Tibbett," she said.

Emmy, whose dish was still full, declined politely.

Edwin said to Henry in a stage whisper, "Have to forgive Aunt Dora, I'm afraid. It's her age, y'know. Wonderful for ninety-three, when you come to think of it."

Quite unabashed Aunt Dora turned suddenly to Sir John Adamson. "*You* know what I mean, don't you, John Adamson—if anybody does." She paused, took a drink from her glass, and then said, "This wine is very delicious, Violet. I think I will have a little more."

"It's not wine, Aunt Dora," said Violet in obvious relief at the change of subject, "it's lemonade."

"I like a good sauterne with my dessert," remarked Aunt Dora implacably.

"Let me get you some more, Miss Manciple." Sir John was on his feet at once in slightly exaggerated gallantry. He picked up Aunt Dora's empty glass and made for the side table where the lemonade stood, cool and green, in a graceful but chipped Waterford glass pitcher.

"Thank you, John," said Aunt Dora. And then, to Sir Claud she added, "I hear that Mr. Mason's son is in Cregwell."

"So I believe," replied Sir Claud. "I haven't met him."

"I understand he is a most unpleasant young man," put in Lady Manciple. Once again, Henry was struck by the beauty of her deep voice. "He has been causing all sorts of trouble. I believe he is a Bolshevik."

Sir John, who had returned to the table with Aunt Dora's recharged glass, said, "People are being less than charitable about the young man. After all, he has a right to his political views, eccentric though they may be, and he has lost his father..."

"As if he cared," said Julian.

"He's delighted that old Mason is dead," said Maud. "He hated his father, and what's more he inherits the business."

"Well, yes. H'r'rump." Sir John cleared his throat noisily as he resumed his seat. "It's normal for an only son to inherit. No need to assume that he wanted to see his father dead. Goodness me," he went on rather more aggressively, "you might as well say that you and Maud were just waiting to bump off poor old George so that you could inherit this house. What d'you say to that, eh young man?"

Julian said nothing. He had gone very white, while Maud had flushed—more, Henry thought, from anger than embarrassment.

George Manciple looked up from his peaches and said, "Bump me off? Bump me off? Who wants to bump me off?"

"Nobody, George." Violet sounded upset. "Really, John, the things you say. Maud, dear, would you get the cheese from the pantry? And there are some cream cookies on the shelves under the stairs..."

It was as they were all filing out of the dining room after lunch that Aunt Dora appeared to see Henry for the first time. "Ah," she said with satisfaction, "there you are. Tibbett. Hang him from a gibbet. I have been looking for you."

"So Mrs. Manciple told me."

"I very much want a word with you, Mr. Tibbett." Aunt Dora sounded positively conspiratorial. "I have some papers which I think will interest you, apropos of our conversation yesterday."

"The—the astral appearance of animals, you mean?"

"The appearance of the astral bodies," Aunt Dora corrected him. "There is no such thing as an astral appearance. I am a little tired now, Mr. Tibbett. I expect it was the second glass of sauterne. As you know, I never sleep in the daytime, but I think I shall put my feet up for a little while. I will see you later."

Before Henry could reply Aunt Dora moved the switch on her hearing aid. Rendered *incommunicada* by the veil of high-pitched sound which resulted, she made her way slowly up the stairs.

Henry had been hoping to get an early interview with Sir John Adamson, but the latter damped his hopes by saying, as he put down his coffee cup, "I'm anxious to have a talk with you, Tibbett, but just now I have to go to Danford on urgent business. Come to my house at five, eh? Then we can talk for as long as you like."

With this Henry had to be content. A few moments later Sir John took his leave, and the Daimler nosed its way down the drive. Sir Claud and Lady Manciple were packed and ready to go back to Bradwood, and Julian offered to drive them to the station. George Manciple was already down on the range, as the distant sound of gunfire testified. The piercing sounds of a clarinet inexpertly played left no doubt as to where the Bishop was, or what he was doing. Violet had her apron on and was clearly itching to get at the washing up. There was no possible reason why Henry and Emmy should stay any longer at Cregwell Grange.

As they drove away down the winding drive and turned into the main road Emmy said, "What marvelous people! From what Isobel said I was afraid that they'd be stage Irish and tiresome. But they're not. They're absolutely real."

Henry hesitated. Then he said, "All of them?"

Emmy looked surprised. "Of course. I mean, a family like that is all of a piece, isn't it?"

"They're not all Manciples, remember," said Henry. "Violet and Julian and Ramona are outsiders."

"Oh, I know," said Emmy. "But, it's like skin-grafting..."

"What on earth do you mean?"

"I was reading somewhere the other day, the graft has to be from the person's own body or else from a close relative. If the new tissue is alien the body simply rejects it."

"You mean that the Manciple family would reject outsiders in the same way?"

"Yes, I'm sure of it. Oh, I don't mean that they all marry blood relatives, just that a stranger who didn't fit in wouldn't last long. The engagement would be broken off or the marriage would go on the rocks. Of course," Emmy added in a burst of enlightenment, "that's what Isobel meant about Julian."

"What about him?"

"Well, she said that the family had gathered this weekend to vet the young man. I thought it sounded dreadful—I'm afraid it prejudiced me against the lot of them. Now I understand. It's not a question of vetting in the ordinary sense; it's just exposing the proposed new member to the full impact of the family to see whether or not the graft takes. For instance"—there was laughter in Emmy's voice—"you obviously took from the word go. You'd fit in at Cregwell Grange like a hand in a glove. What a pity Maud's too young for you!"

"Don't be an idiot," said Henry, but he felt strangely pleased. He went on, "And how do you think Julian has fitted in?"

"Oh, beautifully. He's not a very definite personality, but he's obviously tremendously adaptable, which is what matters. In a year or so he'll be more of a Manciple than the Manciples themselves. You mark my words. I think he and Maud are a wonderful couple." Henry said nothing. Emmy looked sharply at him, and then said, "You don't like Julian, do you?"

"Whatever makes you say that?"

"I don't know. I can just feel it."

"Well, you're wrong," said Henry. "But I will admit that I'm—I'm a bit worried about him."

"Worried about him? Why?"

Very seriously Henry said, "I'd be worried about anybody who was engaged to Maud Manciple."

But when Emmy began to expostulate he shut up like a clam and refused to elaborate his statement. So they drove on in silence until Henry turned to the left in the middle of the Village street.

"Oh," said Emmy, "aren't we going back to the pub?"

"I thought," said Henry, "that we might visit the Thompsons."

"Oh, yes. What a good idea."

"I have a date with Dr. Thompson at four o'clock anyhow, and I shall be interested to meet Aunt Dora's meddling little gossip."

Emmy laughed. "She's not really," she said. "Just ordinarily feminine."

"I wonder," said Henry. "I have quite a respect for Aunt Dora's judgment."

Isobel Thompson greeted Emmy enthusiastically, but looked a little taken aback when she saw Henry.

“Oh, Inspector Tibbett. I’m so delighted to meet you, but I’m afraid Alec is still out on his rounds. He said he wasn’t expecting you until four.”

“He was quite right,” said Henry. “I’m early. I thought perhaps you wouldn’t mind if I waited for him.”

“No—no, of course not.” Mrs. Thompson sounded strangely disappointed. “Can I get you a cup of tea?”

“I’d much rather hear the latest village gossip,” said Emmy.

Isobel looked doubtfully at Henry. “I don’t really think I should,” she began.

Emmy laughed outright. “You can’t fool me, Isobel,” she said. “You are simply bursting with some lovely scandal or other. Come on, out with it. Henry won’t mind. In fact, he’s interested.”

“If you’re really sure,” said Isobel, unable to disguise the eagerness in her voice.

“Of course I’m sure,” said Emmy. “Why else did you think we came?”

“Well,” Isobel turned to Emmy, radiant at the prospect of relaying the newest tittle-tattle. “It’s about Frank Mason, the son. I suppose you know he’s in Cregwell, staying at the Lodge.”

“Yes,” said Emmy, “I’ve seen him in The Viking. Do you know him well?”

“Well? My dear, nobody in Cregwell even knew of his existence until this weekend. Raymond Mason certainly kept quiet about him, and in the circumstances I don’t blame him.”

“In what circumstances?”

“It started on Saturday, with young Mason throwing his weight around in the Village—in The Viking, at the police station, in the shops—anywhere he could get anyone to listen to him. He upset a whole lot of people.”

“Why were they upset?”

Isobel laughed. “Cregwell is the last place on earth for anyone to air violently left-wing ideas,” she said. “He started off by lunching at The Viking and telling old Alfred, the waiter, that he was an outmoded relic of a feudal society and that he should be spitting in the faces of the so-called aristocracy, instead of serving them with soup. Alfred was furious, especially when Mason told him that tipping was degrading to human dignity. Then he got hold of that nice but slightly feeble-minded girl who helps Mrs. Richards at the General Stores. Betty, her name is. He demanded to know why she didn't belong to a union, and how many hours she worked, and if she got paid overtime. He had her in floods of tears in no time and Mrs. Richards says she literally had to drive him out of the shop; and poor Betty was so upset that she had to go and lie down.

"And that wasn't the worst of it. Yesterday he met the Vicar on the way to church and told him that he was a Capitalist lackey pandering to the superstition of fools. And in The Viking at lunchtime he was saying quite openly to all and sundry that Maud Manciple was a degenerate debutante who had vamped his father, and that Julian Manning-Richards was an even more degenerate playboy—damned by his double-barreled name from the start, of course—who had shot Raymond Mason out of jealousy. *And* he accused Sir John Adamson of protecting Manning-Richards under the Old Pals Act."

"What a pity we missed all that," said Emmy wistfully. "We had lunch at The Viking, but we didn't go into the bar. I don't imagine it went down very well with the locals, did it?"

"Not *at all* well," said Isobel with relish. She seemed to have quite forgotten the existence of Henry, who was lying back in an armchair with his eyes shut. "The Manciples are popular here, and everyone adores Maud—most of the Village can remember her as a little girl. As for Julian, they don't know him well, of course, but he's a nice-looking lad, and anyone can see that Maud is mad about him, which is quite enough to make Cregwell love him. Then, the Adamsons have lived in this part of the world for generations, and Sir John is generally respected. In fact, what with one thing and another I think

Frank Mason would have been lucky to get out of Cregwell alive, the way he was carrying on yesterday."

"You talk," said Emmy, "as though that were all past. As though things had changed…"

"But they have!" Isobel was bubbling over with her story. "*That's* what I wanted to tell you. I heard it from Miss Whitehead at the bakery. It seems her young nephew, Tom Harris, had been fishing yesterday afternoon, and in the evening, when he was coming home, he saw Frank Mason walking up through the meadows from the river. And who do you think was with him? Maud Manciple! And her boxer pup! And Miss Whitehead says that Tom says that Mason was being *very* attentive, obviously struck. And then, a little later, there was a terrible row in the bar of The Viking between Frank and Julian. Mabel the barmaid told me."

"I wouldn't call it a terrible row," said Emmy. "They had a bit of a set-to, but…"

"You mean you were actually *there*?" Isobel sounded envious.

"For a bit," said Emmy quickly.

"Well, anyhow," Isobel went on, "it's all around the Village now that Frank Mason has fallen for Maud in a big way, and that he's determined to get Julian out of the way by hook or by crook. Mrs. Penfold was saying in the post office this morning that she wouldn't be surprised if Frank tried to murder Julian, especially if he really thinks Julian killed his father. He's obviously a violent young man. But Mrs. Rudge thinks it's more likely that Julian will end up by attacking Frank. 'Give him a good hiding and serve him right' was how she put it, and there's no doubt that most of the Village agrees with her. Then there's another thing. Mrs. Penfold and Miss Whitehead were saying how odd it was that nobody ever heard of Frank while Raymond Mason was alive. There must have been bad blood between them, they were saying, *and* Frank inherits the business. It makes you think. In fact, Peggy Harris from the dairy was saying right out that Sir John ought to arrest Frank Mason."

"A couple of days ago," said Emmy, "everybody thought that George Manciple had killed..."

"That's just what I mean," said Isobel. "Everything's changed now. I haven't heard anybody mention George at all today. They're all keyed up over the big fight between Frank and Julian—anyone would think it was a heavyweight championship. And..."

It was at that moment that the door opened, and a tall, thin man in his forties came in, saying, "So sorry to keep you waiting, Inspector Tibbett. Had to go out to Fairfield Farm. One of the children—nothing serious. Just flu."

"Alec, darling," said Isobel, "if you'd stop talking long enough to draw breath I'd introduce you to Mrs. Tibbett."

"Delighted to meet you," said Dr. Thompson with hardly a glance at Emmy. "Now, Tibbett, if we go into the surgery we can have a quiet chat. I have to be off again in a few minutes, I'm afraid..."

"I know how busy you must be," said Henry. "I won't take up much of your time..."

"That's a good thing," said Dr. Thompson. It was evidently not his intention to be rude. "This way."

As he followed the Doctor into his office Henry heard Isobel Thompson saying, "And you see, the fascinating thing is that everyone knows Sir John would never *dare* to..."

Alec Thompson shut the door behind him, and Isobel's voice was cut off in mid-sentence.

Thompson sat down at his desk, motioned Henry to a chair, and said, "I really don't see that I can add anything to the post-mortem report I made to Sergeant Duckett. The man was shot from a considerable distance. Bullet entered the right temple. Death instantaneous. Must have been a pretty good shot, whoever fired the gun. Unless it was an unlucky accident, of course. Can't rule that out. Somebody on the shooting range, for instance, who couldn't even see Mason, didn't even know he was there... Still, that's not my department, of course. Well, what do you want to ask me?"

"About your father," said Henry.

"My father?" Alec Thompson sat bolt upright in his chair and looked at Henry as though he considered him eligible for immediate admission to the nearest psychiatric ward. "My *father*?"

Henry grinned. "Yes," he said. "Your father and George Manciple's father."

"But," Dr. Thompson made an impatient gesture. He was obviously making an effort to be polite, and not finding it easy. "My dear Tibbett, what on earth do you want to know about them?"

"I'm not sure," Henry admitted. "Anything you can tell me."

Dr. Thompson looked for a moment as though he would explode. Then, apparently deciding to humor this lunatic, he said, "Well—my father attended the Head for many years. Old Manciple was always known as the Head, you know. They were never very close friends. In fact, toward the end, the Head grew suspicious even of father. Poured his medicine down the drain in case it was poisoned, spat out his pills, refused to allow himself to be examined. You know how these geriatric cases carry on. Senile decay. If it hadn't been for Miss Dora—she used to slip the medicine into the Head's cocoa when he wasn't looking. The only person in the world he trusted, outside of his family, was Arthur Pringle, the solicitor, who killed him in the end, ironically enough. I don't know what else I can tell you."

"When you say senile—was the old man really going mad?"

Thompson hesitated. "Not certifiably," he said at last. "He could be perfectly ordinary in his manner, that is, as ordinary as any Manciple ever manages to be. In academic matters his brain was as sharp as a razor, right to the end. What he had was a persecution complex, which is not unusual in old people. In his case, I understand, it started with the shock of his wife's death, and grew progressively worse until he distrusted everyone, doctors in particular."

"And yet," said Henry, "I understand that he confided in your father on his deathbed."

The Doctor shrugged. "*Faute de mieux*," he said. "There was nobody else there. In any case I'd hardly call it confided. Apparently the old man seemed desperately anxious to contact George, and get some message to him about not selling the house and so on. My father said it was really very moving. The Head was quite a character, you know."

"So I have gathered," said Henry.

"And now, Tibbett, if there's nothing else I can tell you…?"

"Pringle," said Henry, "the solicitor."

"Can't help you there," said Thompson. "The firm packed up soon after old Pringle's death."

"He didn't leave a family?"

"Never married." Alec Thompson smiled, a little wryly. "I think that's why the Head thought so much of him. He was isolated, you see. Any secrets that Arthur Pringle may have known died with him." He looked at his watch. "I'm really sorry. Tibbett, but…"

He was interrupted by the telephone ringing. Quickly, with an impatient movement, he picked it up. "Dr. Thompson here—Who?—Yes—Yes, of course, Mrs. Manciple—Very well, I'll come as soon as I can—I've been somewhat held up this afternoon…" He gave Henry a look which was not altogether friendly. "I have a couple of urgent calls to make, and then—Yes, yes, you told me, but she has these attacks quite frequently, doesn't she?—Yes—Just the usual pills—There's nothing to worry about—I'll be along later—Good-bye, Mrs. Manciple." He rang off, and stood up. "Well, I hope I've been of use to you, Tibbett, but frankly I can't think that—anyhow, you'll have to forgive me now."

"Was that," Henry began. He knew that medical etiquette forbade him questioning Dr. Thompson about his telephone call, but he was very intrigued.

Dr. Thompson, too, was only too clearly familiar with medical etiquette. "Good-bye, Inspector Tibbett," he said firmly. "So nice to have met you." He opened the door and called out, “I’m off, Isobel. Back for supper!” Then he wound an old scarf around his thin neck, struggled into his tweed overcoat, and hurried out to his car.

Henry collected Emmy from the drawing room and drove her back to The Viking. It was time for him to go to Cregwell Manor and speak to Sir John Adamson.

CHAPTER TEN

CREGWELL MANOR, HENRY reflected as he maneuvered his car in the drive, was everything that Cregwell Grange was not. For a start it had been built in the reign of Queen Anne, when architects understood the beauties of proportion and simplicity, whereas the Manciple family home was the brain-child of an overenthusiastic Victorian who was obviously under the influence of Balmoral Castle. To go on with, the gardens of Cregwell Manor were carefully tended with close-cropped green lawns and neat flower beds. And when the elderly white-aproned maid opened the front door in response to Henry's ring, he stepped into a cool, orderly interior, which smelled of lavender and furniture polish. And yet, after the dominating personality of Cregwell Grange, this place was as characterless as a doll's house. Henry was in no doubt as to which he preferred.

Sir John was waiting for him in the book-lined, leathery study. He seemed relaxed and cheerful, and insisted that Henry should take a glass of whiskey with him.

When he had poured the drinks, Sir John said, "Well, Tibbett, it's been nice having you down here. We've all enjoyed it and we shall miss you. But on the other hand, nobody would want to prolong an affair of this sort. It's most creditable that you should have cleared it up so quickly, and we're all very grateful." He raised his glass. "Your very good health. And let's hope that your next visit will be longer—and unofficial."

Henry smiled. "You're very kind, Sir John," he said. "Kinder than I deserve, I'm afraid."

"Not at all. Extremely good work…"

"I mean," said Henry, "that I shan't be leaving Cregwell just yet."

Sir John's dismay was almost comic. "Not," he began. Then he pulled himself together. "Ah, I understand. You're staying on for a few days' holiday, I suppose, your wife being a friend of the Thompsons'."

"Not a holiday, Sir John. I haven't yet finished my investigations."

This time Sir John had himself well under control. Nevertheless, he did not sound pleased. "What an extraordinary thing, Tibbett," he said. "You told me quite plainly on the telephone that you had solved the mystery of Mason's death and that there would be no arrest."

"That was perfectly true."

"Well, then…"

"Sir John," said Henry, "are you a betting man?"

The question clearly caught the man off balance. "I don't know what you mean," he said.

"Do you gamble a lot—on horses, for instance?"

Sir John had gone very red. "Well, I'm damned," he said. "That seems rather an impertinent…"

"I'm sorry if you think I'm being impertinent, Sir John," said Henry. "I do assure you that I wouldn't ask the question if it weren't important."

"I don't pretend to know what you're getting at Tibbett, but if you insist—well—I have a few pounds on the Derby and the National, and so forth. Like most people. I certainly wouldn't describe myself as a betting man."

"You never placed bets with Raymond Mason, for example?"

There was a distinct hesitation before Sir John said, "I've told you, I had a small bet occasionally, and I generally put it on through Mason. After all, when one has a bookie as a next-door neighbor..."

"You never had any dealings with him before he came to Cregwell?"

Sir John looked positively shocked. "Certainly not," he said. There was a little pause, and then he said, "When the fellow first came here, he approached quite a number of people—the Manciples, for instance, and myself—proposing that we should—in other words—not that he was exactly touting for business, but he suggested that we should open accounts with him. He said it would be simple and pleasant for us, as he was a personal friend. I happen to know that George Manciple simply laughed at him; I don't think he or Violet have ever bet a sixpence in their lives. But in my case, I thought that it might be useful..."

"So you opened an account with Raymond Mason Ltd.?"

Again the slight hesitation. Then Sir John said, "No, no, no. Nothing so elaborate. I just contacted Mason when I wished to place a small bet. Really, Tibbett, I don't see where this is leading."

"I visited Mason's London office this morning," said Henry, "and looked at his files."

"Then you must know that I had no account with the firm," said Sir John with some spirit. "Why ask me, eh?"

"You had no account with Raymond Mason Ltd.," said Henry.

"That's what I said."

"But you had what Mason called a private account, with him, personally."

Sir John looked shaken, but rallied gamely. "Isn't that just what I've been telling you?"

Henry said, "Sir John, I must tell you that I have inspected that account."

There was no doubt that Sir John's reaction was anger. "Of all the damned impudence!" he shouted. "I suppose that whippersnapper of a son…"

"Frank Mason had nothing to do with it," said Henry. "He didn't know I was visiting the office; and I doubt whether he knows of the existence of the private accounts."

"Then who…?"

Henry grinned. "I dealt with a Mr. Mumford," he said.

"A Mr. who?"

"Mumford. The general manager. I can assure you that he went to the greatest possible lengths to protect the clients of Raymond Mason, but Scotland Yard is Scotland Yard."

"The general manager wouldn't have known," Sir John began, and then stopped.

"He didn't," said Henry. "He knew of the existence of the private accounts, but he had no key to the files. He was considerably upset when I unlocked the sacred dossiers for myself. It wasn't very difficult; it was just a question of finding the right key from Mason's key ring."

To Henry's surprise Sir John laughed. "So the guilty secret is out," he said. "Naturally, I wasn't keen to bruit about the Village that I had dealings with Mason—he wasn't quite—you understand…"

"I dare say," said Henry, "that you also didn't want to bruit about the village the fact that you owed him three thousand pounds."

"Three thousand…!" Sir John's face registered blank astonishment. "What on earth do you mean?"

Henry was beginning to get a little bored. "You know very well what I mean, Sir John. I looked at your account this morning. You owed Raymond Mason three thousand pounds in unpaid gambling debts."

"But that's ridiculous. I owed him nothing."

"It's there in black and white."

"My dear Tibbett," Sir John replied with spirit, "I know what money I wagered, and which of my horses won or lost.

I may have placed rather more bets than I led you to believe, but…" A new thought seemed to strike him. "Forged, of course," he said. "Falsified documents. I suppose Mason thought it might give him a hold over—and what happens now? When his miserable son demands the money from me…"

"Nobody is going to demand anything from you, Sir John," said Henry. "I have Mr. Mumford's word that all debts from the personal files are to be written off. He said it was what Mr. Mason would have wished."

Sir John sat down abruptly. 'Is that so?" he said.

"It is."

"Which puts me in an even worse position."

"What do you mean, sir?"

"I'm not a fool, young man," replied Sir John belligerently. "Taken at its face value, which is how you are taking it, this blasted personal account gave me a strong motive for murdering Mason. That's what you've been working around to all along, isn't it? Well, I can tell you that…"

He was interrupted by a shrill ringing from the telephone. He picked up the instrument quickly, as though glad of an excuse to end the embarrassing conversation. "Adamson speaking—Who? Oh, yes, George—what is it this time? Not another corpse, I trust…" There was a long burst of talk from the other end of the telephone, during which Sir John went beetroot red. Henry guessed that he had committed a grave gaffe of some sort. At last the flow from the other end of the line dried up to a trickle, and Sir John managed to insert a few words.

"I'm most terribly sorry, George—anything I can do—Yes, yes, poor Violet—No, not entirely unexpected, I suppose, but… Yes, one must think of it that way, but it's always a shock. Tibbett? Yes, as a matter of fact he is with me now—Certainly I'll tell him—Yes—yes—Well, let me know if there's anything—Good-bye, George."

He put down the telephone, took a large handkerchief out of his pocket, and blew his nose loudly. Then he turned to Henry.

"That was George Manciple."

"I gathered as much," said Henry.

"He was ringing about—to tell me—Aunt Dora is dead."

"Aunt Dora," Henry repeated. He felt great distress, but not very much surprise.

"Oh, nothing in your line..." Sir John, who was clearly moved, managed a half-smile. "She was ninety-three, after all; one has to expect these things. Can't live forever. It seems she went up to her room after lunch for her usual nap. Violet had some sort of a committee meeting in the afternoon at the Grange, and so she didn't see anything of Aunt Dora until she went up at about half-past four to see if the old lady wanted some tea. She found her in a coma. She rang Thompson at once, but he was inclined to brush it off, thought it was one of her usual attacks and said he'd call later. He got there a few minutes ago, but too late. The poor old dear was dead."

"I'm very sorry," said Henry lamely.

"She'll be greatly missed," said Sir John, "greatly."

"I'm sure of that."

"Oh, by the way—George says that Aunt Dora was expecting to see you this evening, something about some pamphlets. He asked me to tell you. No point in going now, of course. And the family will naturally want to be left alone..."

"I know," said Henry. He looked and felt very unhappy. "All the same, I think I ought to go around to the Grange..."

Violet Manciple opened the door to Henry. Her eyes were red from recent weeping, but she managed a smile and said, "Oh, Mr. Tibbett. I thought that John had told you..."

"Yes, he did, Mrs. Manciple," said Henry. "I want you to know how terribly sorry I am."

"I'm glad you came," said Violet. She opened the door wider and motioned Henry to enter. "She was so looking forward to her talk with you. She'd have been disappointed if you hadn't come."

"I hate to intrude on you at such a time as this…"

Violet Manciple cut him short. "No, no. It's no intrusion, Mr. Tibbett. In any case, we don't observe mourning in this family."

"You don't?"

"The Head disapproved of it. Of course, Edwin, in his position—however, at heart he agrees with the rest of us. Why, even when George's mother died, the Head refused to have the curtains drawn or to cancel any of his appointments. He was at his desk at Kingsmarsh the next morning, just as usual."

Henry could not help feeling that in view of Augustus Manciple's subsequent behavior it might have been better for him to have indulged in the safety valve of public mourning. However, it was none of his business. He said, "May I see her? Aunt Dora? I'd like to—to pay my respects…"

"Certainly. Mr. Tibbett. She is in the Chapel of Rest attached to Parkins, the undertakers, in Kingsmarsh. You may go there at any time between now and the funeral on Friday."

Henry was taken aback. "You mean—already…?"

"Oh, yes. They are very quick and efficient, you know. Dr. Thompson signed the death certificate soon after five o'clock, and I rang Parkins at once."

Henry felt stumped. He could think of no possible reason for asking to be shown Aunt Dora's room. He looked around him, seeking inspiration, and quite by accident his eye fell on the open kitchen door. Inside, there was considerable confusion.

Violet Manciple blushed. "Oh, please don't look at the kitchen, Mr. Tibbett. I had no time to do the washing up after lunch, with that wretched committee meeting. And I hadn't even made the tea when I went up to see Aunt Dora, and…" Her voice trailed off into miserable silence. Then, on a brisker note, she said, "But of course, you'll be wanting the pamphlets."

"Pamphlets?"

"The ones that Aunt Dora was going to give you. That's what you came for, isn't it? She'd have been so delighted to know that you cared enough. If you'll just wait here, I'll go up and get them. She had them all laid out beside her bed ready for you. I shan't be a minute."

Violet Manciple disappeared upstairs. Quickly Henry went into the kitchen. He had no difficulty in recognizing Aunt Dora's special tumbler, the one which she had drunk from at lunch. It was empty, but bore traces of dried-up lemonade. The lemonade pitcher itself was also there, still half-full. Henry looked around quickly. On a shelf was a small, empty medicine bottle with a cork. He had no idea whether or not it was clean, but there was no time to worry. He poured a little lemonade into the bottle, corked it up, and slipped it into his overcoat pocket. Aunt Dora's glass went into the other pocket. He managed to get out into the hall again before Violet returned, and then saw to his dismay that George Manciple was standing in the doorway of the study, regarding him quizzically.

Before Henry could say a word, George said, "So you came after all. I thought you might."

Henry murmured some words of sympathy, which George ignored. Abruptly he said, "I won't ask what you were doing in the kitchen. That's your business. I only ask you not to distress Violet more than is necessary. This isn't an easy time for her, and there's the Fête on Saturday."

"You'll surely cancel it?"

"Certainly not. Didn't Vi tell you? The Head never approved of mourning. Everything will go on just as usual. Ah, here's Vi," George Manciple withdrew into his study, like a snail into its shell, as his wife came around the bend of the stairway.

"I hope I've found everything, Mr. Tibbett," she said. She was carrying a bulky bundle of printed papers.

Henry took them from her quickly and bundled them into his briefcase. "I'm sure you have, Mrs. Manciple—so kind of you. No, no, please don't bother. I'll see myself out..." Aunt Dora's tumbler was rattling against Henry's pipe in his overcoat pocket, but mercifully Violet Manciple did not seem to notice it. As fast as he decently could, Henry got out through the front door and into his car.

He drove first to Dr. Thompson's house, where, as he had expected, he was considerably less than welcome. A young girl in a white apron, whom Henry had not seen before, informed him in a bad-tempered East Anglian accent that the Doctor and Mrs. Thompson were sitting down to their supper and weren't to be disturbed. Emergencies were to telephone Dr. Brent in Lower Cregwell. The doctor was having an evening off.

It took quite some time for Henry to convince this watchdog that while he was an emergency in his case Dr. Brent would be no substitute for Dr. Thompson. In fact, the girl was still looking extremely doubtful when a door opened, presumably from the dining room, and Isobel Thompson came out looking cross.

"Whatever is the matter, Mary?" she said. "I've rung three times and…" At that moment she saw Henry. "Oh," she said without enthusiasm. "it's you."

"Yes, Mrs. Thompson. I'm sorry to disturb you, but I must see your husband for a moment. I promise it won't take long."

"Oh, honestly. Can't we have a moment's peace? This is the first free evening Alec's had for…"

"I'm really sorry, but this is important."

"What on earth's going on out there, Isobel?" Dr. Thompson, napkin in hand, joined them in the hall.

"He says he's got to see you. It's not my fault." Isobel Thompson turned on her heel and went back into the dining room. The girl called Mary slipped off into the kitchen.

Henry said, "You signed a death certificate this evening for Miss Dora Manciple."

"That's right. Any objection?"

"Only that I'd like to know the cause of death."

Alec Thompson smiled. "My dear Tibbett," he said, "she was ninety-three."

"I know she was, but even people of that age don't die for no reason at all."

"Certainly they don't. The cause was heart failure. She'd had a weak heart for some time. Just a question of wear and tear."

"Did you actually examine her?"

Alec Thompson began to show signs of impatience. "Look here, Tibbett, you were with me in my office when Violet Manciple telephoned. Aunt Dora had had one of her attacks. You heard me telling her to give her the pills I'd prescribed..."

"If this was an ordinary attack, why did Mrs. Manciple phone you?"

Dr. Thompson made an impatient movement with his table napkin. "I suppose it was rather more severe than usual. Slightly different symptoms, apparently. I got around there as soon as I could, after I'd dealt with a more urgent call. But the old lady was already dead. Clearly from heart failure. Anybody could see that."

"I see," said Henry. "Well, that's all. Thank you."

This time Dr. Thompson was really indignant. "You mean to say that you came around here at this hour, interrupting our meal, just to...?"

"I had to know, you see," said Henry, and beat a hasty retreat.

From the Doctor's house Henry drove to the police station. Sergeant Duckett greeted him with warm friendliness and a tepid cup of tea, and eavesdropped with unconcealed curiosity while Henry telephoned to Inspector Robinson at Kingsmarsh. The latter agreed, with professional lack of emotion, to send a car to Cregwell in order to pick up a drinking glass and a small bottle of liquid for analysis in the laboratory.

As Henry rang off Sergeant Duckett said, with elaborate casualness, "That'ud be a drinking glass from Cregwell Lodge, I imagine, sir? Property of the late Mr. Mason."

"No," said Henry, "not from Cregwell Lodge." He brought the glass and medicine bottle out of his pockets and laid them on the table. "Perhaps you could wrap these up carefully, Sergeant, and give them to the driver from Kingsmarsh when he arrives."

"Yes, sir." Duckett eyed the two objects with almost pathetic eagerness. Then, with the air of one who has had a brainwave, he said, "I'd better label them, hadn't I, sir? Just in case of accidents."

"Yes," said Henry, "you'd better."

Licking his lips, the Sergeant picked up a pen and opened a book of stick-on labels. He looked hopefully at Henry.

"Just put for chemical analysis—Chief Inspector Tibbett."

Duckett's disappointment was heart-rending. "No more than that, sir?"

"That's all," said Henry firmly. He stood up. "I'm off back to The Viking now, Sergeant. Ring me there if any news comes through."

Emmy was waiting for Henry in the bar, drinking light ale and complaining of acute hunger. "Did you have to stay so long with Sir John?" she asked plaintively.

"I haven't been with Sir John," said Henry. "Not since before six. I've been at the Grange. Aunt Dora died this evening."

Instantly Emmy's mood changed. "Died? Oh, Henry, how dreadful. She seemed so well at lunchtime."

"I know," said Henry gloomily.

"Goodness, I am sorry," said Emmy. "Poor Mrs. Manciple. First Raymond Mason and now this. Although I suppose it was only to be expected…"

"Why do you say that?"

"Well, she was over ninety…"

Henry nodded abstractedly. "I know," he said. And after a pause, "That's what everyone will say."

"Henry." Emmy put down her glass. "You don't mean…"

"I don't know," said Henry. He suddenly felt very tired. "I really don't know." He smiled at Emmy. "It's my wretched nose again."

"But," Emmy glanced quickly around the bar. Apart from two tweedy men who were discussing pig-breeding in loud voices at the far end of the room, they were alone.

Nevertheless, she lowered her voice as she said, "If Aunt Dora's death was—not natural—then it must mean that Raymond Mason's wasn't either."

"We know it wasn't, darling. He was shot."

"Yes, but you thought it was an accident, I know you did. Now you don't think so. You think he was murdered, and you think Aunt Dora has been killed because she knew too much."

There was a long pause. Then Henry said, "I'm afraid that may be true. Or at least partly true. I hope to God it isn't. Now, let's go and persuade the outmoded relic of a feudal society to give us something to eat."

It was two hours later, when the Tibbetts had dined, taken a final drink in the bar, and climbed the uneven staircase to their room that Henry opened his brief case and took out the sheaf of papers which Mrs. Manciple had given him. He laid them out on the dressing table, pulled up a chair, and began to study them carefully.

"What on earth have you got there?" Emmy, on her way to the bathroom in a white terry cloth dressing-gown, paused to look over his shoulder.

"Aunt Dora's pamphlets," replied Henry.

"*Psychic manifestations in the Animal Kingdom,*" Emmy read. "*Auras and Emanations, Testimony of a Spirit Guide Dog*—surely you don't think you'll find any clues there, do you? The poor old dear was obviously a bit of a crank about spiritualism."

"I don't know what I shall find," said Henry, "but I know I must look for it. Go and have your bath."

Aunt Dora had assembled an odd assortment of literature for Henry's benefit. Long after Emmy was in bed and asleep, he was still wading dutifully through the pronouncements of a Red Indian spirit guide, as revealed to a lady in Ealing, concerning the reincarnation of human spirits as animals, and vice-versa. He was interested to see that Aunt Dora had underlined several passages in purple ink. One of them read, "*The individual human being, as we know him, is not always responsible for his actions in an environment of limited space-time dimensions (i.e. the physical world); he may be driven inevitably to self-destruction by pressures built up in a previous incarnation."* Another underlined passage read: *"Human action is always explicable, but only when all the circumstances are known. This is why it is sheer folly to attempt to live life, let alone interpret it, without the aid of the Spirit World."* This struck Henry as curiously similar to Sir Claud's sentiments about human behavior, although he felt certain that the latter would look to scientific rather than supra-natural aid when it came to determining causes.

Other underlined extracts concerned, respectively, a tortoiseshell cat named Minette, who had twice been seen by her owners after her death, each time apparently trying to raid the larder; and a chestnut gelding who had persistently refused to pass the spot where his mother had been killed in a hunting accident, even though he himself had been far away at the time of the disaster. This last story, inevitably, originated in Ireland.

The pamphlets, however, were not the only things that Violet Manciple had found beside Aunt Dora's bed. There were several yellowing copies of the Bugolaland *Times*, dating variously from two decades earlier to the final number of the previous year, with its banner headline "INDEPENDENCE!". Beside this, Aunt Dora had written: "Poor things. May God bless them!"

A marked paragraph in a year-old paper recorded the retirement, for health reasons, of The Right Rev. Bishop Edwin Manciple, dearly beloved by the people of Bugolaland irrespective of race or creed. The twenty-year-old newspaper appeared at first to have no raison d'être in the collection, until Henry noticed a small paragraph, unmarked by Aunt Dora's pen, which recorded the tragic deaths of Mr. Anthony Manning-Richards and his family, when their car plunged over a precipice while negotiating the notorious Okwabe Pass in East Bugolaland. The paper recalled that Mr. Manning-Richards was the son of

Mr. Humphrey Manning-Richards, who until his recent death had been a well-known figure in Bugolaland.

Henry found it hard to believe that Aunt Dora had really intended these ancient snippets for his consumption; remembering the sentimental story related by Edwin, he felt that it was more likely that the old lady had kept them as souvenirs of her unfulfilled romance. The very last item in the pile of papers, however, interested him considerably, and he would have given a great deal to know whether it was part of Aunt Dora's regular bedside reading or whether it had been put out especially for him.

It consisted of several sheets of writing paper, held together with a rusting pin. The text was written in Aunt Dora's characteristic hand, but the purple ink had faded with the years. The writing was that of a vigorous woman in middle age.

The superscription ran as follows: *This is a copy of the letter written by Dr. Walter Thompson of Cregwell to my nephew, George Manciple, on the occasion of the death of his father, my brother Augustus Manciple, M.A.* Below this, in a shakier but more recent hand, Aunt Dora had written: *In the event of my death, I would like my Great-Niece, Maud Manciple, to be handed this letter so that she may be in no doubt of her Grandfather's last wishes.*

Much intrigued, Henry turned to the document itself. It was headed by the address of the house in Cregwell where Dr. Alec Thompson now lived and practiced, and dated fifteen years previously. It ran as follows:

> *Dear Manciple,*
> *You will have heard by now the tragic news of your father's accident and death. I do not need to tell you how sincere is my sympathy at your bereavement. I can do no more than extend my deepest commiserations to you and to Mrs. Manciple.*
> *As you may know, I had the melancholy duty of*

attending to your father during his last hours, and there can be no doubt that he was anxious to communicate certain things to you. Since his speech was imprecise, I am writing down this account while the incident is still fresh in my mind, so that you may have the best possible opportunity of judging what were The Head's last wishes.

He was unconscious when brought in to the hospital at midday, but recovered consciousness soon after 3 P.M., while I was actually in his room. His first thought, typically, was for his old friend Arthur Pringle. He said the word accident several times, with increasing vigor, and then, "How's Pringle?"

Arthur Pringle was, of course, already dead—he had been killed outright—but I felt that it would do no good to tell your father this sad news, and so I prevaricated, saying something about his being gravely injured. At this, Mr. Manciple said sharply, "Will he live?" And when I hesitated in my reply, he said, "Don't try to fool me, Thompson. He's dead, isn't he?" I am afraid that your father was always too clever and perceptive for me. I was compelled to admit the truth.

The news clearly upset Mr. Manciple greatly. He repeated the words dead and Pringle several times, lying with his eyes closed. I had the impression that he was concentrating—I have seen the same look on his face when he was wrestling with a crossword puzzle. He was also losing strength rapidly, more rapidly, perhaps, than he realized. Next he opened his eyes, looked at me, and said, "Thompson."

"Yes, Mr. Manciple?" I replied. "Send all these people away," he said. "Want to talk to you." There was nobody else in the room except the nurse, but I asked her to wait outside. Then Mr. Manciple said, "George. Tell George. Most important. Must tell

George."

I pointed out as gently as I could that you were half the world away. He seemed irritated at this, and said, "I know. I know. Must tell George." The effort of irritation seemed to have tired him, for there was quite a long silence after that. Then, more feebly, he said, "Tell George—Thompson tell George—my home—my home..."

"What about your home?" I asked.

"Never sell the house," he said quite strongly. "Never—tell George—my home..." He was very weak by then, and there was another long silence. His breathing became labored, and he murmured, "Ill—sick...," several times.

As cheerily as I could, I said, "Certainly you're sick, Mr. Manciple, but we'll soon have you as right as rain." At that he opened his eyes wide and looked straight at me. In a loud, clear voice, he said, "You always were a bloody fool, Thompson," and then, as if the effort had been too much for him, he lapsed into a coma and did not recover consciousness again. He died at 4:37 P.M. I need hardly say that I was deeply moved by the whole incident, and not least by his dying words.

I am sure that I am speaking for all Cregwell when I say that we sincerely hope to see you and Mrs. Manciple home again soon and taking over the reins of Cregwell Grange. There can be no doubt that this was your father's dearest wish.

With my deepest sympathy,
Yours sincerely,
Walter Thompson

Henry read this document over several times. From the bed Emmy's sleep-heavy voice murmured, "Aren't you ever coming to bed?"

Henry stood up. "I've got a crazy idea," he said. "It just could be right."

"And if it is, all the mysteries will be solved…" Emmy was more than half-asleep.

"Oh no," said Henry cheerfully.

"What do you mean?"

"One mystery will be solved, and another will be insoluble."

"Oh, shut up," said Emmy. She turned over on her face and went to sleep.

CHAPTER ELEVEN

THE TELEPHONE CALL from Kingsmarsh came at eight o'clock on the following morning, when Henry had just finished his cup of tea and was gazing at his lathered face in the mirror, preparatory to attacking it with a razor. Quickly he rinsed away the soap, put on his dressing gown, and went downstairs to the phone booth.

In a voice carefully devoid of any curiosity Sergeant Duckett read out the result of laboratory analyses. The contents of the medicine bottle and the dried-up residue left on Aunt Dora's glass were identical: both consisted of lemon juice, sugar, and water, together with a small amount of barbituric acid of the type normally used in sleeping pills. Nothing else. Henry thanked the Sergeant gravely and hung up.

Upstairs again he reapplied the lather with unusual vigor.

"In a hurry?" Emmy asked. She was propped up against the pillows reading her morning newspaper.

"Yes. I think I'm on to something."

"Because of your phone call?"

"No, no. Because of Aunt Dora."

"I give up," said Emmy. "When shall I see you?"

"For lunch here," said Henry, "that is, as far as I know. I really can't say. I just hope I'm not too late."

"For what?" Emmy asked, but he had gone.

Henry's first call was on Dr. Thompson, who was in the middle of his morning office hours and made no secret of the fact that visitors were not welcome. However, he answered the questions which Henry posed and agreed to take certain actions. Henry thanked him, sent his best wishes to Mrs. Thompson, and proceeded on his way to his next port of call.

Cregwell Lodge looked even more hostile than the Doctor's office. The curtains were tightly drawn and the doors bolted. However, in response to Henry's prolonged pealing on the front doorbell, Frank Mason finally appeared, unshaven and yawning in a camel's hair dressing gown, and obviously suffering from a bad cold.

"Wha'd'yar want?" he asked, ungraciously, and proceeded to have a fit of coughing.

"A look around the Lodge," said Henry.

"Gotta warrant?"

"No. But I can get one."

"Thought you'd been through the place with a fine-tooth comb already," grumbled Frank, but he led the way into the study. "Like a cuppa coffee?"

"Thanks, I'd love one," said Henry.

"Back in a tic," said Mason. He blew his nose loudly, and shambled off toward the kitchen.

The study was, at first glance, exactly as it had been when Henry inspected it two days before; but, as he started to look more closely, it became clear that there was a difference. Somebody had made a thorough investigation of the room.

Henry went first to the bookshelves. The leather-bound volumes had clearly been taken down from the shelves, for they were out of order and some of them were upside down. It was as though somebody had pulled them wholesale out of the shelves, perhaps searching for something behind them, and had then made a not-very-successful attempt to put them back in their right order.

The desk, too, showed signs of a hasty search, and the small diary which had interested Henry on his last visit was nowhere to be seen. Henry did not waste any more time on the room itself, but went and sat down in an armchair. He had his pipe going nicely when Frank Mason came back with two cups of coffee on a tray.

Henry said, 'Well, did you find it?"

Frank started so that some of the coffee spilled into the saucers. He did not answer, but put the tray down carefully and disappeared into the kitchen again. A few seconds later he came back with a box of crackers and a cloth with which he wiped up the spilled coffee. Then he handed a cup to Henry and said, "Cracker?"

"No, thanks."

"They're not bad. Sugar?"

"No, thanks."

Frank Mason helped himself to sugar, took a cracker, coughed raucously, sat down opposite Henry, and drank some coffee. Then he said, "Find what?"

Henry indicated the desk and bookcase with the merest twitch of his eyebrows. "Whatever you were looking for."

"I wasn't looking for anything."

"Really? Then who was?"

"I don't understand you."

"Oh, don't be silly," said Henry. "Somebody has been searching this room for something, and I don't imagine you'd allow an outsider to do that without your permission."

"You mean, somebody has been searching *here*?" Mason's tone of shocked surprise was almost entirely convincing.

"Don't tell me you haven't noticed?"

"Noticed what?"

"The books, for one thing," said Henry. He took a drink of coffee. "Somebody has had most of them out of their shelves."

"What on earth for?"

Henry looked quizzically at Mason's apparently innocent young face. "Don't you know?"

Deliberately or not, Mason dodged this question. Instead, his expression began to take on its normal look of explosive anger, and he said, "There's only one person who'd want to come poking around in here, and that's the person who killed my father!"

"Or so it would appear," said Henry. "And what about the gun?"

Frank Mason flushed a dark, angry red, "What gun?"

"The gun in the attic," said Henry patiently. "Major Manciple's gun. Is it still there?"

There was a moment of baffled silence. Then Mason said, "That's like asking a man whether he's stopped beating his wife. Whatever I answer is going to be wrong."

"You knew it was there, of course?"

Mason said nothing.

"You probably found it when you were looking for something else," said Henry persuasively. "Quite by accident, I mean."

In the silence that followed, Henry could almost hear Frank Mason's brain working, calculating the most suitable reply. At last he said, "All right. I found it there yesterday. By accident, like you said. I couldn't know you'd already seen it. I knew it couldn't have any connection with my father's death, because the police had told me that they were holding the gun that shot him. So I—I removed the other gun. I thought it might be embarrassing if…"

"What did you do with it?"

Mason blew his nose. He seemed more at ease as he said, "No mystery about that. It's here in the desk drawer. I was going to…

"To do what?"

"To take it back to Major Manciple. It's his, after all."

"I see. When were you proposing to give it back?"

"Well—I'd thought of going up there today. I thought I might…" Again he paused.

Henry grinned and said, "You thought you might find Miss Maud Manciple at home?"

The flush came back into Frank's face. "You leave her out of this!"

"Very well," said Henry. "But you'll have to find some other excuse for visiting the Grange. I'm taking the gun away with me now."

"Just as you like, Inspector. Here you are. It's..." Frank opened the desk drawer with somewhat of a flourish. It was the drawer in which Henry had originally found the diary, and it was, as he knew, quite empty.

This time Mason's astonishment was even more convincing. "But—I put it there yesterday. It *must* be..."

Henry stood up "You put it there yesterday," he said, "and now it's gone. Unfortunate, but not altogether surprising. I dare say the Homer's *Iliad* is also missing."

"Homer's *Iliad*?"

"That's right. Book Six."

"I haven't the faintest idea what you're talking about."

"I'm delighted to hear it," said Henry. "Nevertheless, I think we'll have difficulty in locating that particular book. Perhaps you could help me look for it."

Augustus Manciple's handsomely-bound edition of Homer consisted of a set of six volumes. All bore the Manciple crest on their finely-tooled leather spines; all were bound in pale beige calf and freely embellished with gold. The first volume contained the *Odyssey* in Greek, with copious and learned notes, while the second was an English translation of the work, again richly annotated. The remaining four volumes comprised the *Iliad*, in Greek and in English. But of these six tomes, only five were to be found, for all Henry's searching. The missing book was the first volume of the *Iliad* in Greek—Vol. III of the set—which had apparently contained Books One to Twelve in Greek, for Vol. IV started at Book Thirteen.

"And you've no idea where it is?" Henry said at last.

Frank Mason ran a hand through his red hair, making it even more unruly than usual. "I tell you, I don't know what it's all about. I can't read Greek. I never knew my father had all these books—I suppose he bought them by the yard for snob effect. I'm bloody sure he never read them. If you're trying to tell me that one of them was so valuable that somebody killed him to get hold of it..."

"I wouldn't exactly say that," said Henry, "but one of them was very valuable, and that one is missing."

"How do you know it's missing? How do you know he ever had it? He wouldn't have known the difference if the set had been one short. For heaven's sake, why don't you go up to the Grange and see if it's not there?" There was a little silence, and the Mason added, "I suppose you know that Manning-Richards is a classical scholar?"

"Is he? No, I didn't know that."

Frank laughed, ill-humoredly. "When I say scholar," he amended, "I mean that he played around at Greek and Latin, as he played with everything else. He seemed to think..." Mason groped for the most damning expression he could find. Eventually, he finished, "He seemed to think that education was for *fun*."

Henry could not repress a smile. "Poor fellow," he said. "He must be one of the last people alive to take that view."

"I'm glad to say," said Mason aggressively, "that we've practically eliminated the privileged class that can afford to study for amusement."

"That's what I mean," said Henry.

"Oh, I can see that you're in the pockets of the Manciples and the Manning-Richards," said Mason. "Just as I'd expect. You're a sad little bourgeois, and you'd give your eyes to be what you call a real gentleman. The fact that one of these precious gentlemen of yours is a murderer doesn't bother you, of course. The king can do no wrong."

Henry looked at him seriously for a moment. Then he said, "If you really believe what you've just said, Mr. Mason, doesn't it strike you that you are in considerable danger from this murderer yourself?"

"I can look after myself."

"I do hope so. Sometimes the most unexpected people turn out to be very vulnerable." Henry paused. Then he added, "If you are thinking of visiting Maud Manciple, I think I should tell you that her great-aunt died last night."

"The ninety-year-old? Well, she'd had her innings, hadn't she?"

"I'm told," said Henry, "that there is to be no mourning, because the Manciples don't go in for it. All the same, I think the old lady will be very much missed. She was greatly loved. I'd be a little tactful, if I were you. And careful."

"Careful?"

"Somebody," said Henry, "has that gun. If it isn't you..." He left the sentence unfinished, and went on. "Have you had many visitors here in the last couple of days?"

"Visitors? Oh, I see what you're driving at. The person who..." Frank laughed, the laugh totally devoid of any sort of joy or amusement, a laugh he seemed to use as a weapon against the Establishment in the same way that a small boy will stick his tongue out at his elders. "You don't imagine that Cregwell has been beating a path to my door, do you? I'm not likely to have had any visitors."

"But did you?"

"I've told you, no."

"Not even the postman or the milkman?"

"Well, yes, of course, they were both here yesterday. But I don't count them."

"That's what I was getting at," said Henry. "Is there anyone else who has been here whom you don't count?"

"Your famous Sergeant Duckett, wizard of the Fenshire force, was around here on Sunday," said Frank with ponderous sarcasm. "Something about checking a statement. And I can do even better. The great Sir John Adamson himself favored me with a brief call on Sunday evening."

"Did he?" Henry deliberately ironed any interest out of his voice. "In connection with the case, I suppose?"

"To tell me that the inquest is to be next Friday," said Mason. "Very solicitous of him. He could perfectly easily have let events take their normal course. I had an official notification from the coroner's office yesterday in any case, which accounts for the visit of the postman, if you're interested. It came by the afternoon mail."

"I expect Sir John thought that you'd rather..."

"He wanted to take a good look at me," said Frank. "Quite understandable. But, of course, simple vulgar curiosity can never be admitted to affect the aristocracy. Oh, no. So he comes here in avuncular mood, dripping patronage."

"If you care to take it that way..." Henry shrugged. "You seem to have caught a nasty cold," he added.

"So would anybody in this benighted hole. What's that to do with...?"

"I just wondered if the Doctor had been up to see you?"

Mason looked surly. "He did drop in yesterday," he said. "I rang to ask when his hours were, and he said that he had a call to make in these parts and that he'd drop by. He gave me a prescription for some cough mixture and aspirins. Anything sinister about that?"

"I don't know," said Henry. "When was this?"

"Yesterday morning, around eleven, I suppose. I didn't make an accurate note of the time."

"It doesn't matter," said Henry seriously. He was too absorbed in his thoughts to worry about the irony in Mason's voice. "Were any of these people left alone in this room for any length of time?"

Mason knitted his brows in thought, and began to cough again. Then he said, "Yes. All of them."

"Really?"

"Well, the telephone rang in the hall outside while Duckett was here, and I had to go and answer it. That must have given him three or four minutes alone in here. Then, Sir John High-

and-Mighty Adamson made it so clear that he expected to be offered a drink that eventually I had to give him one. I went out into the kitchen to get some ice—that must have taken a few minutes. As for old Thompson, he started on about my National Health card, because obviously he's not the G.P. I'm registered with. I happen to know it's not necessary to produce the card for a temporary thing like this, but he made quite a fuss, and so I had to pretend to go and look for it. I knew I didn't have it here, of course. Damned bureaucracy, that's all it is. Men like Thompson think they can push people around, just because they've got a couple of letters tacked onto their names. In a properly-organized society..."

Mercifully, another fit of coughing intervened, for although Henry would have been interested to hear how Mason, who was far from unintelligent, proposed to reconcile a Communist society with the abolition of bureaucracy, he really did not have time for it just then. He waited until the coughing ceased, and then said, "Any other visitors?"

"Not that I know of. But that doesn't mean that people may not have been prowling around."

"Wouldn't you have seen them?"

"Not if I was out."

"But you'd have noticed if any of the doors or windows had been forced..."

"I don't lock doors," said Frank Mason. "I trust my fellow workers."

"There seem to be an awful lot of people you don't trust, all the same," said Henry.

Suddenly, disarmingly, Frank Mason smiled. Henry was amazed to see how a real smile, as opposed to a sneer, could illuminate his face and fill it with interest, as a shaft of sunlight reveals the contours of a landscape. "The people I distrust," said Frank Mason, "are the rich people. And there's nothing in this house worth locking up against people of that sort."

Henry, in his turn, smiled, but a trifle bitterly. "I think you're wrong," he said. "Or at least, you were. There *was* something worth taking, but now it's gone. So I wouldn't bother about locking up. Remember the old proverb about the stable door. Well, I'd better be off. I've a lot to do this morning. And by the way," he hesitated, "I'd like to read your book when it's finished."

"You'd—what? Trying to make something out of *that*, are you?"

"Not in the sense you mean. I've always been interested in Xenophanes. He certainly anticipated a great deal of modern radical thinking, and I'd be interested to see how you relate him to Marx."

"What do you know about it?" said Frank Mason suspiciously.

"Well—take his ridicule of the idea of gods created in men's images," said Henry. "That cleared away more cobwebs of superstition than..."

"You surprise me," said Mason. "I should have thought you'd be a Heraclitean, with your attitude to the Establishment." In spite of his sneering tone he was obviously intrigued.

Henry laughed, "I'm not quite such a die-hard as that," he said. "Of course, *panta rei*..."

"Everything flows," said Mason. "There's a great deal to be..." Then he stopped.

Henry said, "You do read Greek, don't you?"

Mason went a furious red. "So you were simply trying to trick me, were you? Everybody knows what *panta rei* means. You don't need to be a Greek scholar..."

"I wasn't trying to trick you at all," said Henry. "It wasn't necessary."

"What does that mean?"

"Simply that a man as brilliant and as conscientious as you would never embark on such a book if he couldn't read his original sources." Mason said nothing. Henry added, "There was no need to lie about it." He sounded almost sad. "No need at all." He walked out into the windy garden.

Life at Cregwell Grange was evidently continuing its usual course, regardless of Aunt Dora's death. As Henry got out of his car, he could hear the sound of firing from the range, indicating George Manciple's whereabouts. From another part of the garden came the penetrating but tremulous notes of a clarinet, inexpertly played; that could only be the Bishop. The front door stood wide open, and from the inside of the house the whirring of a vacuum cleaner made a continuous obbligato to the soloists in the garden. Nevertheless, for all its air of apparent normality, Henry fancied that he could detect the oppressive atmosphere of a house in mourning. It depressed him profoundly to think that he was about to add a further dimension of distress to that mourning. However, there was nothing to be done about it. He rang the bell.

The tinkling echoes had not died away before there was a clatter of footsteps on the stairs. The vacuum cleaner was switched off, and simultaneously Maud's voice called from above, "I'll go, Mother! It's probably…" At this point she appeared at the bend of the staircase, saw Henry through the open front door, and exclaimed, "Oh! It's you," with obvious surprise.

"I'm afraid so," said Henry. "I'm sorry to have to worry you at a time like this…"

"Don't apologize," said Maud. But her voice was slightly edgy. "I expect Mother told you that we don't go in for mourning."

"Yes," said Henry, "she did." He noticed all the same that Maud was wearing a white dress, and he knew that this was the color of mourning in some countries. It made her look more fragile than ever.

"Well, come in. What do you want?"

Henry went into the hall. At once he was aware of the agreeable, flinty scent of chrysanthemums. The house had been filled with them, great bowls of shaggy blooms, many of them white. It was, of course, September, and the height of the chrysanthemum season; but Henry had remarked that few grew in the gardens of Cregwell Grange, and certainly no specimens like these, whose great heads, the size of grapefruit, proclaimed them as showpieces from an expensive florist. Chrysanthemums, Henry knew, were regarded in most European countries as the flowers of the dead and were by tradition heaped on family graves at the festival of All Souls. It certainly seemed as though somebody at Cregwell Grange was defying the Head's edict and was mourning Aunt Dora. Henry felt somehow pleased at the fact.

"I'm afraid," he said, "that I must have a word with Major and Mrs. Manciple."

Maud gave him a direct look. "Can't you leave them in peace for a moment?" she said. "Raymond Mason is dead. Surely your investigations, or whatever you call them, can at least wait until after Aunt Dora's funeral?"

"What I have to say to your parents has nothing to do with Raymond Mason, Miss Manciple."

"Oh. You mean, it isn't official business?"

"Yes and no."

"What on earth does that mean?"

"It means that I have to talk to Major and Mrs. Manciple."

Maud looked at Henry as though she did not like him at all, and he realized, not for the first time, just how tough she was in spite of her fairy-doll fragility. It also occurred to him what a dangerous enemy she would be, with her beauty, her brains, and her whiplash strength of character—and what a useful ally. He also found himself wondering how George and Violet Manciple had managed to produce such a child, and at once answered his own question. Maud was a direct throw-back to her grandparents. He remembered the photograph which George Manciple had shown him, and marveled that he had not noticed at once the strong resemblance between Maud and the long-dead Rose Manciple. He also glanced, instinctively, at the portrait of the Head, which dominated the hall. Maud, following his eyes, said at once, "Yes, I am very like him."

"You must be a mind-reader," said Henry. He smiled at her, and she smiled back, dissolving miraculously from a deadly member of the Erinyes into a small, vulnerable girl in a white cotton dress.

As she opened the drawing-room door for him, Maud said, "People often tell me how frightening I can be. I don't mean it, you know. It must be a trick of the light playing on the Manciple bone structure. Just wait in here and I'll call Father."

The drawing room, too, had been embellished by two big bowls of chrysanthemums. Henry watched from the window as Maud made her way down the garden toward the shooting range. As she disappeared behind the privet hedge, Edwin Manciple came up toward the house from the opposite direction. He was wearing khaki shorts and he carried his clarinet, a collapsible music stand, and an untidy collection of sheet music. He saw Henry standing at the window and waved his clarinet in a welcoming manner before disappearing around the corner of the house in the direction of the front door.

A moment later Maud and her father came out from the shelter of the hedge and walked up toward the house. They both looked grave and were deep in conversation. On the lawn outside the drawing-room window, Maud stopped, said something to George, and went off down the garden again. George Manciple sighed, tucked his gun under his arm, and came in through the French windows to the drawing room.

"Maud says you want to see me, Tibbett," he said.

"I fear so," said Henry, "you and Mrs. Manciple."

"Together?"

"That's largely up to you," said Henry.

"To me? What do you mean?"

"it's about Miss Manciple."

"About Maud?" The Major looked really alarmed.

"No, no. Miss Dora Manciple."

"Poor Aunt Dora. Surely she may be left in peace, now that she's dead?"

"I'm afraid she can't," said Henry. "I know it will be very distressing for you, but I have to tell you. I'm not at all satisfied about her death and I think there should be a post-mortem examination."

For a moment George Manciple gaped at Henry as though he were some sort of imbecile. Then he let rip. Henry, he said, in an ever-thickening Irish brogue, had been called in to investigate the death of Raymond Mason. This he had not done. Had as good as told Sir John Adamson that Mason committed suicide, which was arrant nonsense, as anybody with a modicum of intelligence could see. He, Henry, had then proceeded to hang around Cregwell, doing nothing, upsetting everybody, and coming to no sensible conclusions. Now, to crown it all, he was making unfounded and positively indecent suggestions concerning poor Aunt Dora, who had done no more than die quietly in her bed of a weak heart, God rest her soul, and if she hadn't a right to do that at ninety-three, he, George, would like to know who had.

At this point he paused to take a much-needed breath, but Henry had no time to say more than, "Major Manciple, I..." before the flood was unloosed again.

A post-mortem indeed? And why, might George be allowed to ask? Was Henry suggesting that Aunt Dora had been murdered? While Raymond Mason had committed suicide, at the range of a hundred yards or more? Was that it? Really, George began to think that his brother Edwin had been quite right when he expressed doubts as to Henry's mental stability. Good God, if anybody had been murdered, it was Mason, wasn't it? George knew that he, George, was not considered to be very bright, but he at least had eyes and ears in his head and could use them. Henry could rest assured that never, under any circumstances, would the family consent to a post mortem on Aunt Dora. Thompson had signed the death certificate, hadn't he? Everything was straightforward and above board, and things were worrying enough for Violet as it was. He certainly wasn't going to have her upset by nonsense of this sort, and...

He was interrupted by the arrival of Violet, flustered as usual, and apologizing to Henry for having been detained by some household chore. It was not until she was actually inside the room that she appeared to realize that she had interrupted a tirade. However, one look at her husband told her all. Abruptly she switched her attention from Henry to Major Manciple, and said, "What's the matter, George?"

"Matter? Nothing. Nothing whatsoever, my dear. Now, just you go and…"

"Of course there's something the matter," said Mrs. Manciple. She did not speak sharply, but with the calm conviction of one in full grasp of the facts. "You are all upset, George. I haven't seen you like this since Mr. Mason complained to the Council about the range."

"That has nothing to do with it," said Major Manciple crossly.

Violet appealed to Henry. "Will *you* tell me, Mr. Tibbett? What has been happening?"

"Don't say a word, Tibbett," rapped out the Major.

Henry said, "I was just telling your husband that I'm not satisfied that Miss Dora Manciple's death was entirely natural."

To his surprise Violet Manciple said at once, "Oh, I am glad that you feel that, Mr. Tibbett. I absolutely agree with you."

"Violet," began the Major on an explosive note.

His wife took no notice. Addressing herself to Henry, she said, "She used to have these attacks, you see, but this was different. If only I hadn't had that wretched meeting about the Fête, I might have—but by the time I went up to her, it was too late. And I couldn't make the Doctor understand that it wasn't just an ordinary attack. To tell you the truth, Mr. Tibbett, I've been trying to pluck up my courage to ask you if we couldn't have a post-mortem examination. She—it was almost as though she'd been drugged, you see."

Henry nodded. "I think she very likely was," he said. "She never took sleeping pills, did she?"

"Sleeping pills? Oh, certainly not. She always slept like a log. But in any case, the Doctor told me that she must on no account ever be allowed to take even the mildest of barbiturates. He said that with her heart in its present state…"

"Did the other members of your family know this, Mrs. Manciple? That sleeping pills could be dangerous for Aunt Dora, I mean."

"Of course," said Violet at once. "Everybody knew, because it's so easy to get medicines mixed up, and we had to be especially careful. You see, Ramona takes sleeping pills—far too many, in my opinion, but I suppose it's none of my business. And so does George, of course."

"Do you, Major Manciple?" Henry asked.

George Manciple was now the color of a ripe tomato. "What if I do?" he demanded. "Thompson prescribed them a few months ago, when I was so worried over the Mason business. I don't see that it has anything to do with…"

"I suppose," said Henry, "that anybody could have gotten at your bottle of pills? Or at Lady Manciple's?"

"I suppose so. Mine are in my bathroom cabinet. Thought they were safe enough there, because Aunt Dora had her own bathroom. Never used ours. Heaven knows where Ramona kept hers. But if you're suggesting that Aunt Dora deliberately went and took sleeping pills, when she knew very well that Thompson had forbidden them…"

"I'm not suggesting anything of the sort, I'm afraid," said Henry. "I wonder if you'd go and take a look at your bottle of pills, Major Manciple, just to see if any are missing."

"My dear man, I don't count them. They're not poisonous."

"But at least you'd know whether the bottle was full or half full or…"

"As a matter of fact," Manciple conceded with a bad grace, "now you come to mention it, I should have a brand-new bottle. I ran out last week, and Thompson wrote me a new prescription. Maud and Julian got the new tablets from the druggist yesterday morning. So…"

He ambled out of the room, leaving the sentence unfinished.

Violet Manciple said, "Do you know for certain that Aunt Dora had taken...?"

"We can't possibly know for certain until after the post-mortem," said Henry.

Violet nodded, gravely.

"But I can tell you that there were traces of barbiturate in the glass which Miss Manciple used at lunch yesterday."

Mrs. Manciple looked puzzled. "Where is that glass, do you know, Mr. Tibbett? I was certain I had taken it out of the dining room, but when I came to do the washing up yesterday evening I couldn't find it anywhere. I thought perhaps it was broken."

Henry said, with some embarrassment, "I'm afraid I am the guilty party, Mrs. Manciple. I took the glass from the kitchen while you were upstairs. I wanted to have it analysed, you see, and I didn't want to upset you unnecessarily..."

"So you suspected," said Violet, "Even yesterday."

"Yes," said Henry. "So..."

The door opened and Major Manciple came back. He walked jauntily, carrying a small package in his hand. Triumphantly, he said, "Here you are! See? Still done up in the druggist's wrapping. Seal not even broken. Are you satisfied now?"

"Let's open the wrapping, all the same," said Henry. "Somebody might have..."

"Of all the nonsense!" cried George Manciple in great good humor. "Still, if it makes you happy..." He broke the small red seal and unwrapped the white paper. "There!" He held out a small bottle, a bottle which Henry recognized as being identical with the one he had taken from the kitchen shelf on the previous day. The top of the bottle was sealed with plastic, and it was full of small white pills.

"I'll have to take those pills away for analysis, I'm afraid," said Henry, "but it certainly looks as though..."

The telephone cut him short in mid-sentence. Violet hurried out into the hall to answer it, leaving the door open.

"Hello—Yes—Yes, Ramona dear—How kind of you to ring—Oh, yes, we're managing—No, no, of course not—Tell Claud he mustn't dream of... Yes, Friday—at least, as far as I know—Yes, Friday at half-past two at the parish church, and afterward at the crematorium—yes, of course we'll be delighted to put you both up—What? Oh..."

She caught her breath as if in dismay, and the two men in the drawing room exchanged a glance. Then Violet recovered and went on.

"Yes, I'll—I'll look, of course—Where did you see them last? I see—well, certainly I'll... Yes, dear—no, no, it's no trouble—I mean, it may be import... That is, you must want them—I'll look—Yes—Good-bye, Ramona..."

She hung up and came back into the drawing room. "That was Ramona," she said.

"We had gathered that," said George. "What did she say?"

"She was calling about—about the funeral, and so on. I told her..." She glanced in inquiry at Henry. "I suppose the funeral arrangements can go ahead, Mr. Tibbett?"

"As far as I know," said Henry. "There's no need to change anything at this point."

"Get on with what Ramona said," put in George Manciple impatiently.

"Well, then she said, just as an afterthought, had I seen her sleeping pills?"

Major Manciple took a step toward his wife.

Violet continued, "She said she had had an almost full bottle, which was on the table beside her bed. She hadn't noticed when she was packing, but when she got back to Bradwood, she found she didn't have them. She thinks she must have forgotten them, and that they are still on her bedside table. But..." Violet looked at Henry with a desperate sort of appeal. "But I've just been cleaning out the room they had, and there's nothing there. Nothing at all."

CHAPTER TWELVE

"I CAN'T UNDERSTAND IT, Tibbett," said Sir John Adamson. "I simply can't. I thought the whole thing was over and done with."

"So did I," said Henry. It was only teatime, but he felt very tired already. "But there it is. There were traces of barbiturates in both the specimens of lemonade that I sent for analysis. It's true that I poured the lemonade from the jug into a bottle which had previously contained Major Manciple's pills, so that proves little, one way or the other. But the barbiturate in the drinking glass can't be accidental. Dr. Thompson has confirmed that even a small amount of the drug would have been fatal to Miss Manciple with her heart condition. And Lady Manciple's sleeping pills have disappeared; there's no sign of them, and nobody at Cregwell Grange will admit to having seen or touched the bottle, though they all agree that they knew of its existence. Well, as I told you, Major Manciple finally agreed to a post-mortem examination, and—there's the result." Henry tapped the file which lay on Sir John's desk. "Miss Manciple died from heart failure as a direct result of swallowing a couple of sleeping pills, which would not have harmed any ordinary person. They were undoubtedly administered in the lemonade."

"Why, Tibbett? That's what beats me. Why?"

"I can only suppose," said Henry, "that it was because Miss Manciple had announced her intention of having a talk with me later in the day."

"About the supernatural manifestations of parrots? Bah!" said Sir John forcefully.

Henry sighed. "I know, sir," he said. "It does sound silly when you put it like that, but..."

Sir John picked up a metal ruler and began beating a tattoo on the leather desk top. "Mason," he said, "let's get back to Mason. That's why you're here, after all. Let's have an end to this hedging and ditching. Tell me straight out what happened to Mason."

Henry hesitated for a moment. Then he said, "I think that Raymond Mason's death was accidental."

"You mean, somebody killed him by mistake? Is that it?"

"No."

"Then what in heaven's name..."

"I think that he killed himself by mistake."

For a moment it seemed that Sir John would explode. Then, with a great effort at self-control, he said, "I think you will have to make yourself a little clearer, Tibbett."

Henry grinned. "Certainly," he said. "I'll start at the beginning—or as near the beginning as I've been able to trace so far. Raymond Mason wanted to buy Cregwell Grange."

"We all knew that."

"He wanted to buy it with a sort of desperation, something far more powerful than the ordinary desire of a man who has seen a house that suits him and hopes to get it. For some reason Cregwell Grange had become an obsession with Raymond Mason."

"Wanted to establish himself as a landed gent." said Sir John. He laughed shortly. "Some hope!"

Henry looked at him. "Yes," he said. "Well, he started by making a generous offer for the house, and when it was turned down he increased his bid. Apparently it took some time to penetrate Mason's brain with the fact that George Manciple was simply not prepared to sell at any price. This undoubtedly infuriated Mason, and made him more determined than ever to get the Grange for himself.

"His next line of attack was to try to make George Manciple's life such misery that he would be happy to sell the place and move to get a little peace and quiet. Mason's best hope lay in getting the shooting range banned, because he was shrewd enough to realize that it was Major Manciple's chief joy in life and that without it he might well be tempted to—anyhow, Mason failed. Major Manciple had too many friends in high places."

Sir John cleared his throat noisily and said, 'Very interesting theory. Go on."

"Mason's next gambit," said Henry, "was to propose to Miss Maud Manciple. A pretty far-flung hope that was, but she's a beautiful girl and I imagine that he really fell in love with her. No reason why he shouldn't have. Unfortunately for him, she was secretly engaged already, and he was not only turned down and snubbed in what must have been a very hurting manner, but he was insulted and even threatened by her fiancé. After that, I think he got really desperate. He was determined to get his own back from the Manciple family, to get them out of that house at all costs."

"That's all very well," said Sir John, "but how did he think he was going to do it?"

"Very sensibly," said Henry. "He went back to the shooting range idea. Previously he'd claimed that the range might, in theory, be dangerous—and he'd been overruled. Now, supposing that an accident should take place on the range, a potentially fatal accident. Not all Major Manciple's influential friends would be able to defend it then. Naturally, Mason knew all about Manciple's patent tennis-ball traps, just as everyone else did. He also found it quite easy to filch one of Manciple's guns in order to do some experiments."

"How on earth do you know all this?"

"Major Manciple had reported a gun missing a couple of weeks ago and I found it in Mason's house. There was a piece of string still tied around the trigger. Mason had obviously been experimenting with firing it by remote control."

Sir John was beginning to look interested. "Had he, by Jove? And did it work?"

"I think it did," said Henry. "It doesn't take any great pressure on the trigger to fire the gun, just a short, sharp pull. Mason's idea, as I see it, was to stage an accident, with himself cast in the role of potential victim, who might easily have been maimed or even killed but for a lucky chance."

"Taking a bit of a risk, wasn't he?"

"Oh, no. He had it all worked out. His idea was that at a time when he knew Major Manciple to be down at the range a shot should be fired which *might* have hit somebody in the drive. In fact, the errant shot would be fired out of the window of the downstairs lavatory, that little Gothic slit that looks out into the shrubbery beside the front door. Mason himself, the possible victim, would be in the drive, but by great good fortune he would be protected by the open hood of his car, which he would have happened to raise in order to investigate a fault in the engine, a fault which, of course, he had engineered himself. Protected by a ton and a half of Mercedes Benz, he would have been perfectly safe. But the bullet would have struck the car, providing just the evidence Mason needed. Manciple's shooting range would never have survived an incident like that."

"Who was to fire the shot then? Did he have an accomplice?"

"No, no. I told you, he was experimenting with remote control. In fact, before leaving the Grange that day he spent quite a long time in that downstairs cloakroom, much longer than would have been required in the normal course of nature, as Mrs. Manciple noticed; but of course she would never have mentioned so indelicate a matter if I hadn't dragged it out of her. Actually, of course, Mason was rigging up the gun. He had it pointing out of the window with a string around the trigger attached to one of Manciple's spring traps.

"We'll never know exactly how the gun was supported, because Mrs. Manciple tidied up the cloakroom and put everything away before I realized the significance of it. One thing is clear, however. Those traps work off a burning fuse. As Mason left the cloakroom, he lit the fuse. He knew exactly how much time that would give him before the trap sprang and fired the gun. I imagine that he intended the gun to fall back into the cloakroom; he could easily enough have found an excuse to go in there afterward and tidy everything up. But as it happened, he must have found it necessary to prop up the gun with something solid, another box or a book, perhaps. So, when the gun jumped backward with the recoil, it hit against this solid object and fell forward instead and out of the window. Mason hadn't counted on that."

"He hadn't counted on killing himself, either," said Sir John. "What went wrong?"

"Aunt Dora," said Henry.

"Aunt Dora?"

"I think," said Henry, "that Mason was genuinely fond of the old lady. In any case it was no part of his plan that anybody should get hurt, let alone killed. He had the hood of the car open; he was snugly protected behind it, just waiting for the shot, when Aunt Dora came out of the house and down the steps, waving her pamphlets at him. Mason must have been appalled. She was walking directly through the line of fire only a few feet from the gun. Mason knew that she was deaf and wouldn't hear if he called to her. There was no way of stopping her except by signs, and that meant coming out into the open himself. She told me that when he saw her coming, he ran out from behind the car, obviously alarmed and waving his arms at her. He was trying to warn her to go back. Mercifully, she stopped, but he had no time to get back into shelter before the gun went off. And so he was killed—accidentally. The fact that the single bullet got him through the head and killed him outright was just simple bad luck."

There was a silence, and then Sir John said, "Are you sure of all this, Tibbett?"

"As sure as I can be. I found the remains of Mason's booby trap in the cloakroom, even though it had been tidied up quite innocently by Mrs. Manciple—she's used to clearing up the mess that the Major makes in there with his traps and tennis balls. The shot was definitely fired through that window, and nobody was or could have been in there at the time. Mason had only just come out, and the only two people in the house were Mrs. Manciple and the Bishop. She was in the hall, telephoning to her grocer and in full view of the cloakroom door; and the Bishop was upstairs, and came down immediately after the shot had been fired."

"So Violet herself was the only person who could have fired the shot deliberately, was she?" said Sir John.

"I suppose that would have been just possible, but very far-fetched," said Henry. "I've checked with Mr. Rigley, the grocer, and he confirms that she was speaking to him when she suddenly said she must ring off as her aunt was calling her. Of course, he can't pin down the time to within a couple of minutes, but, in any case, she still had the telephone in her hand when the Bishop came downstairs."

"So that's that." Sir John sighed with unambiguous relief. "All over and done with. Just an accident, the result of a stupid trick which misfired. Literally. No mystery, after all."

"On the contrary," said Henry.

"What do you mean?"

"There are two mysteries," said Henry, "which may or may not be connected. The first is why was Raymond Mason so keen on buying Cregwell Grange? The second, who killed Dora Manciple, and why?"

Sir John made a small, impatient gesture. "I've told you. Mason wanted to join the ranks of the landed gentry. The man was nothing more nor less than a jumped-up nouveau-riche…"

"I wonder," said Henry, "just how rich he was."

"How rich?" Sir John laughed shortly. "Rolling in money."

There was a short pause and then Henry said, "Did you ever pay him any gambling debts, Sir John?"

"I—I just happened to be lucky in my few little flutters."

"Yet you owed Mason three thousand pounds."

"So you said before, and I say that it's a monstrous lie. I have never dreamed of gambling in that sort of money. And in any case, if I had owed Mason money, why did he never ask for it?"

"That's what I'd like to know," said Henry. He leaned forward. "Look here, Sir John. I know this is a painful subject for you, but I must get to the bottom of it. You're not the only person to have had one of these special accounts, you know, and I want to know how they were worked. It may be important." He paused. "You say you're not a great betting man, but surely you take enough interest to know how much money you've staked, and whether or not the horse has won and at what odds. You *must* know your position with Mason, at least approximately. Or else the files that he kept must be complete works of fiction."

There was a long silence. Sir John lit his pipe with a great deal of unnecessary attention to detail. At last he said, "Well, Tibbett, it was like this. Mason was in a position to get the very best inside information—red-hot tips from trainers and owners and so forth. Very often at the last moment. Of course, occasionally I would fancy a horse very strongly and I'd put a few pounds on him, win or lose. But more often than not, Mason would telephone me and say that he expected to have some good things for a certain meeting that day. 'Just tell me how much you're prepared to stake,' he'd say. 'Ten, twenty, fifty pounds? You name it. Then trust me to invest it right for you. I'm guaranteeing nothing, of course, but I think I can say you're not likely to lose.'"

"And you didn't?"

"Once or twice I'd be a couple of pounds down, but more often he'd do extremely well for me. He'd come along the next day with my winnings in cash, anything up to a couple of hundred. Naturally, he always gave me a full account of which horses he'd backed for me, the odds, and so on."

"I see," said Henry. "And what did you do in return?"

"In return? I don't know what you mean, Tibbett. Nothing whatsoever. It was a perfectly straightforward business arrangement."

"Except, of course, that you felt in honor bound to invite him to dinner, and to introduce him to..."

"He was a neighbor," said Sir John in furious embarrassment. "Couldn't be rude."

"All the same, without that inducement I don't believe you'd have allowed him to set foot inside your house. By the way, did you keep a record of these transactions, which horses he'd backed for you?"

"Good Lord, no. Why should I? It was all perfectly simple and innocent."

Henry sighed. "It was all perfectly simple and innocent from your point of view, Sir John," he said. "I don't doubt that. The fact remains that Mason wasn't a simple or innocent person. He told you one story, and he gave you money. In his office, on the other hand, he kept a file which showed a very different picture—that you had lost heavily and owed him a considerable sum. If it had come to a showdown, you'd have been in a very awkward position indeed. Your unsupported word against Mason's records kept in black and white. And I know that there are some people who regard unpaid gaming debts as even more shameful than unpaid bills. I've never been able to understand why, but there it is."

"You're not suggesting that he would have blackmailed me?" Sir John was outraged.

"Indeed he would have, if it had been to his advantage," said Henry equably. "As a matter of fact, I doubt if he ever did put the pressure on in that way, although of course I shall try to check up. I think myself that all his private customers played along very nicely. He was prepared to pay handsomely for the privilege of dining in the right houses and sitting on the right committees. But it must have cost him a great deal of money."

"What do you mean, cost him? Those were winnings that he paid out."

"So he said. It's easy to know after a race which horse won, and to claim that you staked money on it. My guess is that he simply dug into his firm's bank account and wrote it off as general expenses. I dare say he could have done with some extra money. No wonder he was so keen to buy Cregwell Grange."

"That would hardly have put money in his pocket. Gracious me, Tibbett, he offered George Manciple a ridiculous price for the house, far more than it was worth. And then he'd have had endless expenses, putting the place to rights. Quite honestly, in my opinion Cregwell Grange is more of a liability than an asset."

"Ah," said Henry, "that's where you are wrong. Cregwell Grange is a very valuable property."

"Valuable?"

"If you know where to look."

"And where is that?"

"I don't know," Henry admitted. "By the way, Sir John, did you ever borrow any books from Mason?"

"Books?" Sir John sounded shocked. "*Books?* Certainly not. What would I want with the sort of pornographic rubbish that a man like Mason would have in his house?"

"He has a lot of the Manciple books, mostly classical."

"If you think, Tibbett, that I settle down after a hard day's work to read Greek and Latin in the originals, you are very sadly mistaken." Sir John's irony was elephantine.

"Oh well," said Henry, "it must be somewhere."

"What must be?"

"Homer's *Iliad*, Book Six."

Sir John looked at Henry with grave misgivings. Then he said, "If I were you, Tibbett, I'd go back to The Viking and put your feet up. You've had a tiring time with this case, we all understand that, and then you've been spending a lot of time at the Grange. Nothing against the Manciples, of course, but not what you would call a *balanced* family. And these things can be contagious." He cleared his throat. "Your reconstruction of the circumstances of Mason's death seems to me to be masterly. Really masterly. I presume that you'll submit your official report tomorrow, and that will be that. As for the other matters—well—I think you'll find that after a good night's sleep they fall into proper perspective. Anybody may mislay a bottle of sleeping pills. I dare say Lady Manciple will have found them by tomorrow."

"There is also a gun missing," Henry reminded him.

"An unloaded gun, as you told me yourself," said Sir John. "I expect young Mason just forgot where he had put it. It'll be back in Manciple's armory by tomorrow, you mark my words." He stood up and held out his hand. "Most interesting and stimulating experience, working with you, Tibbett. Can't thank you enough. Most satisfactory outcome to a nasty affair. Good-bye, then. Hope you'll come and see us again in happier circumstances."

"Good-bye, Sir John," said Henry. He shook hands and walked out to his car; as he did so he rubbed the back of his neck with one hand, a gesture which always indicated that he was worried about something. In this case it was the fact that he would almost certainly have to apply for a warrant to search the Chief Constable's house, and he was far from enthusiastic at the prospect.

"Ah well," he said to himself as he drove back to The Viking, "perhaps it won't be necessary. Perhaps I'll find what I'm looking for elsewhere."

At the Inn, Henry was greeted by Mabel, the barmaid. She wondered, she said, whether Mr. Tibbett would like his bill now or in the morning.

"My bill?" said Henry surprised.

"Well, you'll be going tomorrow, won't you? You and Mrs. Tibbett?"

"What makes you think that?"

Mabel went a little pink and prevaricated. It soon became obvious, however, that Village gossip had established that the case of Raymond Mason was closed, and that the Scotland Yard gentleman would be leaving.

Henry grinned. "Sorry to disappoint you, Mabel," he said, "we're staying."

"Staying?"

"For several days at least. Until the end of the week."

Enlightenment dawned on Mabel's plump face. "Ah, you'll be here for Miss Dora's funeral I expect. Friday."

"That's right."

"And you wouldn't want to miss the Fête, Saturday."

"I certainly wouldn't," said Henry.

The next morning, Wednesday, Henry decided to step up his search for the missing objects which were so much on his mind: the sleeping pills, the gun, and—an incongruous third—Homer's *Iliad*, Book Six, in the original Greek.

He found the family at Cregwell Grange only too willing to co-operate. They were all subdued and distressed over Aunt Dora's death and the mystery surrounding it; more shocked, Henry felt, at the idea of the post-mortem examination itself than at its findings.

Edwin and George were both of the opinion, which they stated several times over, that Aunt Dora would have been perfectly capable of taking the pills herself in mistake for something else. They could not, however, explain what she had mistaken them for or what had become of the bottle. Maud and Julian both offered to help Henry in his searching of the house, an offer which he was regretfully compelled to turn down. George Manciple confirmed his original statement about the disappearance of the gun, and nobody could add anything useful to it. George and Violet both declared emphatically that if Volumes I, II, IV, V, and VI of the Head's Homer had been sold to Mason, then Volume III would certainly have been with them. No sets were split up, and all were complete when Mason bought them. He refused to buy any incomplete sets. None of the family put forward the smallest objection to the house being thoroughly searched.

So Henry and Sergeant Duckett spent a weary and fruitless morning wading knee-deep through the accumulated bric-a-brac of a large family house They got very tired, filthy, and disgruntled. They found nothing.

In the afternoon Henry and the Sergeant transferred their attention to the Doctor's house. Neither Dr. Thompson nor his wife were at all pleased about this, and Henry felt reasonably certain that even the memory of mutual schooldays would not be sufficient to save Emmy's friendship with Isobel, which was a pity, because he found absolutely nothing of interest in the house.

Once again Henry found himself face to face with the unpleasant prospect of searching Cregwell Manor, and he could not believe that he would be accorded the same good-natured co-operation by Sir John Adamson that he had been given by everybody at the Grange. After all, when a Chief Constable exercises his privilege of calling in Scotland Yard to help with an investigation, he seldom assumes he will be on the receiving end of it himself.

Henry, however, was not easily intimidated, for all his apparent mildness; and it was not cowardice but close reasoning that made him decide to postpone his visit to Cregwell Manor for the moment and to start on the following day, Thursday, with further talks with certain members of the Manciple family. In the quiet, almost literally funereal atmosphere of Cregwell Grange, he counted on being able to talk at length and in tranquility with people who could help him.

Consequently, when Henry drove up the winding drive to the Grange at a quarter past nine on Thursday morning, he was surprised and not over-pleased to see that he was not the first visitor. Several cars were parked in the drive, and he was able to identify Dr. Thompson's among them. Henry felt a twinge of worry. What had happened? Had somebody else at the Grange been taken ill? Or even…

He parked his car quickly and got out. The front door stood open and before Henry could reach it, the Doctor came hurrying out. He looked anxious.

"What…?" Henry began.

"Sorry. Can't stop. Urgent." The Doctor opened the door of his car and took out what appeared to be an old pillow-case stuffed with bulky objects. Carrying this in his arms—it seemed to be heavy—he hurried into the house again. Henry followed him, only to collide in the doorway with a stout lady whom he identified as Mrs. Richards, proprietress of the General Stores.

"Pardon," said Mrs. Richards. "Didn't see you. Have you come about the lemonade?"

"In a way," said Henry.

"Poisonous stuff," said Mrs. Richards severely. "We don't want *that* again."

"I quite agree," said Henry.

"Well, I hope you'll see to it. Several people were sick last time." Mrs. Richards bustled out into the drive and got into one of the cars. From the depths of the house Violet Manciple's voice called, "Jumble in the study!"

A figure loomed up in the doorway behind Henry. He turned to see Sir John Adamson framed against the sunshine outside. He was carrying a large box and he called out, on a note of interrogation, "Jams and jellies?"

Like a jack-in-the-box Maud appeared at a run from the cloak room.

"Dining room bottled fruit, drawing room jams and jellies, jumble in the study," she said, and then to Henry, "Hello. What do you want?"

She had gone before Henry could reply, and her place was taken by Edwin Manciple, who came out of the drawing room saying, "Harry Penfold wants to know what to do with the Lucky Dip."

"Excuse me, Tibbett," said Sir John, pushing past Henry. "Got six more boxes in the car." He disappeared into the drawing room.

Violet Manciple appeared at the kitchen door. "Lucky Dip in the garage, Hoop-la in the morning room," she said briskly, and retreated into the kitchen again.

Dr. Thompson came out of the study empty-handed. "One more lot," he remarked cheerfully as he made his way out to his car.

Behind Henry, Julian Manning-Richards came into the hall carrying a large, fully-charged sack. "Lucky Dip?" he asked.

"In the garage," said Henry.

"Thanks," said Julian. He went out through the back door.

Mabel and Alfred from The Viking arrived together, each carrying a bulky load. "Home-made jam?" Mabel asked.

"Drawing room," said Henry.

"Ta."

"Jumble?" queried Alfred.

"In the study." Henry began to feel as though he were on point duty.

"And get a move on, Alfred," remarked Dr. Thompson. He had come in from the car with another pillowcase full. "This is my last lot." To Henry, he said, "Tell Violet that Isobel will be along later with the bottled fruit."

Behind Henry a throat was cleared noisily, and Frank Mason said, "I've brought some jumble. Do you know where...?"

Maud came down the stairs. "Jumble in the study." she said.

"Oh, Miss Manciple—I wondered..."

"In the study," said Maud heartlessly. "Anybody seen the Vicar?"

"He rang up," Violet called from the kitchen. "His car's broken down."

"Would you like me to go and fetch him?" asked Frank Mason eagerly.

"Have you got a car?" Maud showed a glimmer of interest for the first time.

"Yes, of course. Outside in the drive. I mean…"

"Well, dump your jumble in the study and then you can drive me to the vicarage."

"Oh, *yes*, Miss Manciple."

"Why on earth don't you call me Maud? Everyone else does."

"Well, I…"

Maud winked at Henry. To Frank she said, "Queen Victoria is dead, you know. And so is Karl Marx. The world goes on."

"Panta rei," said Henry. He felt it was rather unkind, but he could not resist it.

Violet Manciple came out of the kitchen with Julian. "But he *promised* to let me have the bran for the tub," she was saying. "*And* the Hoop-la rings."

"He says his wife isn't well," said Julian.

"That has nothing to do with it. Oh, it's too provoking. Where's George?"

As if in answer a series of shots rang out from the range.

"Really," said Violet Manciple, "at a time like this the least he could do—oh, dear, I wish Claud and Ramona were here…"

"Sir Claud said they'd be arriving about lunchtime," said Julian.

"As if that helped," said Violet. She sounded as nearly bad-tempered as Henry could imagine, for a person of her singularly sweet disposition. "Two more mouths to feed and the worst will be over by then. Now, Julian dear, will you please go and find Maud and ask her to bring me the list of booths and helpers. I'll be in the kitchen."

"Right you are, Mrs. Manciple."

"I think," said Henry, "that Miss Manciple has gone to the vicarage."

"Oh, no, she can't have," said Julian easily. "It's too far to walk and her car's in the garage. I've just been unloading it."

Oh, well, thought Henry, it's none of my business. Aloud, he said, "Frank Mason gave her a lift in his car."

For a moment it looked as though Julian were going to be really angry; or, rather, as though he were going to show it, for Henry had no doubt about the reality of the fury that flashed into his blue eyes. However, the dangerous moment passed. In a split second Julian had his anger under control, and he managed an apparently unforced smile as he said, "Oh, well, I dare say she won't be long. I'll go and give the Bishop a hand with the Lucky Dip."

"Thank you, Julian," said Violet. "And tell Harry Penfold that the tub is no use without the bran. He must see that."

"I'll tell him," said Julian. He went out into the back yard.

Violet Manciple looked seriously at Henry for a moment, and then said, "You must forgive me, Mr. Tibbett, but just for the moment I can't remember why I asked you to come up here this morning."

"You didn't," said Henry.

"Ah, that would account for it. But—yes, I did!"

"Really, you didn't, Mrs. Manciple. It was I..."

"Your charming wife," said Violet Manciple firmly. There was a note in her voice that Henry recognized and feared: the voice of an organizing woman in the process of organizing. "Guessing the Vicar's weight."

"I beg your pardon?"

"The Vicar's weight. Sixpence a guess, and one of Miss Whitehead's home-made cakes as a prize for the person who comes closest."

"But..."

Violet Manciple laid a hand on Henry's arm, "I was at my wit's end this morning," she said, "when Harry Penfold told me that Elizabeth had come down with flu. I couldn't imagine who would be able to look after the Vicar's weight, all my helpers are fully booked-up you see. And then, suddenly, I said to myself, Mrs. Tibbett! Mrs. Tibbett is the answer!"

"You mean that…?"

"I know she won't refuse," said Mrs. Manciple in a voice of pure honey. "It's quite simple. All she has to do is to take the sixpences and write down each person's guess with their names. And make sure that the children are kept away from the cake. Last year two of the prizes were eaten before they could be distributed. I never caught the culprits, but I have my own ideas. Why, look!" Violet sounded really surprised. "Here's my list that I was asking Julian to ask Maud to—and it's here on the hall table after all. I'll just write it down. Let me see—here it is, Vicar's Weight Contest. I'll just cross out Mrs. Penfold and put in Mrs. Tibbett."

"I'll have to ask her," said Henry dubiously.

"Of *course* you will," said Mrs. Manciple, generous in victory. "But I know she won't refuse."

"Meanwhile," Henry pursued doggedly, "there are a few things I'd like to talk to you about, you and Major Manciple."

"Jumble?" asked a cheerful voice,

"In the study," said Henry automatically.

The kitchen door opened and a ruddy-faced man in tweeds looked out into the hall. "About that bran, Mrs. M.," he said.

"Yes Harry, what about it? You promised…"

"Well, it's like this, see. If you can send someone up to the big barn at Tom Rodd's place…"

Violet Manciple turned to Henry. "You see how it is, Mr. Tibbett," she said. "I really *can't*. Come back at teatime; we'll be quieter then. And Claud and Ramona will be here," she added, as if promising a rare treat.

Henry hesitated, and in the moment of his hesitation four separate people appeared with problems which only Mrs. Manciple could resolve and which concerned matters as diverse as sheets to cover the tables in the refreshment marquee, sacks for the choir boys' sack race, the placing of the fortune teller's tent, and the composition of the bouquet to be presented to Lady Fenshire. Meanwhile, Harry Penfold was repeating patiently, "The big barn up at Tom Rodd's place, Mrs. Manciple, but it means someone going up there for it. Bess was going to take the Jeep, but now she's been taken bad..."

Henry gave in. "I see how it is, Mrs. Manciple," he said. "I'll go and ask Emmy about the Vicar's weight."

Violet Manciple did not even hear him.

CHAPTER THIRTEEN

AS A MATTER OF FACT Henry had had every intention of returning to Cregwell Grange that afternoon, once the frenzy of preparation for the Fête had died down; but things did not work out like that.

On arriving back at The Viking, he first of all put to Emmy Violet Manciple's proposition that she should take over from the ailing Mrs. Penfold and assume charge of the Vicar's weight. Emmy, outwardly amused but secretly flattered, said she would try anything once.

"Well, you'd better ring Mrs. Manciple and tell her so," said Henry. "It's like a madhouse up there, but I expect you'll be able to get the message through to her. It'll set her mind at rest."

"You don't think I should go up and see her?"

"Heavens, no. I tell you, it's like Piccadilly Circus at the rush hour. Just call her."

Emmy disappeared down the corridor into the small, dark box under the stairs which housed The Viking's telephone, and Henry applied himself to compiling his official report on the death of Raymond Mason. In a few minutes Emmy was back.

"Did you get her?" Henry asked.

Emmy laughed. "I did in the end," she said. "Madhouse is about right. But after I'd spoken to her, Major Manciple came on the line, wanting to speak to you. He's waiting now."

"Oh blast," said Henry. "Did he say what it was about?"

"No, he wouldn't tell me. Another of his crack-brained theories, I expect."

"Oh, well, I'd better go and see what he wants."

"Tibbett?" George Manciple's voice made a gruff solo against the accompaniment of shrill sounds that floated down the wire from the Grange.

"Speaking," said Henry.

In the background a feminine voice said, "Where's Frank Mason? He promised..."

"You were up here yesterday," Manciple went on, "searching the place, looking for things."

"That's right," said Henry.

"Jumble in the study!" came the ghostly echo of Violet's voice from far away.

"And one of the things you were looking for was my gun. The one I reported missing."

"Right again."

"Well, I just thought you'd like to know that it's turned up."

"It's—what?"

"Turned up. Can't you hear me?"

There was a crash from somewhere in the background and Maud's voice said, "*Everything* for the Lucky Dip has to be *wrapped*..."

Henry said, "Where has it turned up?"

"Why, in its proper place. In the rack in the cloakroom with the others."

"Oh, damnation," said Henry.

"What's that? I thought you'd be pleased."

"Well, I'm not. Everybody in Cregwell has been milling around your house this morning, and any of them could have slipped the gun back. I don't like it."

"Well, I can't help that, Tibbett." George sounded nettled that his good news had not been better received. "Anyhow, I reported it missing, and now I'm reporting it back again."

"Well, I suppose there's a hope of fingerprints. Now, listen carefully, Major Manciple. I want you to wrap that gun up in…"

"Too late for that, I'm afraid," said George.

"What do you mean, too late?"

"Well, I wouldn't have known the thing had been returned, with all the rush and to-do, if it hadn't been for Edwin."

"What has the Bishop to do with it?"

"He's helping me on the range on Saturday, you see. He's a surprisingly good shot, for a clarinet player. I always say these things run in families."

"Please, Major Manciple, would you just give me the facts?" Henry was experiencing the now-familiar woolly sensation.

"I lend the range every year, you see," said George, who was evidently in no hurry. "Partly philanthropy, of course, but I won't hide from you the fact that I welcome the chance of demonstrating to all and sundry that it's perfectly safe—after that unpleasant business with the Council. We don't use the traps, of course. Too difficult for amateurs, and too cumbersome to prepare. No, we set up ordinary targets—outers, inners, and bulls—and charge half-a-crown for six shots. There's a small prize for the winning score at the end of the afternoon."

Again Violet's voice floated distantly by. "Well, if Julian has taken Maud's car, and Frank has gone, you'll just have to see if Mrs. Thompson will…"

"Could we get back to the missing gun?" asked Henry.

"Oh, indeed. Yes, to be sure. As I was saying, Edwin is helping me on the range on Saturday, so I asked him today, would he do the usual maintenance job on the guns? Cleaning, oiling, and loading—all ready for the fray. He came to me just now and said, 'Well, that's done, George, all five of them.' 'All five?' I said. 'But there's only four. The police still have the gun that shot poor Mason and another one is missing.' 'There's five as sure as I'm standing here,' he said. 'Come and see for yourself.' It seems Edwin hadn't realized there was one missing, you see. So I went along to the cloakroom and there they were..."

"All nicely cleaned and polished by the Bishop," said Henry bitterly.

"Yes, he'd made a very nice job of them, I'll say that for him. Now he's quite positive that all five were in the rack when he started on them about an hour ago. And I'm sure that there were only four first thing this morning. So..."

"Yes," said Henry, "I can draw a deduction from that."

"Well, there we are. That's all I wanted to tell you. I thought you'd be interested. What's that? Yes, dear, tell your mother I'll be along in a minute. Good-bye for now, Tibbett."

Henry walked back to his room with mixed feelings. On the face of it, it was a good thing that the gun had been returned to its rightful owner; at least it was not being concealed for some sinister purpose. On the other hand, it had been placed in the most convenient position for speedy use, and Henry had some misgivings about leaving five loaded guns freely available in a house where he was reasonably sure that one murder had been committed. The thought of the shooting range and its equipment being open to all on Saturday was also an uneasy one. He returned to his report and worked on it steadily, pausing only for a quick lunch.

It was at half-past four, when Henry had put the finishing touches to his report and was contemplating another assault on Cregwell Grange, that he was again summoned to the telephone. This time it was Scotland Yard. According to the sergeant in London, a Mr. Mumford had been persistently trying to get in touch with Henry. Other than his name he had refused to disclose any particulars of himself or his business, simply insisting that he must speak to Chief Inspector Tibbett, and that the matter was confidential. He had first telephoned at about three o'clock. Every effort had been made to persuade him to talk to somebody else or to explain what he wanted, but to no avail. All that took time, as Henry would appreciate. Finally, Mr. Mumford had admitted that he had important information concerning the Raymond Mason case. At which the sergeant had decided that Henry should be contacted. He passed on Mr. Mumford's telephone number—a Mayfair one, which Henry recognized as being that of Raymond Mason Ltd.—and suggested that Henry might like to ring Mr. Mumford directly. Henry said that he would.

"Oh, Inspector Tibbett, thank heavens I've been able to get in touch with you at last!" Mr. Mumford was more than agitated; he was terrified, and his terror shivered down the telephone line like cracking ice. "I really am at my wits' end. Nothing like this has ever happened before. Never. And of course I can't call in the police. That would be quite impossible."

"What has happened?" Henry asked.

"I hardly like to tell you over the telephone."

"Just give me some idea."

"Well," Mr. Mumford gulped. "First of all you may remember that when you were here the other day, we had some—er—unwelcome visitors."

"I remember," said Henry.

"I have been waiting with some apprehension, as you can imagine, for the—em—the results of their visitation."

"I haven't seen anything in the papers myself," Henry remarked.

Mr. Mumford drew in his breath sharply at such plain speaking on a public telephone line. He said, "There has been nothing to see—until today. You have not noticed—anything—today?"

"No," said Henry, "but I've been busy."

"There is a most scurrilous, a most—well—you'll just have to read it, Chief Inspector. In the—em—one of our most popular dailies. I won't mention its name. It concerns itself with—em—with my late employer. It hints, definitely implies that there was an irregularity between Mr.—my late employer—and some of his clients. It has been cleverly written, for I immediately contacted the firm's solicitor, but he gives it as his opinion that we cannot sue. The insinuations are all too oblique, if you see what I mean. That makes it none the more pleasant."

"I'm very sorry to hear about this, Mr. Mumford," said Henry, "but I really don't see what I can do to help you."

"Nobody can help me," said Mr. Mumford with epic resignation. "Not over that matter, at any rate. It was not primarily about that that I telephoned you. It was bad enough to read all that in the paper this morning, but I had no idea then what was in store for me later in the day. This has been a day I shall not lightly forget, Chief Inspector."

"What happened later in the day?"

"I arrived back at the office later than usual after lunch," said Mr. Mumford. "The reason being that I had spent a long time with the solicitor, as I told you, and did not get to Fuller's for my customary modest meal until two o'clock. At three I was back at the office. At first I noticed nothing wrong. But then..."

"Then what?"

"I really don't know if I should tell you over the telephone."

"I'm afraid you'll have to," said Henry.

There was a little pause. Then Mr. Mumford brought out a single word like a bullet. "Robbery!"

"You mean your office has been burgled?"

"Precisely. Straightforward burglary!"

"What has been taken?"

"That's the point, Chief Inspector. That is the terrible thing. The—the *very private* files belonging to my late employer. I hope I need not say more. You will understand."

"If you have been robbed," said Henry, "you should have called in the police at once. Why didn't you?"

"I fear I have not made myself clear, Chief Inspector. You see, I know who is responsible for this robbery."

"You do?"

"Of course. My—my late employer's son. I can say no more. No more at all. Chief Inspector, you must come to London and see for yourself."

"Yes," said Henry, "yes, I think I should do that." He looked at his watch. "It's a quarter to five now. I can be with you in about an hour, or better say an hour and a half to allow for the rush-hour traffic. What time does your office close?"

"Six o'clock, thank God," said Mr. Mumford, showing a gleam of humanity. "I'll wait here for you. That way we shall be quite alone here. I can't thank you enough, Chief Inspector."

Henry went back to the bedroom and broke the news to Emmy that he had to leave for London at once, and did not know when he would be back.

"Is it bad?" Emmy asked.

"It's most peculiar," said Henry.

"What does that mean?"

"Just what it says. I don't understand what is happening, but I have a nasty feeling that I may have been a bloody fool. And that's a feeling I don't like." He put on his coat. "Will you be an angel and call Sergeant Duckett for me? Tell him I've had to go to London, but that I'll see him tomorrow. And don't wait up for me. I may be late."

The drive to London took longer than Henry had anticipated, for he hit the suburban rush-hour traffic fair and square. After a frustrating series of crawls and jams he eventually found himself at the offices of Raymond Mason Ltd. just before seven o'clock. The street door was firmly locked, but Henry's ring brought a harassed Mr. Mumford at a run to open it. Together, they walked through the inner office, past the shrouded typewriters and calculating machines, and into the manager's sanctum.

The first thing that Henry noticed—he could hardly miss it—was the fact that Raymond Mason's private filing cabinet was open, and that it was empty. Mumford, following Henry's glance, sat down heavily in the big swivel chair behind the desk and said, "You see? You see? Empty. All gone. Everything."

"Tell me about it," said Henry.

"There's very little to tell. As I told you, I didn't get back until about three. As I came through the big office, Miss

Jenkins said, 'You've just missed Mr. Frank, Mr. Mumford. He was waiting for you, but he left a few.' Frankly, Chief Inspector, I was pleased rather than sorry. As you know, my relationship with Mr. Frank has never been—well—let us just say that he is not the man his father was. Let us just say that."

"By all means," said Henry. "So, Mr. Frank had just left."

"That's right. He had been waiting in my office to see me. Arrived about half-past two, as far as I could make out, and left about ten to three. I said something to Miss Jenkins about it being too bad—I don't believe in letting the staff know if there is any slight—em—friction in the upper echelons. It makes for bad discipline. Anyhow, I came in here, and saw—what you have just seen. I was appalled. That is not too strong a word, Chief Inspector. Appalled. I didn't know what to do." Mr. Mumford sounded amazed as he made this admission. Henry supposed that it was probably the first time in his life that he had found himself in such a predicament.

Mumford went on. "Loth as I was to divulge anything to the staff, I felt compelled—I called in Miss Jenkins, who is the senior typist, and asked her whether Mr. Frank had taken any documents with him when he left the office. 'Oh, yes,' she said, quite unconcerned. 'He had quite an armful. Files and boxes and things. He said to tell you he was taking some things of his father's.' So you see, Chief Inspector…"

"I notice," said Henry, "that he took the money as well as the files, not to mention the whiskey. And the…"

"Where did he get the key?" demanded Mumford in a sort of wail. "Where? *You* had the key, which you said was on Mr. Mason's own key ring…"

"That's right," said Henry, "and it still is."

"Then how did Mr. Frank…?"

Henry sighed. "He has been living in his father's house, Cregwell Lodge, for the past week," he said. "It's perfectly possible that Raymond Mason kept a duplicate key somewhere and that Frank Mason found it."

"Those files were confidential, Chief Inspector. Supposing that he…? I don't like to think about it. You know the names involved. People of the very highest standing."

"You mean," said Henry, "that those files would be extremely useful to a blackmailer."

"To a…? What a terrible word, Chief Inspector!"

"By the way," Henry added, "do you have a copy of that newspaper handy, the one you were telling me about?"

"I certainly do!" Momentarily, Mumford's indignation got the better of his fright. "Of all the disgraceful… Oh, if I knew who was to blame!"

"The journalist concerned, I suppose," said Henry.

"No, no. Who was to blame for setting the press on to us in the first place. Somebody must have drawn their attention to…"

"Yes. It's interesting, isn't it?" said Henry. "Let's have a look at that paper."

Mumford opened a drawer in his desk and pulled out the current copy of a best-selling daily newspaper. It was open at an inside page article entitled, "The Life and Death of a Gambler," which featured a large photograph of the late Raymond Mason. There were also photographs of some of Mason's more aristocratic clients, but none of them, Henry noted, was a "private" client. Each time that the name of a titled or celebrated person was mentioned in the text it appeared in heavy type, even though the connection might be as tenuous as the mention of a John Smith who was "a kinsman of the **Earl of Fenshire.**" In this way the writer had managed to pepper his story with illustrious names. He had also spiced it, very cleverly, with the most gossamer of innuendoes. Phrases like "walking a financial tightrope, like all of the bookmaking fraternity," "steering an unimpeachable course between the pitfalls of near-legality and downright roguery which have besmirched the good name of this profession," and "profitable sidelines, generously helped along by influential acquaintances," all added up to create a certain effect.

The story was, in fact, a rags-to-riches epic. The poor boy from the East End of London who wound up as "a friend to Dukes and Earls." And yet this success story had ended in tragedy and mystery. The writer pointed out that Scotland Yard had been called in to investigate Mason's death, that although no statement had been made, the police were actively pursuing their inquiries, and that the inquest on Friday should be an interesting affair. It occurred to Henry that the writer of the article would have a great deal more juicy material had he had access to Mason's private files, and he wondered whether in a subsequent piece he might have the benefit of their aid.

Mumford was saying, "You will know the legal position better than I…"

Henry said, "I thought that you had consulted your solicitor and that he told you that this article gave you no grounds for taking legal action."

"No, no, no. I am talking about Mr. Frank. The will, you see."

"What about the will?"

"The solicitor told me today. Mr. Mason's will is horribly simple. *Everything* is left to Mr. Frank. Everything. So, you see, Mr. Frank obviously felt that he was entitled to walk in here and take anything he wanted. But is that so, Chief Inspector?"

"No," said Henry, "it isn't. The will hasn't been proved yet. Frank Mason has no right to anything, for the moment. Of course, executors often advance money to heirs, if they need it to tide them over until the will is admitted to probate, but the heirs have no legal right. None at all."

"So I could sue Mr. Frank for theft?"

"You could," said Henry, "but I wouldn't, if I were you. The will will be proved long before you could get the case into court, and—well—I can't imagine that you'd welcome the sort of publicity that it would bring."

"That's just the point, Chief Inspector. I'm not a fool, I realize the position I am in, that the firm is in. That's why I telephoned you rather than the police."

Henry hardly knew whether or not to be flattered at this distinction. Mumford went on. "I knew you would understand and be able to advise me. What am I to do now?"

"The best advice I can give you," said Henry, "is to do absolutely nothing."

"Nothing? But those files…"

"There's nothing useful you can do, except go home and try to have a good night's sleep, and carry on as usual in the office tomorrow. If you are seriously troubled by the press, call the police. If anything else interesting happens, call me." Henry scribbled the numbers of The Viking and the Cregwell police station on a piece of paper, and handed it to Mumford.

"But, Chief Inspector…"

"Meanwhile," said Henry, "*I* will do something." He looked at his watch. "It's five to eight. The roads will be clear now, so I should be back in Cregwell by nine, with any luck. I shall visit Mr. Frank Mason."

Mr. Mumford's face lit up as though some unseen hand had pressed a switch. "You will? And you'll get the files…"

"I don't know what I shall get," said Henry, "but I'll do my best."

Henry was relieved to see that lights were burning in Cregwell Lodge, when he parked his car outside the house soon after nine o'clock. He was also intrigued to see that the heavy red velvet curtains of the study were tightly drawn, for Frank Mason had given him the impression of a man who had no use for such bourgeois devices.

Henry rang the front doorbell loudly. This had an interesting effect. First, the curtain was drawn aside fractionally, as though someone were looking out to see who was ringing. Then there was a slight scuffling sound inside the house, and all the lights went out. A palpitating silence followed.

Henry rang again. When this had no effect, he walked to the study window, unable to resist the thought of the occasion when the Bishop of Bugolaland had done the same thing. The curtains were tightly closed and the light was out, but a smaller, more erratic light flickered behind them. Henry, moving quietly, tried the handle of the French window which opened into the garden. As he had hoped, it was not locked. It opened easily, and Henry slipped between the curtains and into the study.

Frank Mason was standing by the door which led to the hallway listening anxiously. He evidently expected another summons from the front doorbell. In the large open fireplace a pile of logs burned merrily, making the room insufferably hot, for the September evening was mild. On the desk lay what remained of Raymond Mason's confidential files. The others were in the process of being reduced to ash in the fireplace.

"Good evening," said Henry.

Mason wheeled around as though he had been stung. For a moment he looked at Henry with real panic in his face; then, suddenly, he grinned.

"I forgot the garden door," he said.

"Luckily for me," said Henry. "You might as well put the lights on again."

Frank Mason did so. Then he said, "Sorry I was unsociable. No special reason, you know. I just didn't feel like company." He paused, and then added awkwardly, "I was burning some old papers."

"So I see," said Henry. He sat down in a leather armchair. "Why did you set the hounds of the press on to poor Mr. Mumford?"

"I didn't."

"Oh yes you did. There was nobody else who…"

"I didn't set them on to Mumford. He has nothing to do with it. He's a sycophantic cipher. Mumford isn't worth a minute of anybody's time." Frank paused. Then he said, "I thought the world ought to know about people like my father."

"You seem to me," said Henry, "to be in a very muddled frame of mind. Only a few days ago you were claiming that your father had been murdered, and demanding justice and revenge."

"You don't have to murder a man simply because you disapprove of his way of life," said Mason. He smiled suddenly. "Not even if you're a revolutionary Communist. Besides, he was my father. You said just now that I was demanding justice. Well, I am. Justice for the person who killed him, and justice for the community at large by warning them against other men like him. I don't call that muddled thinking."

"You and I," said Henry, "should get a few things straight. For a start, nobody killed your father."

"But…"

"I'll explain," said Henry. He did.

When he had finished, Frank Mason said slowly, "I suppose you must be right. Which means that I owe Manning-Richards an apology, but I'm damned if he's going to get it." After a pause he added, "A bit ironic, isn't it? Dad got himself shot to save old Miss Manciple's life, and now she's dead anyway, not a week later. He needn't have bothered."

Henry looked at him curiously. "Nobody could possibly have known that Miss Manciple was going to die," he said, "could they?"

"No. No, of course not."

"Right," said Henry. "Now we'll go on from there. Starting with the gun. What did you do with it?"

"I told you. I put it in this drawer…"

"You didn't take it back to Cregwell Grange this morning when you called there with your jumble for the Fête?"

"Certainly I didn't. Why, has it turned up?"

"Yes," said Henry.

"Oh well, that's a good thing. One more mystery out of the way."

"Perhaps," said Henry. "Now, about the things you took from your father's private filing cabinet today."

Frank Mason looked decidedly rattled. "How did you…?"

"You don't think that Mr. Mumford would let a thing like that pass, do you? He got in touch with me at once. He's extremely upset."

Mason grinned. "Good," he said.

"Why on earth," Henry asked, "didn't you simply lock up the cabinet again? Then he'd never have known that the things had disappeared."

"Because I wanted him to be upset, of course," said Mason. "I hope he bursts a blood vessel. He can shout all the imprecations he can think of at the top of his tiny voice and brandish his tiny fists. There's not a damned thing he can do about it."

"What makes you so sure of that?"

"Well, everything in that office is my property now, isn't it? Including Mumford, come to that."

"No," said Henry, "it isn't."

"But my father's will…"

"Has not yet been proved. Legally, you aren't entitled to anything yet. Your action today was just as much burglary as if you'd put a nylon stocking over your face and robbed a bank."

Frank Mason looked alarmed. "Are you sure? You mean—he can't actually do anything about it, can he?"

"He could," said Henry, "but I don't think he will. Not if you are sensible."

"What do you mean by sensible?"

"First thing tomorrow," said Henry, "you must go up to London, apologize to Mumford, and return everything that you took out of the cabinet."

"But," instinctively, Mason's eyes went to the fire.

"I do appreciate your difficulty," said Henry. "Why are you destroying them?"

"You know what they are?"

"Yes, I do."

"Well, wouldn't you destroy them?"

"*I* might feel inclined to," said Henry, "but I should have thought that they'd be just the thing to give to the press if you are set on blackening your father's memory."

Mason flushed, "He was my father," he said.

"You mean, there are limits?"

Mason said, "I hold no brief for the useless parasites concerned, but I'm neither a toady nor a blackmailer. When I take over the business, it's going to be honestly run."

"And profitably?"

"Why not? In a competitive society one has to compete."

After a pause Henry said, "I should go ahead and burn the lot. I imagine that all those dossiers show the client in a state of indebtedness, don't they?"

"Of course. That was the whole filthy idea."

"Then nobody is going to complain."

"But Mumford…"

"Least of all Mumford," said Henry. He added, "When you take over, don't sack him. He's an honest man and extremely useful to the firm. You'll never make a profit without him."

Mason stared at Henry. "You're a curious character," he said.

"In every sense of the word," said Henry. "Among other things I'm curious about why your father was so keen on buying Cregwell Grange."

"Snobbery." The word came out like a reflex action.

"No other reason?"

"Not that I know of. What other reason could there be?"

"He never said anything to you…?"

"Never when he could help it," said Frank shortly. He picked up a file from the desk. Henry saw that it had Sir John Adamson written neatly on its label. "Well, another for the holocaust."

As the flames licked around the buff cardboard and its contents, Henry felt a momentary pang of doubt, but he put it aside. He said, "When did you find out about these secret flies?"

"When I found the spare key to the cabinet. It was in a drawer in my father's dressing table, and it was rather indiscreetly labeled. I put it into my pocket the day I arrived here—before you started your snooping around—but I didn't think much about it until I connected it up with a list of names that I found in an old diary of his. Then I decided to investigate. I was delighted to find that Mumford was out. That gave me an opportunity for a cozy little that with Sarah Jenkins. She's a bright girl, and she knew a lot more about what went on in that office than Mumford did."

"Do you still have the key?"

"Yes. It's here," Mason pulled a small key out of his pocket. It bore no label of any sort and Henry remarked on this. Mason said, "I burned the label."

"Can you remember what it said?"

"No."

"Not even in general terms?"

"Oh, something about this being the key to the private account files."

"Nothing else?"

"No."

"Oh well," said Henry, "that's that. But it's very important that you should take the other things back tomorrow."

"The money, you mean?"

"The money, the whiskey, and the book. By the way—may I see the book?"

Mason looked surprised. "I didn't know that you went in for pornography, Inspector."

Henry said blandly, "It's a book that is banned in this country. I should take it into custody."

Mason got up. "Curiouser and curiouser," he said. He opened a drawer in the desk. "Here it is. But I'm afraid you'll be disappointed."

"What do you mean?"

"It's only the dust cover that is wicked. I suppose Dad thought it would give him a certain standing with some of his less attractive customers to have a notorious piece of banned filth lying around in his office. He had that sort of mentality."

He tossed the book over to Henry. Inside the lurid cover was a sensational but morally unimpeachable detective story. Watching Henry's face, Mason said, "I was disappointed myself. That's ruined your bedtime reading for tonight, hasn't it?"

"Yes," said Henry. He grinned. "Yes, it has."

Mabel was just shutting up the bar when Henry got back to The Viking. It had been a busy evening, she said. Sir Claud Manciple had been in with his niece and that nice young man of hers. They'd had a drink with Mrs. Tibbett. Only left a few minutes ago—what a shame Henry had missed them. They were here for the funeral tomorrow, of course. Poor Miss Dora—it was sad, wasn't it, but she'd had a good life after all. Mrs. Tibbett had gone upstairs to bed. Would Henry like a nightcap, him being a resident? No? Then she wished him a very good night.

Emmy was already in bed when Henry got upstairs. He told her briefly what had happened in London and at Cregwell Lodge, and she replied with an account of the pleasant evening she had spent with Maud, Julian, and Sir Claud.

"Oh, I knew there was something I had to tell you, Henry. Sir Claud said that Violet had asked him to tell you, if he saw you, that it was all a mistake about Lady Manciple's sleeping pills. She's found them. She'd apparently quite forgotten having packed them in her cosmetic bag; usually she has some other special place for them. So that clears *that* up."

Henry sat down on his bed looking glum. "Yes," he said.

"You ought to be pleased." said Emmy. "First the gun and now the pills. All your mysteries are turning out to be no mysteries at all."

"That," said Henry, "is exactly what worries me."

CHAPTER FOURTEEN

FRIDAY WAS TO BE the occasion for two melancholy events: in the morning, the inquest on Raymond Mason; and in the afternoon, the funeral of Miss Dora Manciple. Only Major and Mrs. Manciple had been told the disquieting news that at a later date there would also have to be an inquest on Aunt Dora. Following the post-mortem examination and its findings, the Kingsmarsh coroner had expressed his willingness to admit sworn statements of identification and medical evidence, and had agreed to let the funeral arrangements go ahead as planned. Henry was pleased at this, for he was anxious to spare the Manciple family as much unpleasantness as possible.

The inquest on Mason had attracted quite a fair sprinkling of journalists from London, thanks to the hints of sensation dropped by Frank and picked up by the press. Consequently, the police evidence caused considerable disappointment. Henry carefully outlined his theory of Mason's death, and nobody seemed inclined to challenge it. Several witnesses attested to Mason's fervent desire to purchase Cregwell Grange, and to his previous attempts to discredit George Manciple's shooting range. The missing gun was mentioned, and by good luck Sergeant Duckett had unearthed a local errand boy who had actually seen Mason experimenting with it in his garden. He had said nothing about it at the time, he affirmed, because he thought it was just a game or a practical joke—"Mr. Mason being that sort of gentleman."

A certain amount of amusement was caused by the demonstration of one of Major Manciple's patent tennis-ball traps, and the press had to be content to make what they could out of that. The gun and bullet were laboriously identified by experts, and Henry was able to demonstrate how the gun must have been propped in the lavatory window and how it had fallen into the shrubbery. Frank Mason confirmed that he had found the experimental gun in his father's house. When the coroner, who was inclined to fuss over details, asked where this gun was now, Henry replied blandly and truthfully that it had been returned to its rightful owner.

Violet and Edwin Manciple were then called to give evidence that nobody could possibly have been in the cloakroom when the shot was fired, and Violet, very embarrassed, also confirmed that Mr. Mason had spent an unusually long time "washing his hands" before leaving the house. The gas cut-out device on the car was described, and Henry made it clear that this must have been operated by Mason himself in order to make the car stop. Aunt Dora's unexpected presence in the line of fire was also proved, providing the motive which impelled Mason to come out from the shelter of the Mercedes.

The coroner, who seemed anxious above all to end the whole matter in a quiet and seemly manner, indicated to the jury that they might think that Mr. Mason was a man given to practical jokes, although the evidence for this was very slim. In any case, he pointed out, it was no concern of theirs to determine just why Mason had set this booby trap. They were merely asked to say, on the evidence, whether he had done so, and thus, by an unlucky chance, caused his own death. If so, the proper verdict should be accidental death.

The jury needed very little prompting. It took them less than half an hour to return with the verdict indicated, and the journalists took themselves off to the Kingsmarsh Arms in a gloomy mood and did their best to make bricks without straw. There was no doubt that the great mystery of Raymond Mason's death had fizzled out like a dud rocket. It would not rate more than a small paragraph.

Meanwhile, in the watery sunshine of late September, the Manciple family stood in the ancient High Street of Kingsmarsh outside the Town Hall where the inquest had been held, and discussed the question of transportation back to Cregwell. George and Violet had brought Claud and Ramona over in their car, while Edwin had squeezed his considerable frame with some discomfort into the back seat of Maud's tiny vehicle. Now, however, Violet had shopping to do in Kingsmarsh, things, she explained earnestly, which were urgently needed for the Fête tomorrow. It would undoubtedly take her some time, and the others were anxious to get home.

At once Henry volunteered to come to the rescue. He had driven over by himself in a large police car and there would be plenty of room for Sir Claud and Lady Manciple and for the Major as well. Henry's offer was gratefully accepted, and the four of them walked off toward the parking lot while Edwin gloomily agreed to return the way he had come, with Maud and Julian.

In the car Henry remarked to Lady Manciple that he was glad to hear that her sleeping pills had been recovered. She raised her eyebrows.

"Recovered is hardly the word, Mr. Tibbett. They were never missing. I can't imagine what made me put them into my cosmetic bag; as Claud will tell you, I always carry them in my trinket box for safety's sake."

"You keep it locked, do you?" Henry asked.

"Oh dear me, no. I don't have expensive jewelry," said Ramona with the faintest emphasis on the personal pronoun. "It's simply that things tend to get lost in a cosmetic bag, whereas..."

"Was the bottle full?"

"Full? What extraordinary questions you do ask, Mr. Tibbett. What makes you so interested in my poor little pills?"

Before Henry could answer, George Manciple said, "The Inspector has a reason, Ramona. Just tell him what he wants to know."

"Dear me," said Sir Claud. He did not sound at all pleased. "I thought your work here was over and done with, Chief Inspector. By the way, I greatly admired your handling of this morning's sad business. Your reasoning was faultless and lucidly expounded."

"Thank you, Sir Claud," said Henry.

"So," Claud persisted, "that's that, isn't it?"

"Very nearly," said Henry. "Lady Manciple, was the bottle of sleeping pills full?"

"No," said Ramona promptly, "about half full, I suppose."

"You wouldn't know if any were missing?"

"Of course not. I don't count them. They aren't poisonous, you know. Just soothing and soporific."

"And also poisonous if taken in large quantities," Henry pointed out.

"But I have never taken them in large quantities," Ramona protested. "If Violet has been saying that I do, it's too bad of her. Just because she hasn't a nerve in her body and sleeps like a log every night she seems to think that there is something immoral about a sleeping pill. It's really none of her business."

A slightly strained silence ensued, which was broken by George Manciple clearing his throat loudly and saying, "Sorry we can't invite you to lunch, Tibbett, but what with the funeral and the Fête, Vi's a bit pushed, you understand..."

"Of course I do, Major Manciple. I wouldn't dream of giving her any extra work at a time like this."

"But we expect to see you at the funeral, of course. And I trust that you and your wife will come back to the house with us afterward. Just a simple tea."

"That's very kind of you," said Henry. "We'd be delighted."

Maud, Julian, and the Bishop had already arrived at Cregwell Grange when Henry turned the nose of his black Wolsley into the drive. The little pale blue minicar, which Maud had christened the Scarab, was parked near the front door. Henry had been planning simply to deliver the Manciples home and then go straight back to The Viking, where Emmy and lunch would be waiting for him, but George Manciple was adamant. Having explained again, and at length, about Violet's inability to offer a meal, he insisted, positively insisted, that Henry should at least take a preprandial drink at the Grange. Refusals and excuses were brushed aside. The Major would not take no for an answer. In the end Henry felt that he would waste more time by arguing than by accepting. So he gave in.

The house was unrecognizable. Through the open door of the study Henry could see piles of assorted jumble, a motley collection of old clothes, knickknacks, lampshades, books, kitchen utensils, children's toys. There was even a battered perambulator. Some of the junk had overflowed into the hall, and the Head's portrait was now draped with an assortment of patently hand-knitted scarves, as well as a fringed silk shawl which must have been quite lovely in the twenties when it was new.

Maud came out of the drawing room, regarded the confusion, and wrinkled her pretty nose. "Isn't it awful?" she said. "You know, we get the same things year after year. Mrs. A. buys Mrs. B.'s old hat, which would disgrace a scarecrow, just so as to contribute to the Church Roof Fund or whatever it may be. Next year, of course, Mrs. A. brings the hat along again as jumble, and Mrs. C. buys it—and so on. By now, the hat is no more than a ritual object. It would be so much easier for everyone if people could just make a financial donation and leave it at that. But, oh no. There always has been a Fête, and there always will be a Fête." She grinned. "The drawing room isn't so bad. Jams, jellies, and cakes. Some of them are really quite good. The trouble is, I expect they'll all get eaten by mistake at Aunt Dora's wake." Quite seriously she added,

"It's a shame she has to miss it. It's the sort of thing she really enjoyed, a nice funeral and a slap-up tea afterward. Come on in. I expect you can do with a drink."

Edwin was already established in the drawing room drinking a glass of beer and studying *The Times* crossword puzzle with dedicated care. He had cleared himself a small space among the jams, jellies, and cakes, and in it he had planted his favorite armchair, which faced pointedly out toward the bow window, turning its chintz-covered back to the rest of the room. It required no great perspicacity to realize that the Bishop was in no mood for conversation. He did not even look up from his paper when Maud and Henry came in.

"Sherry, whiskey, or beer?" Maud asked.

"Sherry, please," said Henry.

He watched her as she walked to the side table, shifted some jellies, and began dealing with the decanters and glasses. Suddenly he could picture her very clearly in her laboratory—white-coated, deft, expert, impersonal, no longer a pretty, fragile girl but a highly-professional scientist. Cool, too. Unsentimental. Henry, who had only the haziest idea of what went on in an atomic research center, found himself wondering whether she ever dealt with animals for vivisection or experimental purposes—and found no difficulty in imagining her doing so.

The dispassionate, detached female scientist turned from her work among the vials and filters and abruptly became Maud Manciple again—small, blonde, and enchanting. She held out a glass and said, "One dry sherry." She handed it to Henry, picked up her own, and said, "I think we should drink to Aunt Dora. She was very partial to a nip of the right stuff now and then."

"To Aunt Dora," said Henry, and raised his glass.

"Amen," said Maud.

"Stuff and nonsense," said Edwin loudly, and he turned a page of his paper with a marked rustling.

"The chrysanthemums are beautiful," said Henry. "Are they from the garden?"

Maud looked a little embarrassed. "No," she said. "We never have any luck with them here. Something to do with the soil."

"They're for Aunt Dora, aren't they?" said Henry.

There was a tiny pause and then Maud said, "You don't have to be so oblique. Yes, I bought them in Kingsmarsh and arranged them myself. Yes, they are traditional flowers of mourning. Don't forget that I lived in Paris for a year. I felt that something should be done."

"And nobody but you would do it?"

"Nobody else," Maud began, and then stopped. "I was very fond of Aunt Dora."

"Yes," said Henry, "I know you were."

Ramona, Claud, and George Manciple came in together, having divested themselves of the strange assortment of shapeless tweed overcoats, knitted scarves, and porkpie hats which they had considered as suitable outerwear for the inquest. Maud once again busied herself with the drinks, and when everyone had been served went out through the French windows to join Julian, who was wandering aimlessly in the garden.

"And the wildflowers, Mr. Tibbett," inquired Lady Manciple. She was smiling, but there was a distinct undertone of menace.

Quickly and mendaciously Henry said, "Oh, they're coming along. Nothing very exciting yet, I'm afraid. Just buttercups and so on."

Ramona's face relaxed into approval. "In every collection there must be the congregation as well as the preacher," she said. "Your most precious *trouvailles* need the company of the homely buttercup and daisy, so that they may shine the brighter by contrast. I trust that you will keep up the good work when you leave here."

"I shall try," said Henry. He did not mention that the flora of Chelsea was sparse, to say the least. After all, there might still be some willow-herb on the last of the bombed sites.

George was saying to Claud, "It's no use your trying to explain such things to me, Claud. You should know that. My mind simply doesn't work the same way as…"

"The quantum theory," said Claud, "is assimilated without trouble by bird-brained undergraduates. I can't see any difficulty…"

"That is very unjust, Claud," Ramona put in severely.

"What is?"

"The way you disparage the brains of birds. You know as well as I do that a number of them are remarkably well-developed."

"True, my dear," agreed Sir Claud, "a nicely taken point. So much of our idiom is slipshod and inaccurate, even if picturesque. Now, if I were to say 'chicken-brained,' I think you would agree that the epithet was justified."

"Chicken?" remarked Edwin from the depths of his chair. "Again? Violet's being a bit extravagant, isn't she?"

"Chicken-brained, Edwin," said Ramona, enunciating even more clearly than usual.

"Chicken brain? What a bizarre notion." Intrigued, Edwin laid his puzzle on his lap and slewed around in his chair to face the room. "Chicken livers I have had frequently, even in Bugolaland. But never chicken brain. You'd need more than one to make a decent meal, I imagine. Perhaps you were thinking of calves' brains."

"I was thinking of nothing of the sort," said Claud briskly. "George and I were discussing the quantum theory."

"The connection with chicken brain," said Edwin, "seems remote." He set a pair of pince-nez on his hawk-like nose.

"I don't understand a word of it," said George plaintively. "Claud should discuss that sort of thing with Maud and Julian."

"Peaches," said Edwin. He looked sternly at Henry.

"I beg your pardon, sir?" said Henry.

"Peaches. Reminded me of Julian. Other way around, I should say. A hundred in bad shape, including English."

Henry had just begun to say, "You mean, a hundred peaches went rotten," when his eye fell on the crossword puzzle. "Ah," he said, "peaches."

"That's right. 14 down."

"Where does the English part of it come in?"

"E," said Edwin.

"E?"

"Yes, of course. Recognized abbreviation for English. All the compilers use it. C is a hundred, of course. Roman numeral."

"And the rest of the word is an anagram of shape?"

"Naturally. I had just filled it in when George mentioned Julian, and that reminded me."

"Reminded you of what, sir?"

"By Jove!" Edwin exclaimed suddenly. He sounded really excited. "Listen to this, Claud. Push along with a pole…"

"What?"

"Wait a minute, wait a minute. I haven't finished. Push along with a pole? Well—er—it's a theory."

"Quantum!" exclaimed Claud.

"Quantum!" cried Edwin, filling in the letters in bold black ink on the checkered squares.

"Quantum!" agreed Henry, struck by the coincidence.

"Don't understand a word of it," said George.

"Humphrey," said Edwin, "couldn't abide peaches. Wouldn't have them in the house. The boy was the same. Most peculiar. Runs in families. Of course, they had Christmas pudding in the east. I was just telling Mr. Tibbett. A hundred in bad shape…"

"Yes, I heard you," said Claud. He walked over to his brother, looked down at the puzzle, and said, "Seventeen across is antidote."

"How do you make that out?"

"A female relative, we hear, died, with a broken toe. But this should cure her."

"Yes—yes, you're right. Wait till I write it in. How remarkable. The man who compiled this puzzle must be an Irishman. The English say 'Arnty' rather than 'Anty.'"

"Or an American," said Claud. "Americans say 'Anty.'"

"I don't think so," said Edwin, "No, I don't think so. An American wouldn't know what a quant pole was."

"An Irishman might not know what a quant pole was either," said George. "It's an East Anglian term."

"Which means," said Edwin triumphantly, "that this puzzle was compiled either by an American or an Irishman who lives in East Anglia. In view of the use of C for a hundred, E for English, and D for died, I am certain that the fellow is Irish. Those abbreviations are not typically American."

"What would an American be doing in East Anglia anyway?" said Ramona.

"Air bases," said Claud. "Plenty of them in Norfolk."

"Nonsense," said Edwin. "Who ever heard of an American airman contributing to *The Times*? No, the man is Irish. The whole of his work proclaims his nationality." There was a little pause, and then Edwin added, "Poor Aunt Dora. She would have enjoyed the funeral so much. Ah, well, we must trust that she will be with us in spirit."

Henry had always, in his long career with the C.I.D., tried hard to be a conscientious officer. He had followed the procedures laid down; he had made the interminable and often fruitless routine inquiries; he had paid attention to detail; he had used and trusted the excellent facilities for scientific analysis available to Scotland Yard; and he knew that more murderers are caught by tracing a dry-cleaner's label or analyzing the fluff in a trouser cuff than by all the haphazard intuition of fiction. Nevertheless, there remained his "nose." And as he stood in the drawing room of Cregwell Grange, with a glass of pale sherry in his hand, watching the three Manciple brothers—so alike physically, so different in character and mentality, and yet all of them so indelibly Manciples—something clicked inside his brain. Whether it was intuition or deduction or observation, he could not be sure; perhaps it was an amalgam of all three. But a picture had presented itself to his mind, and it was not a picture he liked.

Not for the first time Henry found himself faced with the sort of decision which he loathed. His idea was only a hunch. He was under no obligation to continue with inquiries of any kind. He could go quietly back to London and forget the whole thing. On the other hand, the truth was the truth, and the future was the future, and if his idea should prove to be right…

The Manciples, of course, had no notion of Henry's moment of revelation, nor of the inward struggle that followed it. So they all looked considerably surprised when he put his glass down on the table with a clatter and said, "I'm afraid I have to go now, Major Manciple."

"Already? My dear fellow, it's early. Vi will be back in a jiffy. Have another drink."

Henry's throat felt dry, and he would have welcomed a refilled glass; but he said, "No, I'm afraid I must go."

"Well, we shall see you at the funeral. Two-thirty sharp at the Village church…"

"I'm afraid," said Henry, "that I shan't be able to come to the funeral after all. I'm very sorry."

"Not come to the funeral?" Ramona sounded outraged. "But Mr. Tibbett, you said in the car…"

"And tea afterward," added Edwin enticingly.

"Violet will be *most* upset," said George.

"I really am sorry," said Henry, "but I can't. My time isn't my own, you see. I'm a working man, and I have no more to do in Cregwell. I'm going back to London."

So Henry Tibbett went back to London. But Emmy Tibbett stayed in Cregwell. Because, as she said, a promise was a promise, and she couldn't let Mrs. Manciple down. Somebody had to cope with the Vicar's weight, and that was that. She also went to the funeral and was the only person who cried. The tea afterward was excellent.

CHAPTER FIFTEEN

SATURDAY MORNING DAWNED with thin, horizontal streaks of cloud in the blue sky, and over a hundred or more breakfast tables in and around Cregwell there was anxious speculation. Would the fine weather hold for the Fête or were the elements planning a typical *coup de théâtre* in order to wreck Cregwell's biggest day of the year?

Opinion in The Viking was pessimistic. Alfred, as he served Emmy's breakfast egg, remarked that it had started just the same way four years back, that time there'd been the thunderstorm and the refreshment tent got struck by lightning. Mabel, polishing glasses and tables in the bar, said they'd never had a fine day for the Fête yet, not that she could remember, so she didn't see why they should start now.

"Them's the sort of clouds that build up for heavy rain," she said sagely, adding, "My boy friend's in the American Air Force up Norfolk way. That's how I know, see."

Under the dampening influence of these prognostications, Emmy decided to prepare for the worst. She put on a woolen suit, with which she wore sensible, mudproof shoes and a stout raincoat; but she enlivened this rather somber outfit with a pair of brightly-patterned stockings, which combined the twin merits of warmth and cheerfulness. By nine o'clock, she was ready, and waiting at the main door of The Viking for Isobel Thompson to pick her up.

Isobel, by contrast, was on the side of the optimists. As she braked her battered Ford outside the Inn, Emmy saw that she was wearing a sleeveless cotton shift, no stockings, and sandals. This seemed to Emmy to be tempting fate, and she said as much; but Isobel maintained that having the car she could always nip home and get something warmer if the need arose, and that meanwhile there was always so much rushing around to be done that coolness and comfort were paramount considerations.

"You'll just swelter," she added.

"I can't see why guessing the Vicar's weight should be energetic," said Emmy, as she climbed into the car.

"Just you wait," said Isobel ominously. They drove up to the Grange.

The scene of confusion which Henry had interrupted on Thursday, as the various festive ingredients were carried into the house, was as nothing compared with Saturday morning, when they were all brought out again. A contingent of masculine helpers was engaged in setting up the trestle tables which were to serve as booths, and—as frequently happens on such occasions—were proving more trouble than they were worth. Thumbs were being hit by hammers and fingers caught in collapsible furniture, and what with the swearing and the sweating and the dropping and the breaking and the trampling and the misplacing, Violet Manciple was already beginning to consider sacking the male workers, which was exactly what the male workers were hoping for. They always bet confidently to be discharged with ignominy—and snug in the bar of The Viking by eleven-thirty, which was opening time.

Meanwhile, scurrying female helpers trotted like so many ants in and out of the house and the garage, carrying armfuls of assorted objects, which they laid down in disorganized piles on the lawn. Violet herself was already dangerously near to distraction. Like an oracle besieged by overzealous devotees, she was surrounded by a swarm of importunate ladies, each demanding guidance as to where this was to go, or what was to be done with that, or when something else was expected to arrive, or who was responsible for what. Violet kept them at bay by brandishing a fistful of lists and instructions, as though they were magic talismans; but it was clear that she was fighting a losing battle and must soon be overwhelmed.

She caught sight of Emmy and Isobel, and waved a list at them over the heads of the pack. Then, somehow disentangling herself, she made her way over to them.

"How very kind of you, Mrs. Tibbett. Really, I didn't expect you to give up your morning as well. I do appreciate it." She beamed at Emmy. "Isobel, of course, is always a tower of strength. Isobel, dear, if you want to save my life, go and stop Harry Penfold from putting up the Hoop-la in the middle of George's favorite rosebed. He simply won't listen to me, and you're so tactful. And then, would you help Mrs. Richards get the jams and preserves nicely set out? You always make that booth look so pretty. Thank you, dear."

"What shall I do, Mrs. Manciple?" Emmy asked.

"Well, now, if you go indoors, you'll find Maud with the sheets."

"The sheets?"

"We use old sheets as tablecloths for the trestles in the refreshment tent. You pin them in a special way. Maud will show you. And then there are all the glasses and teacups to be set out. No, Mrs. Berridge, that ash tray is *jumble.* Everything for the Lucky Dip is *wrapped*, because of the bran..." Violet was submerged again.

Emmy made her way with some difficulty into the house. In the hall she nearly collided with Julian, who was carrying a large barrel full of bran, which was presumably the Lucky Dip.

"Hello, Mrs. Tibbett," he said. "I hear your husband's gone back to London."

"Yes."

"Don't blame him. This place is more like a sinking ship than a human habitation. Heaven help the poor sailors." He disappeared with his load into the garden.

Frank Mason came out of the study. His red hair was standing spikily on end, and he carried a lot of assorted bric-a-brac on a battered tray. He was saying, "I know it was there."

"Well, it's not there now, young man. You can see that for yourself." Ramona's voice from inside the study was commanding and displeased.

"It's very important," Frank shouted over his shoulder to her.

"*Everything* is important on the day of the Fête," said Ramona. She appeared in the study doorway, her face invisible behind an armful of old clothes. "Can you take these, Maud dear?"

"No, Aunt Ramona, I can't," said Maud firmly. She was in the hall, trying to fold a sheet several times larger than herself.

"Let me, Lady Manciple," said Emmy.

"Oh, thank you. How kind." Ramona thrust the unappetizing pile into Emmy's arms. "Down the lawn and under the sycamore. They should have the booth up by now."

As Emmy went into the garden she heard Maud say, "What was Frank so worked up about?"

"Oh, some book or other..." Ramona's voice was lost.

The booth under the sycamore tree was not up. That is to say, Emmy arrived in time to watch the collapse of its collapsible legs. It subsided to the ground with a certain slow dignity, neatly nipping the fingers of a male helper as it went. There were bellows of rage and pain, and shouts for adhesive tape. Resigned, Emmy laid her cargo in yet another heap on the grass nearby, and went back to help Maud with the sheets. It was ten o'clock.

At ten past ten, the quiet, assured man in the anonymous government office was saying, "We'll try to help you, of course, Chief Inspector, but it may not be easy. They're a funny lot, these newly independent countries. And, as you know, the present regime leans heavily toward the East. We are—" he cleared his throat—"not exactly persona grata in Bugolaland these days."

"But some of the old colonial families must have stayed on, surely," said Henry. "Working for the new regime, I mean."

"Oh, yes. Yes, indeed. When I said we, I meant we rather precisely. Information is not easy to obtain."

"The information I'm after isn't secret in any way," said Henry. "Just a question of consulting records."

"You don't know these laddies," said the man sadly.

"And if my hunch should be right, your department should be very interested," Henry added.

The man sighed. "It takes a lot to interest us, you know," he said. He pulled a scribbling pad toward him, and carefully removed the cap from his fountain pen. "Fire away then. Full details of the information you want..."

❀❀❀

Half-past eleven. The jumble booth was up; the Hoop-la had been removed from the rosebed, the fortune teller's tent had fallen down for the second time, nearly suffocating Ramona who, as the annual incumbent, had been inside inspecting her quarters. The male helpers had been dismissed, to everyone's relief, and were even now outside The Viking in a solid phalanx, waiting for the bar door to open.

Only Frank Mason remained, fetching and carrying for Maud, and complaining at intervals. "I brought it by mistake, you see. I must get it back. It was with the jumble."

"My dear Frank," said Maud unfeelingly, "by the time today is over, you'll be lucky if you haven't had your gold watch sold for sixpence and your pants raffled. Stop making a fuss about your silly book, and help me get these pitchers of lemonade out to the marquee."

Edwin wandered into the kitchen, crossword puzzle in hand, and said, "Violet sent me with a message."

"Oh yes? What was it, Uncle Edwin?"

"I really can't remember," said Edwin. "Something about the Mother's Union booth. I can't believe it was important." He poured himself a glass of lemonade. Maud snatched it out of his hand."

"Oh no, you don't! That's for this afternoon!" She poured the lemonade back into the pitcher. Edwin regarded his empty hand with some surprise.

Julian put his head around the door. "The band's here," he said with a sort of desperation.

"Good," said Maud. "Take them up to the old nursery to change into their uniforms."

"Half of them haven't got their uniforms," said Julian. "Some of them haven't got their instruments either, and two of them are drunk already."

"They always are," said Maud. "Don't worry."

Julian withdrew.

Edwin said, "Who are always what?"

"Drunk, Uncle Edwin."

"Drunk? The Mother's Union? How very surprising. I thought that stuff was only lemonade."

"Oh, *really*," said Maud. There were times when it was trying, being a Manciple. She hustled Frank and the lemonade out into the garden.

Edwin picked up a plate of small jam tarts, which bore a label saying, "Mrs. Berridge. First Prize, Pastries and Flans." Munching absentmindedly, he wandered down to the shooting range. Here, paradoxically, quiet reigned. Serenely, out of the swing of the sea, George and Claud Manciple prepared the targets, ammunition, and guns for the afternoon's sport. Edwin sat down on the garden bench, from which spectators could watch the shooting, and offered the plate of tarts to his brothers. They accepted gratefully. For a while, they all munched in silence. Then Edwin said, "Maud has just told me the most extraordinary thing."

"Really?" remarked George, his mouth full of jam tart.

"Yes. She says that the Mother's Union members in Cregwell are habitually intoxicated."

"Really?" Claud was intrigued.

"It's a very up-to-date branch, of course," George remarked. "Vi was saying so only the other day. Go ahead. Perhaps that's what she meant."

"Our Mothers in Bugolaland were very seldom drunk," said the Bishop. "I can only remember one or two isolated cases. They were black, of course. Better behaved on the whole."

"That may explain it," said George.

"Mass intoxication," remarked Claud, "is a psychological phenomenon springing from basic insecurity, the desire at once to identify with a group and yet to submerge the personality. Curious that it should appear among the mothers of Cregwell."

The three brothers considered the matter seriously as they quietly demolished Mrs. Berridge's plate of prize-winning tartlets. The shrill yelps, the shouts, the confusion and the babble of the preparations for the Fête reached them muted and subdued by the thick privet hedges.

Twelve o'clock. The quiet man said, "Nothing definite yet, I'm afraid, Tibbett. These laddies are sticky, as I told you, and you're asking to go back a long way, old son. Let's face it, one hell of a long way. We've chased it up from this end, of course, but there's nothing. Absolutely nothing. You'll just have to wait."

One o'clock. The mass of exhausted helpers had dispersed, making their way home in order to feed their husbands—or such of them as could be persuaded to leave The Viking—and change into their best clothes, for the Fête was to be opened by Lady Fenshire at half-past two.

At Cregwell Grange the Manciple family were having what Violet called a "stand-up lunch" in the kitchen. This simply meant that everyone raided the larder and the refrigerator, took what they could find, and ate it in an upright position without benefit of knife, fork, or plate. Violet had pressed Emmy to stay and join the family in this unorthodox meal; and Emmy, finding that Isobel had departed in her car some time ago, had accepted gratefully. The only other outsider was Frank Mason. Nobody had actually invited him; he had elected to stay for several reasons of his own, and everybody concluded that somebody else must have issued the invitation.

It was during the course of this unusual lunch—of which Emmy's share was the tail of a cold salmon, a stewed peach, a spoonful of cold mashed potato, and a sausage, in that order—that Emmy found an opportunity of asking Frank Mason about the book he had mislaid.

He looked embarrassed. "Oh, it's nothing, just a book of my father's. I had it with me when I brought up the jumble from the Lodge, and I must have left it in the study with the other things. I'm sure it's with the jumble, but Lady Manciple simply wouldn't let me take a good look."

"I've been dealing with some of the jumble," said Emmy. "What's the book called?"

Frank hesitated palpably. Then he said, "It's not called anything. I mean, it's in a plain brown paper cover, sort of wrapped in brown paper."

Emmy laughed. "When I was young," she said, "that would have meant *Ulysses* or *Lady Chatterley's Lover*. I had them both in brown paper covers. Now you can buy them in paperback."

"You can't buy this one," said Frank Mason. He stood up from the edge of the kitchen table where he had perched to eat an apple. "I think I'll just go and..."

He left the sentence very deliberately unfinished as he strolled out into the hall, but Emmy saw him go into the study.

At two o'clock Lord and Lady Fenshire arrived with Sir John Adamson. They had all lunched together at Cregwell Manor, and seemed in high good humor in spite of the fact that their arrival coincided with the first drops of rain. These, however, appeared to come from a transitory patch of dark cloud and nobody was very depressed. The sun was still making a brave effort to shine, and, as was remarked some hundreds of times, it was a far better day than last year.

At a quarter past two Maud and Julian went down to open the gates. Already, quite a crowd had collected outside. Some of them carried umbrellas, and one or two had even put them up; but, on the whole, summer dresses were the order of the day, and Cregwell seemed determined to regard the weather as fine, despite appearances to the contrary. Within a few minutes all the helpers were installed in their appointed places. Mrs. Richards presided beatifically over the jams and jellies, while Mrs. Berridge scowled bad-temperedly behind the pickles and preserves booth. The respective frames of mind of these two ladies were simply explained. Upon the discovery of the empty plate and discarded prize card at the shooting range, a new card had hastily been written out giving First Prize to Mrs. Richards' apple flan. Violet would have been very angry indeed with her husband and brothers-in-law, if she had had the time.

Ramona, equipped with a dog-eared pack of Tarot cards and a crystal ball improvised from an up-ended goldfish bowl, was ensconced in her uncertainly-based tent, preparing to foretell the future for a shilling a time. She wore earrings made from large brass curtain rings, and a scarlet silk headscarf, "to be in character," as she put it. In fact, she need not have bothered. She looked perfectly in character without any such aids. Isobel Thompson, assisted by Violet, presided over the jumble booth, which was in many ways the heart of the Fête. Sir Claud Manciple, by tradition, was in charge of the Lucky Dip. Emmy wondered wryly whether this might not be a very suitable piece of casting for an atomic scientist. George and Edwin were already at the shooting range. Maud, assisted by Julian, hurried back from the gate to take charge of the refreshment tent. The Vicar's wife supervised the Hoop-la, while the harassed school-teachers from the Village school had a domain of their own in the children's sports section. Emmy sat at her table, notebook and cash box at the ready, prepared to take bets on the Vicar's weight. Frank Mason roamed disconsolately, looking for his lost book. Everything was ready.

At half-past two, Lord and Lady Fenshire came out through the French windows into the garden accompanied by Sir John Adamson and Violet Manciple. Amid a little burst of applause they mounted the rickety rostrum which had been constructed with much acrimony that morning by men who were now happily sozzled in The Viking.

"I am delighted," said Lady Fenshire penetratingly, "to declare well and truly open the annual Fête of the Village of Cregwell."

"One, two, three," said a loud and slightly slurred voice, and with a crash of cymbals and a wail of trombones, the Cregwell band launched into their highly personal rendering of "Anchors Aweigh." At the same moment it began to rain in earnest. It was exactly two-thirty-two.

At two-thirty-five the quiet man said, "Seems you're in luck, Tibbett. We've been able to trace the information you wanted. Not through Bugolaland at all; they were most unhelpful, but one expects that nowadays. However, it seems that there are libraries in this country which preserve old copies of newspapers. I believe you said your clipping was from the Bugolaland *Times* of twenty years ago."

"That's right."

"Well, this one is from the East Bugolaland *Mail*, the local paper of the region where the family lived, so the account is more detailed. It's not an official record, of course, but it makes it quite clear that the little boy was killed along with his parents—all three of them in that car smash. Read it for yourself. What you intend to make of it, I can't imagine."

"One hundred and forty-nine pounds, two ounces," said the stout lady slowly. The Vicar, who was standing rather self-consciously on a small platform made out of seed boxes, looked pleased.

"One hundred and forty-nine pounds, two ounces," Emmy repeated, writing on a slip of paper. "Your name, please?"

"Mrs. Barton, Hole End Farm."

"Thank you, Mrs. Barton. Here's your stub. Sixpence, please."

The man with her—presumably Mr. Barton—was a small, stringy creature who might have been a superannuated jockey. He said loudly, "A hundred and sixty-two pounds." The Vicar's face dropped. Emmy filled in the form, and the couple departed.

The Vicar said to Emmy in a stage whisper, "Actually, Mrs. Tibbett, I weigh…"

"Don't tell me, please," Emmy begged. "I might give something away if I knew."

"I was only going to say," said the Vicar with dignity, "that I weigh less than a hundred and sixty pounds." He sighed, looked down at his comfortably rounded silhouette, and added, "I play some cricket in the summer. Not enough, I fear."

"Most people have guessed around a hundred and forty-five pounds," said Emmy comfortingly.

"A hundred and forty-five pounds, ten ounces is the average estimate," said the Vicar, who had acute hearing. "I have been working it out in my head. A hundred and forty-five pounds, ten ounces. It is a lesson in humility."

A small girl in a dirty cotton dress came up and said importantly, "Here's sixpence, and my mum says two hundred and twenty pounds and three ounce."

"Two hundred and twenty pounds?" echoed Emmy. "Are you sure?"

"That's what my mum says. Two hundred and twenty pounds, three ounce," she added at the top of her voice. Several passers-by showed a tendency to giggle. The Vicar went very red.

Emmy made out the slip of paper, took the sixpence, and dismissed the small girl. Then she said to the Vicar, "The child obviously doesn't know the difference between a pound and a..."

"That has nothing to do with it," replied the Vicar with some heat. "That was Elsie Beddows, and I have recently had cause to take issue with her mother on the subject of her Sunday School attendance. Elsie's, of course. This is her way of scoring a cheap revenge. Really, I question whether I should have exposed myself to this sort of thing, even in aid of the church roof."

He was interrupted by the arrival of a small, hard-bitten man in corduroy breeches and leggings. He was chewing a straw, and looked as though he had spent a lifetime on and around racetracks. He appraised the Vicar in silence for some time, chewing steadily. Then he walked around and studied him from the back. Finally, he squatted down on his haunches and ran his eye expertly up the ecclesiastical curves, missing nothing. At last he said, "A hundred and fifty-one pounds and six."

"One hundred and fifty-one pounds, six ounces?" said Emmy.

"S'right."

"Your name, please?"

"Harrow. Sam Harrow."

"You are not from these parts, my man," remarked the Vicar.

Sam Harrow regarded him coldly. "I work the fairs," he said. "Buying and selling. Horses, mostly. Having a flutter. Nothing worth having here, but I was in Kingsmarsh for the market." He fixed the Vicar with a wicked eye. "I don't make mistakes," he said. He pocketed his stub and walked off.

The Vicar said to Emmy, "It's this suit, I fear. Made some years ago, when I was stouter. It gives an—em—misleading impression." He laughed with embarrassment. "You never want to judge a parcel by its wrapping, you know."

It was at this moment that Isobel Thompson arrived. "Tea break," she said cheerfully to Emmy.

"Oh really, Isobel, I..."

"No argument," said Isobel. "Violet has taken over the jumble, I am to relieve you for half an hour, and you are to get yourself some tea. And I'd hurry, if I were you," she added.

Indeed, the rain had begun to fail again in large splashy drops. Emmy noticed that Isobel was now wearing a raincoat over her cotton dress. Emmy said gratefully, "Thank you. In that case, I'll go at once."

"I think," said the Vicar plaintively, "that I should put on my mackintosh."

"That would be most unfair, Mr. Dishforth," said Isobel, cheerfully but firmly. "You must let the customers get a good look at you."

"You make me sound like a freak at a sideshow, Mrs. Thompson."

"Well, freak or not, you're certainly a sideshow," said Isobel. "And think of the church roof."

"Your husband wouldn't approve of my catching my death of cold."

"I don't mind holding an umbrella over your head, but you are not to put on a raincoat. Mrs. Manciple said so."

"Really, Mrs. Manciple has no authority to..."

Emmy left them to it and made her way to the shelter of the refreshment marquee.

As she sipped a cup of hot, strong tea, and ate one of Mrs. Richards' excellent cakes, something that the Vicar had said came suddenly back into her mind. And with it, inspiration. She looked around, hoping to see Frank Mason; but there was no sign of him. She peeped out through the tent flap. It was raining harder than ever, and Emmy did not feel inclined to waste her precious half-hour's respite trudging in the damp. She did, however, see Maud, and called to her.

"Hello, Mrs. Tibbett," said Maud. She was wearing Wellington boots, a shiny black oilskin coat, and a sou'wester, and she looked as though no amount of rain could daunt her. "What can I do for you?"

"Have you seen Frank Mason?"

"Not recently, but he's around somewhere. Do you want him?"

"Not specially. But if you see him, tell him from me that his book is probably in the Lucky Dip."

"You mean, the book he brought by mistake for the jumble?"

"That's right. He told me at lunchtime that it was wrapped in brown paper. And your mother said several times that all the Lucky Dip things were wrapped, while the jumble wasn't. So I'm sure it must have gotten put into the tub."

Maud made a face. "Some hope of finding it in that case," she said. "Anyhow, I'll tell him if I see him."

"Thanks," said Emmy. She returned to the dry warmth of the marquee with the added glow of having done her good deed for the day. It was four o'clock.

The quiet man was beginning to show a certain amount of enthusiasm. That is, he had assembled several files and papers on his desk, and was allowing a cigarette to burn unattended in his ash tray while he studied them. He said to Henry, "You may have something here, Tibbett."

"I hesitated for a long time," said Henry. "I simply couldn't believe it."

"In this department we can believe anything," said the man with a certain gloomy pride. "Look at the Lonsdale case.

A complete personality built up over twenty years in several different countries…"

"I'd thought of that," said Henry. "But this boy is so young…"

The quiet man tapped a typewritten paper which had just been laid on his desk. "The step-grandmother," he said, "Magda Manning-Richards, nee Borthy. Hungarian. Came to London as a cabaret dancer more than fifty years ago. Met and married Humphrey Manning-Richards, who was at that time a district officer in Bugolaland. Went out there with him, and was badly received by the British community. Conceived an intense dislike for all things British. After the death of her husband and the marriage of her stepson, Tony, she returned to Hungary, where she became an active revolutionary. With her knowledge of Bugolaland, she was naturally in touch with the most violent left-wing elements in that country before the days of independence. Twenty years ago Tony Manning-Richards was killed in that car smash in Bugolaland, along with his wife and five-year-old boy. It was ten years later that Magda turned up in Alimumba, the town where she had first lived with her husband in Western Bugolaland. Naturally, she didn't dare go back to the East, where Tony and his family had been well-known, because she had this fifteen-year-old lad with her whom she described as her orphaned grandson."

"Who is he?" Henry asked. He felt a little sick. He was thinking of Maud.

The quiet man shrugged. "Your guess is as good as mine, old boy. Almost certainly Hungarian, maybe a genuine relative of Magda's. A child of the revolution, that's for sure, and carefully groomed for his job as a secret agent. His ultra-conservative, die-hard colonialist pose was cleverly done, to judge by the reports we have on him."

"He," Henry was aware of grasping at a straw, "he knows who he is, does he?"

"I'd say rather," said the quiet man, "that he knows who he *isn't*. He knows that he's not Julian Manning-Richards. His meeting with Maud Manciple was no coincidence, nor was his engagement to her. His instructions were to get that job at Bradwood. Think of it." He sat back in his chair and spoke almost admiringly. "If they could have gotten an agent in there. Sir Claud's personal aide, married to his physicist niece. Access to every secret document in the place; nothing to do but pass on the information at his leisure; and so firmly entrenched that it would have taken a Royal Commission before anybody dared point a finger of suspicion at him."

"And Magda?" Henry asked.

"Died last year in Bugolaland. Had, of course, given up all political activity since returning to Bugolaland ten years ago. Of course. Ostensibly. A dear little old lady with her charming grandson. Very much persona grata with the new regime, but politics? Oh, dear me no. Nobody ever mentioned her years in Hungary after the war. Even our people seemed to take it for granted that she'd never left Bugolaland, until they looked into it." The quiet man looked curiously at Henry. "What beats me," he said, "is how you rumbled him."

"It was Aunt Dora," said Henry.

"Aunt Dora?"

"Old Miss Manciple, who died last week. She—she knew Humphrey Manning-Richards well. She didn't recognize Julian."

"Any reason why she should have?"

"She knew he was wrong," said Henry.

The quiet man raised his eyebrows.

"He didn't fit. It wasn't so much that she didn't recognize him. She quite definitely anti-recognized him, if you follow me."

"No, I don't," said the quiet man.

"And then," said Henry, "there were the peaches."

"The peaches?"

"It's too complicated to explain," said Henry. "But from one or two things he said, I felt pretty certain that his childhood memories of Bugolaland were pretty hazy, to say the least of it. Yet I knew he'd lived there. Then I realized—he knew about West Bugolaland, where it's very hot and humid, but he knew very little about East Bugolaland, where he was supposed to have been born and reared and where the climate is quite different."

"And you deduced all this from a remark about peaches?"

Henry shrugged. "Just call it a hunch," he said, "a correct one, I'm afraid."

"You're afraid?"

"Well, he is such a charming young man," said Henry.

The quiet man did not bother to reply to this. He was already telephoning instructions with chilling efficiency.

CHAPTER SIXTEEN

AT FIVE O'CLOCK Emmy emerged from the tea tent to make her way back to her post. Miraculously, the rain had cleared, and a watery sun was doing its best to send out a few farewell shafts before it sank behind the flat, marshy horizon.

In this unexpectedly bright light the Fête looked bedraggled. The setting sun gilded the few unsavory remnants still left in the jumble booth; the Hoopla was down to its last Christmas-cracker rings and brooches; and the jams and jellies had been completely cleared, leaving only the trestle table partially covered by its tailing and jam-smeared sheet. From the shooting range, sporadic shots indicated that business was still reasonably brisk. The schoolchildren, who had been immaculately scrubbed and starched for the opening of the Fête, now wandered in small groups, grubby and tired, but apparently happy. Some of them clutched the prizes they had won in the various sporting events; some of them still trailed the sacks of potatoes which had formed part of their racing equipment; all of them were chewing or sucking candy of some sort, and several of them looked as though they might soon be sick.

In fact, the afternoon was drawing predictably to its close, and Emmy hurried across the lawn to her table. Any moment now the secret of the Vicar's weight would be revealed, together with the numbers of the winning raffle tickets, the lucky program and the highest scorecard from the shooting range. Then Lady Fenshire would emerge once more from the house, where she and her husband were enjoying, respectively, a cup of tea and a whiskey, with Sir John Adamson; she would again mount the rostrum, names would be called out, and prizes distributed. And at last the Village would feel free to disperse to its various firesides, armed with the ammunition for many evenings of gossip, while the hard core of helpers rallied around Violet Manciple and made a start at clearing up the mess.

With no sense of foreboding whatsoever Emmy walked across the damp grass; and still no warning bell of trouble rang in her mind when she saw Mrs. Manciple emerge, looking worried, from a little knot of people clustered around the Lucky Dip.

"Oh, Mrs. Tibbett," Violet began.

"Yes, Mrs. Manciple?" said Emmy politely. "I must congratulate you. Everything has gone off splendidly."

"It's that Mason boy," said Violet. "He says it was your idea."

"What was?" Emmy felt slightly alarmed.

From the center of the group of people Sir Claud's voice rose in half-amused exasperation. "Mr. Mason, I really must…"

"Go on!" Frank Mason was shouting. "Go on! Take it! There's no law against it! Go on!"

Other voices began to rise from the group, and Violet Manciple said, "Oh please, Mrs. Tibbett, he may listen to you."

Reluctantly Emmy pushed toward the bran tub.

Sir Claud Manciple and Frank Mason were facing each other, separated only by the tub. Sir Claud looked as nearly flustered as it is possible for a leading atomic scientist to do. Clearly, Frank Mason was exhibiting a behavior pattern which deviated from the norm, and, with the inadequate facts at his disposal, Sir Claud was unable to form a reasonable hypothesis to account for it. Meanwhile, the Lucky Dip was in danger of fission.

Frank's red hair was standing on end and his sharp face was white with anger and emotion. He was waving a five-pound note in the air, and as Emmy approached, he shouted again, "Take it! Take it!"

Around this strange couple a selection of Cregwell's citizens were standing and staring with that impenetrable inertia which descends on the English, like a cloak of invisibility, when they wish to observe events without being personally implicated. Emmy realized, with a pang of envy, that if any of these onlookers should be appealed to by either side they would simply melt into the landscape and disappear, only to reappear to watch the fun when the threat of involvement had passed. She, however, was in a different position; she had allowed herself to be drawn into the arena.

Frank Mason saw her and was diverted. "Mrs. Tibbett, it was your idea. You must make him see sense!"

"What was my idea?"

"That my book would be in the Lucky Dip."

"Well, yes. It occurred to me…"

"You're right, of course. And I've got to get it back."

"Mrs. Tibbett," said Sir Claud a little desperately, "please reason with this young man. I am in charge of the Lucky Dip, and…"

"Take it!" yelled Frank, attempting to ram the five-pound note into Sir Claud's waistcoat pocket.

"He wishes," Sir Claud explained to Emmy, "to buy up the contents of the barrel. Five pounds at sixpence a time would give him two hundred dips, and there cannot be more than twenty objects left in the tub. In any case, everyone should be entitled to his turn…"

"You said nobody had taken out a book," shouted Frank.

"Nobody while I've been in charge," said Sir Claud with dignity. "However, I was relieved for a short spell by my niece Maud, and…"

"Oh, to hell with the lot of you!" Frank Mason had reached the breaking point. He flung the five-pound note at Sir Claud's face and overturned the bran tub.

The bran rose into the air like a cloud, and, behind its protective cover, several villagers applauded, while others shouted disapproval. Sir Claud let out a bellow of baffled intellectual rage, and Violet moaned, "Oh dear, oh dear. I *knew* something like this would happen!"

"Get Maud," said Emmy urgently to Violet.

"Get who?"

"Maud. She'll be able to deal with this."

"*Maud?* But..."

"Get her!" said Emmy fiercely.

Frank Mason, who had gone down on the ground with the barrel, arose like a loaf in a hot oven, his clothes and face whitened with bran, his hair like a red crust. He held a square, paper-wrapped package in his hand. "This is it!" he cried. A few people cheered. Frank scrabbled at the wrapping paper and tore it off. Inside was a jigsaw puzzle in a gaudy box. Frank flung it at Sir Claud with a howl of fury.

"It's not here! Somebody did get it!"

"Somebody got what?" Maud had pushed her way into the circle.

"My book!"

"Oh, was that your book?" Maud sounded faintly amused. Frank glowered at her through his mask of bran. With enormous restraint, he said, "Yes."

"Well, I was deputizing for Uncle Claud," said Maud, "and Alfred from The Viking came along to take a Lucky Dip. He pulled out this book. He seemed a bit fed up."

"Fed up? Certainly I was fed up!" Alfred's voice, thin and indignant, came from the outskirts of the crowd. "Call that a Lucky Dip! It was all in some foreign sort of writing."

"What d'you expect for sixpence, Alf?" queried a local wit. "James Bond?"

"What did you do with it?" shouted Frank.

"Do with it? I gave it to the jumble."

"Jumble!"

Frank Mason made a dive into the crowd.

Maud cried, "Frank"—and went after him.

Sir Claud remarked, "The young man is mad," but he followed, picking pieces of jigsaw off his jacket as he went.

Violet grabbed Emmy's arm, and cried, "Stop him, Mrs. Tibbett! Lady Fenshire will be out at any moment!" And the two of them set off in pursuit. It is hardly necessary to add that the faceless crowd came trailing along behind.

Isobel Thompson was taken by surprise. The jumble, or what remained of it, was at the far end of the lawn, and with so little stock left to sell, Mrs. Thompson was not taking her guardianship of the booth very seriously. In fact, when the invasion arrived, she was having a quiet cigarette and a chat with her husband, who had just completed his afternoon round of calls and was paying his duty visit to the Fête.

The Thompsons' first intimation that the comparative peace of the evening was shattered forever was Frank's hunting cry of "Where is it? Where is it?" And then bedlam broke loose. The trestle table was overturned, the remaining feathered hats and decorated pots flew in all directions; Isobel Thompson screamed; Alec Thompson swore; and Violet Manciple burst into tears.

In the midst of the confusion Maud said clearly and coldly, "It's not here, Frank. You can see that for yourself."

"What's the matter? What do you all want?" Isobel's voice was a squeak of alarm and emotion.

Maud said, "Alfred brought you a book to sell..."

Isobel's face cleared a little. "Yes, that's right. He'd gotten it in the Lucky Dip, and he said he couldn't make head nor tail of it, and that I could have it for jumble..."

"All in foreign writing," added Alfred from the outskirts.

"What happened to it?" demanded Frank. Sweat was beginning to run down his face, making furrows in the bran.

"Lady Manciple bought it," said Isobel.

"Aunt Ramona?" Maud queried.

"That's right. She said something about it being a Manciple book. She was having her tea break. She took it with her, back into the fortune teller's tent."

There was a moment of bated breath, while every head turned toward the frail canvas structure embellished with golden paper stars and mysterious zodiacal signs. Then the hunt was off again in full cry.

Inside the tent Ramona had laid out a row of grubby cards and was gazing earnestly into the upturned fish bowl. It was curious, she thought to herself, how she sometimes *did* have an intuition about these things. Not that she subscribed to any of Aunt Dora's ridiculous superstitions, of course. She and Claud were both devout atheists, materialists, and humanists. They believed in what they could see and hear and smell and touch. Nevertheless, playing this childish game of fortune-telling, Ramona sometimes had strange misgivings. The cards and the gold fish bowl did, more and more frequently, seem to raise images in her mind. Purely subjective, of course. Ramona wondered whether she might be imagining things as a result of guilt feelings, a consciousness of betraying her convictions by supporting so barbaric and outdated a cause as the Church Roof Restoration Fund, The church, of course, fulfilled a certain social function; she and Claud were agreed on that. But they were both convinced that as the age of scientific enlightenment dawned, the church would wither away spontaneously, her usefulness outlived and her bigoted dogmas swallowed up in the light of pure reason. Edwin, of course, would never understand this point of view, and it had given rise to many stimulating discussions within the family circle.

"Nature I loved, and after Nature, Art..." murmured Ramona like an incantation.

"Eh?" said her client, a plump and comely farmer's daughter called Lily.

Ramona pulled herself together. "I can see," she began, and then stopped. The usual patter about the handsome young man and the short journey simply would not come. It stuck in her throat. Suddenly it seemed to Ramona that everything went dark, like blood, before her eyes. Only the mesmeric surface of the shining bowl grew brighter, compelling attention, and in the shimmering brightness she seemed to see a face. She heard her own voice saying, "Dark—dark—dark and fair—dark and light—he brings the darkness—there is darkness in the light—there are people—I see people—many people…"

"Eh?" said Lily again. She had heard people say that Lady Manciple was a little touched, and she was beginning to think it an understatement.

"Evil," moaned Lady Manciple, "coming nearer—darkness—people—people are coming—"

"I *can* hear a funny noise, now you mention it," said Lily, "like people running."

Ramona stood up, her eyes wild, "Fly!" she cried, "Fly from the evil! Fly from…"

She got no further. Neither she nor Lily had time to act on this very sensible advice, for the mob was upon them. The tent, of course, never had a chance. Frank Mason's entry ripped the flap from its moorings; Violet tripped over a guy rope and uprooted one peg; and the whole thing collapsed with a certain slow grace. The darkness, as Ramona had prophesied, descended.

It took a considerable time to disentangle the tent from its occupants. Lily, who had jumped to the not unreasonable conclusion that the end of the world had come, was having hysterics somewhere beneath the canvas folds. Another part of the wreckage, which was behaving like an active and blasphemous sack of potatoes, was Frank Mason. The guy rope had brought Violet down, and she was now sitting, rubbing her ankle, on what appeared to be a comfortable cushion covered in canvas. It was, in fact, Ramona.

Sir Claud was shouting for his wife. He had given up all thoughts of rational and predictable behavior by now and was solely concerned with getting out of the Fête alive. As for the crowd, it had swelled to include virtually everyone left within the grounds of Cregwell Grange. Only those privileged few who had been in on the affair from the beginning had even the haziest idea of what it was all about. Rumor ran riot. They were chasing a dangerous burglar. Young Mr. Mason had gone off his head and attacked Sir Claud. Something was on fire. The Communists were at the bottom of it. Somebody had been shot—the sound of firing from the range reinforced this theory. Mrs. Richards was tearfully begging the Vicar to intervene, and the Reverend Herbert Dishforth advanced—all hundred and fifty-one pounds and six ounces of him—to take part in the affray.

"Er—is something wrong, Mrs. Manciple?" he inquired.

"Where's Ramona?" shouted Sir Claud.

"Oh, Vicar," Violet began woefully.

"Somebody," said a deep, clear voice from beneath her, "is sitting on me."

Violet jumped up as though stung.

"Ramona!" yelled Claud. "Speak to me!"

"Get me out of this bloody tent!" bellowed Frank.

"Help!" screamed Lily.

"Get my wife out of there, Violet!"

"Who the hell are you?" came a muffled roar from Frank.

It was answered by Lily's shrill, "Take your hands off of me!"

The tent appeared to undergo some sort of convulsive fit. At the end of it, Lady Manciple emerged. Her hair was tangled and her dress torn and she had lost one earring, but she was surprisingly serene. She got to her feet with her husband's help, and said, "I have just had the most extraordinary experience, Claud."

"I can see that," said Sir Claud grimly. "Come out of there, young Mason. I want a word with you."

The tent heaved again. From beneath it Lily giggled and cried, "Oh, you are a one!" She seemed to have made a rapid reappraisal of the situation and decided that the world had not ended for the time being. Perhaps fortunately, all that could be heard of Frank Mason's reply was an urgent demand to "Get out of my way, damn you, you…" The rest was inaudible.

Ramona said calmly, "A *spiritual* experience, Claud. In the light of it, I shall have to reconsider my whole attitude to psychic phenomena. What a pity Aunt Dora could not be with us."

Mason emerged from the wreckage of the tent like a cork from a champagne bottle. His appearance had not been improved by his most recent experience. Mingled with the bran was now a quantity of mud, and several cabbalistic signs in colored paper adhered to various parts of his person. Addressing Ramona, he said, "Where's my book?"

"Your what, Mr. Mason?"

"My book! My book! The one you bought from the jumble booth! The leather-bound…"

"Oh, the book from the Manciple library? That's not your book, Mr. Mason." Ramona sounded perfectly calm.

"It damn well is. It's from my father's library. He bought it, and it was his, and now it's mine, and I want it."

"*I* bought it," Ramona corrected him gently, "from the jumble booth."

"It shouldn't have been there. It was all a mistake…"

"In any case," Lady Manciple went on, "I haven't got it any more."

"What d'you mean, you haven't got it?"

"Julian has it. He came to visit me in my tent, saw the book, and took it away with him. I don't know why he seemed so interested in it."

Mason let out a howl of fury. "Let me get at him! Where is he? Where is he?"

As if in answer, a shot rang out from the range, and the Vicar said, "I saw Mr. Manning-Richards making his way toward the shooting range not many minutes ago. I think he must be there with Major Manciple and the Bishop."

Once again there was a moment of silence, of scenting and pointing, as all heads turned toward the privet hedge. And then the pack was off.

There were several quiet men in the car with Henry, and they all looked grave, not to say grim. They also looked curiously alike, one to the other, as impersonal as Erinyes, and as implacable. Henry sat miserably in the driving seat, wishing himself a thousand miles away.

He said, "There's a Village Fête going on in the grounds, as I told you. I think we should be able to get him without attracting too much attention." The quiet men remained quiet. "I'd be grateful," said Henry, "if you could do this with as little—as little fuss as possible. It'll be bad enough for the Manciples. without..."

Again the silence. At last one quiet man said, "The girl will have to be thoroughly investigated. You understand that, Tibbett?"

"Of course. But I feel sure..."

"We'll be sure when we're sure."

Another silence.

Then Henry said, "I suppose we'll never know his contact at the Soviet Embassy."

The quiet man almost smiled. "I could tell you his name," he said. "But we'll never prove it, of course." He paused, and then added, "The Manning-Richards boy was known to the jewelers because he brought in pieces to sell. That was how he was paid. Quite ingenious. It was clever of you to think of making inquiries there."

"When I heard that he hadn't gone in to buy the ring until after lunch on Saturday," said Henry, "I realized that he'd been somewhere else in London in the morning. The jeweler was just intended to provide an excuse for his trip to London. I suppose he was worried about Mason's death and wanted to get instructions."

"I dare say," said the quiet man. "Again, we'll never prove where he was on Saturday morning. Not that it matters. There was enough in his apartment…" He lit a cigarette. "Ingenious, those tiny microfilm copiers and the radio transmitter in the camera case. Yes, we've got enough to put him away for a long, long time." He sighed. "One can't help feeling almost sorry for them. All those years of preparation, and now we get him before he can start on the job. Seems a waste, doesn't it?"

"Yes," said Henry, "yes, it does." He was thinking of Maud.

There were several cars parked in the drive of Cregwell Grange when they arrived, but the gardens seemed curiously deserted. Henry, followed by his posse of quiet men, made his way to the deserted lawn, which exhibited many of the characteristics of a battlefield on the morning after. A tangle of torn canvas and twisted ropes was all that remained of the fortune teller's tent. The bran tub lay empty on its side, its remaining treasures scattered over a rosebed. The jumble booth had been overturned, and numerous broken glasses and teacups spoke mutely of havoc in the refreshment tent. The resemblance to a battlefield was weakened, however, by the absence of dead and wounded. There was not a soul in sight.

The quiet men looked at Henry, and raised their eyebrows slightly.

Henry said, irritably, "Well, *I* don't know what's happened. It might be anything. You don't know the Manciples."

"Looks like the Fête is over, at all events," said one quiet man. "Perhaps our bird has flown." He seemed unaware that he sounded like a character from a very minor film indeed.

It was at this point that a small, very dirty child emerged from what was left of the refreshment tent. Her face was pale, and she said to Henry, "I think I'm going to be sick." She was clutching a jam cake in one hand and an ice-cream cone in the other.

Henry squatted down beside her. "Where is everyone?" he asked.

"There's nobody in the tent," the child confided. "I've had five ice creams and three cakes and some marshmallows and jam and I think I'm going to be..." Whereupon she was.

Henry held her head and wiped her mouth and comforted her. The quiet men stood in a circle, sneering. Henry said, "Do you feel better now?"

"Yes, thanks," said the child cheerfully. "Shall we go back and see if there's any more cake left?"

"I'd rather know," said Henry, "where everybody is."

The child gestured vaguely. "They all went that way," she said.

"To the shooting range," said Henry.

"I 'spect so," said the child. The quiet men stiffened. "There was a whole box of marshmallows. Shall we go and see?"

"Not just now," said Henry. He stood up and said to the quiet men, "This way."

George Manciple had just handed Julian the loaded gun when the hunt broke through the gap in the privet hedge. Julian was taking careful aim at the roundels of the target, which stood against the lower wall of the range. Edwin Manciple was sitting on the bench, peacefully sorting through the target cards which had been shot at during the afternoon. Beside him, lying on the bench in the pale sunshine, was a leather-bound volume of Homer's *Iliad* with the Manciple crest on its spine.

Frank Mason saw it at once, and shouted, "There it is!"

Julian wheeled around, the gun in his hand. "What on earth," he began.

"You won't get away with this," said Frank. "I know all about you, Manning-Richards, and what you're after." He took a step forward.

"Stand still." Julian's voice was like a whip.

Frank stood still. The others crowded eagerly behind him, trying to get through the gap in the hedge.

Gently, lovingly, Julian said, "Maud, darling, would you come here a moment?"

"Maud," Emmy tried to grab her arm, but it was too late. Maud, with a ravishing smile, pushed her way past Frank and went over to Julian.

"What is all this about darling?" she said.

In a flash the gun was at Maud's temple. She looked mildly surprised, amused. "Julian darling, what…?"

"If anybody moves," said Julian, "I shall shoot Miss Manciple."

"Julian," Maud still sounded as though it were a joke.

"Shut up, you silly bitch," said Julian. "Get in front of me."

Expressionless, Maud stood in front of him, between him and the silent crowd. Julian began to walk slowly backward, toward the gap in the far hedge. As he went, he snatched up the book in his free hand. Each time he took a step backward, Maud did the same. Always the gun was at her head, and she was between Julian and Frank.

It was in the thicket of this dead silence that Julian and Maud stepped slowly, pace by pace, backward—and into the arms of Henry and the quiet men. Julian realized his danger a split second too late. Henry had time to strike out at his arm before he fired, and the gun went off harmlessly into the air.

As though the shot had been the signal for the start of a race, pandemonium broke loose. It was still raging as Sir John Adamson and Lord and Lady Fenshire came out innocently into the garden, beaming with refreshment and good will, and all ready to distribute prizes. The prizes were never distributed. The crowd roared like flame over the lawns and down the drive and eventually into The Viking, where everybody had a story to cap the next man's. All were wildly inaccurate, but that did not matter in the least.

Julian Manning-Richards—he was charged under that name, for nobody ever established his true one—was in custody, accused of espionage. The Manciple family was in its castle, nursing its shock in decent seclusion. Frank Mason was at Cregwell Lodge, raging noisily against the Establishment, which apparently comprised the whole world with the exception of F. Mason and M. Manciple. And M. Manciple herself was at Cregwell police station facing Chief Inspector Henry Tibbett across a bare, scrubbed table.

Henry said, "You met him in Paris and then later on in London. You had no reason to suspect that he was anything other than..."

Maud said, "You seem very sure."

Henry looked at her. "You would never," he said, "have contemplated helping a spy to get into Bradwood."

"No," said Maud, "no, I wouldn't."

"And as regards Miss Dora Manciple, the verdict, I think, will be accidental death. It can never be proved who gave her the sleeping pills or, indeed, that she did not take them herself by accident. However—I feel that I must tell you this, Miss Manciple—I personally am convinced that it was Manning-Richards who put the pills into her drink. He served her with her first glass of lemonade, if you remember, and she particularly remarked on the taste of the first glass."

"I remember," said Maud.

"The reason, of course, was that he realized that she constituted a danger. By some strange mixture of memory and instinct, Aunt Dora knew that he was an impostor. She may even have known, at one time, that the real Julian had been killed as a small boy. At any rate, she took the trouble to look up that particular newspaper clipping for me." There was a silence, and then Henry said, "I'm telling you all this very brutally, I know, but it's for your own good. Once you get it into your head just how calculating and cynical he was, how he was prepared to lie to you and cheat you—and kill you, if necessary—he wouldn't have hesitated, you know..."

"I know that," said Maud.

"You're a very sensible girl," said Henry. "It's all a terrible shock now, but you're young and you'll get over it. If you face things squarely now you'll find that in time the wound will heal."

"In time," said Maud. There was no expression in her voice.

"That's right," said Henry, "in time."

"I don't understand," said Maud, "about the book."

CHAPTER SEVENTEEN

"I DON'T UNDERSTAND," said Sir Claud, "about the book."

"What book?" asked the Bishop. "Thank you, Violet, I would enjoy another cup of coffee. Maud is very late coming home this evening."

"Maud is at the police station, Edwin," said George Manciple. He felt very tired. It was nine o'clock at night, and he still had not fully assimilated the happenings of the afternoon.

"Police station? Why the police station?"

"Because of Julian," said Ramona, "her young man. He turned out to be a Russian."

"A *Russian*? But he's Humphrey Manning-Richards' grandson."

"No, he isn't, Edwin," said Violet patiently. "He was just pretending to be."

Edwin sighed. "It's all beyond me," he said. "Why was that young fellow Mason making such a to-do this afternoon? Bran all over his face."

"That was because of the book, Edwin," said Violet.

"What book?"

"Some book from the Head's library," put in George. "It's all very mysterious."

"I don't understand about the book," said Sir Claud again.

"Where is it now anyway?" Ramona asked.

"I don't know. Tibbett has it. We keep going around in circles," said George Manciple irritably. "Ever since last week there's been nothing but trouble and bother. I'm damned, Violet, if I'll lend the garden next year for this blasted Fête of yours, if this sort of thing is going to happen."

"Well, really, George! You can't blame the Fête for..."

"Manning-Richards isn't a Russian name," said the Bishop. "If Tibbett thinks it is, it just shows that he's an ignoramus."

"It's all very confusing, I agree," said Ramona. "And I don't believe he made any real effort with his wildflower collection, for all that he said."

"Julian never collected wildflowers, my dear," said Sir Claud. "Let us be charitable and give credit where it is due."

"Not Julian, Claud," said Violet, "Inspector Tibbett."

"Tibbett isn't a Russian name either," said Edwin. The conversation, having reached an impasse, stopped. And Henry walked in, preceded by Maud.

"Ah, there you are, Maud," said Edwin. "I've been keeping this for you. Haven't looked at it myself yet." He held out the current copy of *The Times*, carefully folded to display the crossword puzzle.

At this gesture Maud's ironclad composure cracked like old plaster under a chisel. The tears came faster than she could control, and her voice broke as the said, "Thank you, Uncle Edwin." She grabbed the paper and ran out of the room.

Edwin looked genuinely surprised. "What's the matter with Maud?" he asked.

Ramona said gently, "It's because of Julian being a Russian, Edwin. She's bound to be upset."

"Julian? I thought Claud said it was Tibbett..."

Violet said, "Poor little Maud. Do you think I should go to her...?"

"I wouldn't, Mrs. Manciple," said Henry. "I think she'd rather be left alone."

"Oh, Inspector Tibbett, or Mr. Tibbett, I should say—I never get it right. I'm afraid you find us in rather a confused state. Do let me give you some coffee. You may have heard something of what happened this afternoon..."

"Yes," said Henry, "I did hear something of it. And I've brought you this book."

"Book? What book? *The* book?" Claud put on a pair of rimless spectacles and peered at Henry over the top of them.

"Yes," said Henry, "a book belonging to your late father, Augustus Manciple. One of the volumes of Homer's *Iliad*."

"But that isn't our book, Tibbett," said George Manciple.

"Not yours?"

"No, no. I recognize it. It is one of the books from the Head's library which I sold to Raymond Mason some time ago. It must now belong to his son, Frank."

Henry smiled. "That's quite right, technically," he said. "However, on another technical point you might say that it belongs to Lady Manciple, for she bought it for sixpence from the jumble booth this afternoon. Isn't that right?" he added to Ramona.

"Quite correct, Mr. Tibbett. I told the young man..."

"What on earth was it doing at the jumble booth?" asked George Manciple.

"Alfred from The Viking donated it. He had picked it out of the Lucky Dip, and not being a Greek scholar..."

"Oh, Mr. Tibbett, you are being tiresome," said Violet. "Do get down to *facts*. Why was it in the Lucky Dip?"

Ramona said, "Ah, now I begin to understand. Frank Mason brought it up here with some jumble, by a mistake..."

"No," said Henry.

"But Mr. Tibbett, he told me..."

"It was no mistake," said Henry. "He brought it here to hide it—and a very good hiding place it was, too. He intended to take it back quietly, but owing to its brown paper wrapper it got put into the Lucky Dip and he couldn't find it."

"To hide it from whom?" Edwin asked.

"From me."

"I don't understand," said Sir Claud for the third time.

"I'll explain," said Henry. "That's what I came here for. Frank Mason has been looking for this book ever since his father's death."

"But why on earth should he..." began George.

"That's the funny part," said Henry. "He had no idea why the book was so valuable. He simply knew that it was, because his father told him so. And then he discovered that I was looking for it, too. So, having found it, he decided to hide it from me."

"I thought, Tibbett," said the Bishop heavily, "that you were going to *explain*."

"I am," said Henry.

"Well, where did young Mason find the book for a start?"

"In his father's office in London, in Mason's private filing cabinet. The maddening thing is that I actually looked into that filing cabinet myself before young Mason did, and I never spotted the book. Raymond Mason had put it into a lurid, pornographic jacket."

Edwin looked shocked. "Homer? The Head wouldn't have liked that."

"I'm sure he wouldn't," said Henry. "Anyhow, Frank Mason found it and brought it back to Cregwell Lodge. Shortly afterward, I called at the Lodge. When he saw me coming, he hastily removed the Homer from the dust jacket, and put another book in its place. And before I could search the house again, he wrapped the Homer in brown paper and brought it up here with his jumble."

"This is all very well," said Sir Claud, "but when are you going to come to the point? What's so special about this book, and how did you know about it at all?"

"I'm just coming to that," said Henry. "I found an entry in Raymond Mason's personal diary which puzzled me. It was his car registration number."

"Never heard such nonsense," said Edwin. He glared at Henry and added, in an undertone to Claud, "Told you the man was unbalanced."

Henry said, "Mason's car was numbered RM1—typically. But in his diary he had entered the number as BK6P82. It was obviously not his car number but some other number which he wished to remember, something important. It didn't take much imagination to come to the conclusion that it meant Book Six, page eighty-two. I had no idea what it referred to, but my—that is, I had a feeling that it was important. And then I read Aunt Dora's copy of old Dr. Thompson's letter to Major Manciple."

"Better ring young Dr. Thompson," said Edwin audibly to Claud. "Fellow's off his rocker."

"I don't see," said Violet.

"From that letter, written just after old Mr. Manciple's death, it was clear that on his deathbed Mr. Manciple had been trying very hard to communicate to Dr. Thompson some message to be passed on to his son, George. I couldn't believe that it was simply about not selling the house; that was understood among the family and was mentioned in his will. Nor did I believe that the Head would have wasted his precious last breaths in mumbling that he was ill and sick. His final remark to Dr. Thompson was also revealing."

"What final remark?" Ramona asked.

"That Dr. Thompson was a fool. Meaning that he had not grasped what the Head was trying to tell him. However, fortunately, Dr. Thompson was conscientious enough to report to Major Manciple verbatim what his father had said, so that it's possible for us to interpret it. In fact, it was not 'my home,' but 'my Homer.' And what Thompson took for the words 'ill' and 'sick' were actually '*Iliad*' and 'Six,' Book Six, that is. This at once tied up with the entry in Mason's diary. Book Six of the

Iliad contains, on page eighty-two, a special message left by Mr. Augustus Manciple to his son George.

"I have been told by several people," Henry went on, "that old Mr. Manciple became extremely suspicious of outsiders as he grew older, that he was convinced that he was being cheated, and that he trusted nobody except his solicitor, Arthur Pringle. Pringle undoubtedly had instructions to pass on to George the secret of the *Iliad*, but he died before he could do so. On hearing of Pringle's death the Head did his best to get the message over himself, but he was misunderstood. For years the book sat here on the library shelf, unread—for none of you are classical scholars. Eventually it was sold with a number of similar volumes to Raymond Mason, who wished to make a brave show of leather-bound volumes in his study.

"What made him look at the book we shall never know—although I gather that he made a pretense of reading these weighty works in order to impress people like Sir John Adamson. At any rate he opened the book, which is more than any of you had done, and he found the secret of page eighty-two. Which explains why he was so desperate to buy this house. Why he tried every trick he could think of to make Major Manciple sell—and why he finally killed himself in a desperate effort to do so."

George Manciple was looking much as he did when Claud and Edwin started on a metaphysical discussion. He said, "I don't understand a word of what you've been saying, Tibbett. What has Mason's registration number got to do with it? I always disliked that car of his."

"I think," said Henry, "that the time has come to let you take a look at this."

He held out the leather-bound book to George, who took it gingerly. It was open to page eighty-two. George said, "All Greek to me, old man."

"Look more closely," said Henry, "between the pages."

They all watched as George examined the open book, and there was a dead silence as he held it up to show that pages eighty-two and eighty-three had, in fact, been pasted together. Apparently, at some recent date, they had been carefully cut open with a sharp knife for the cut showed clearly, but they had been refastened with transparent tape.

Henry held out a pocket knife. “Open it up, Major Manciple,” he said.

George cut the pages apart, and as he did so, a flimsy paper with writing on it in faded ink fluttered to the ground. Edwin stooped to pick it up.

“That’s the Head’s handwriting,” he said.

Henry nodded. “It’s addressed to his son, George,” he said. And to Major Manciple, “Read it, sir.”

George Manciple slowly smoothed the paper. Then he began to read aloud.

Dear George,

By the time you read this I shall be in my grave, thanks mainly to the ministrations of that old fool Thompson and his cronies. Arthur Pringle, who is the only honest man in England, will have told you where to find this letter. When you read it, you will see that I have taken steps to safeguard your inheritance. Had I not taken these steps you can be certain that you would never have had the means to maintain Cregwell Grange, which, as you know, I have charged you to do in perpetuity.

For some years now my suspicions have been growing concerning Masterman, the bank manager, and I am now convinced of his dishonesty. I considered moving your dear mother’s jewels to a safer spot, but in these days where is safety to be found? One bank is as perfidious as the next, and all of them are thieves and rogues.

However, I think I may say that I have fooled them. Over a period of years I have been removing items of jewelry from the bank safe, one at a time, having them copied in worthless paste, and replacing the fake pieces in the bank. The real jewels I have concealed at Cregwell Grange, where I can keep them under my own eye. Just last week I completed the final transfer—the diamond sunburst brooch. So, when Masterman and his gang of crooks come to rifle the strongbox, they will find only pinchbeck and glass. I confess that this thought gives me considerable satisfaction.

Now, it only remains for me to tell you how to locate the real jewels. They are buried beneath a flagstone in the wine cellar of the Grange. From the doorway count ten flagstones forward, and three to the left. The stone itself is beneath the bin containing my vintage port. I trust that the wine has not been unduly disturbed each time that I have had to move it in order to bury another piece, but I should advise leaving it to rest for several months before drinking it. You will note—with amusement, I hope—that in my will I have specifically left to you "Cregwell Grange and all its contents." Thus your title to the jewelry is unassailable.

I most strongly advise you to leave the jewels where they are, removing one piece at a time to sell as and when you may need money. On no account should you entrust it to a bank, any more than you should entrust your investments to a stockbroker or your person to the medical profession. Consider, after all, what has happened to me.

Your loving father,
Augustus Manciple

George's voice trailed away into a sort of astonished whistle, and for a moment there was dead silence.

Then Henry said, quickly, "You'll obviously want to talk this over, and, I imagine, to go and dig in the cellar. I suppose there's no doubt that the jewels will be there?"

"If he left them there, they're there still," said George. "There are even a few bottles of the Head's port left. And, of course, they are never disturbed."

Henry held out his hand to George. "Well," he said, "I congratulate you, Major Manciple. That jewelry must be worth many thousands of pounds."

George was looking dazed. He shook Henry's hand and said, "Who brought back my gun then?"

"I don't know for certain," said Henry, "but I think it was probably Sir John Adamson."

"But why…"

"Just as a kindly gesture," said Henry hastily. He did not feel compelled to explain Sir John's reasons for wishing the death of Raymond Mason to be cleared up quickly and quietly.

"And Aunt Dora?"

"I think," said Henry, "that it will be regarded as an accident." He paused, and then said, "I hope you won't be too distressed over the unfortunate business of Miss Manciple and that young man. She'll get over it, you know. Youth is very resilient."

It was in the hall that Henry met Maud again. In fact, she was waiting for him. She said, "You know I bought the chrysanthemums."

"Yes," said Henry.

"I had to try to make amends, you see. Because I…"

"Please," said Henry, "don't say any more."

"I love him," said Maud. She was dry-eyed now. "I wouldn't have cared if he'd shot me, if it had helped him to get away. I shall wait for him. They can't send him to prison forever."

Henry said brutally, "He never cared a rap for you. He only proposed to you to get that job at Bradwood."

Maud turned on him like a small tiger. "Do you think that makes any difference? Do you think that to love someone you have to be loved in return?"

"Another thing you should consider," said Henry, "is that in a few years' time, he may well be exchanged for a British agent and repatriated to Russia. What will you do then?"

"Go with him, if he'll take me," said Maud.

Henry said, "It's natural that you should feel like this now. But I do beg you not to isolate yourself. Frank Mason is really a very intelligent young man, you know, under that rather unfortunate manner of his. He asked me if I thought he might come and see you..."

"I won't be here," said Maud. "I'm going away."

"Away?"

"I obviously can't go back to Bradwood, and I can't stay here. I wanted to ask you, Inspector Tibbett, do you know to which prison they have taken Julian? Because I shall take a room somewhere nearby and find a job. I suppose they'll let me visit him."

"I suppose they will," said Henry. "But..."

"You needn't imagine," said Maud, "that I'm going to fit into your cozy little happy ending."

"Then I can only hope," said Henry, "that you find your own."

His last view of her was standing alone in the big, empty hall with a bowl of chrysanthemums behind her.